# Six Strokes
# Under

# Six Strokes Under

# Roberta Isleib

**WHEELER**
CHIVERS

This Large Print edition is published by Wheeler Publishing, Waterville, Maine USA and by BBC Audiobooks, Ltd, Bath, England.

Published in 2004 in the U.S. by arrangement with The Berkley Publishing Group, a member of Penguin Group (USA) Inc.

Published in 2004 in the U.K. by arrangement with The Berkley Publishing Group, a division of Penguin Group (USA) Inc.

U.S.  Softcover  1-58724-664-3 (Cozy Mystery)
U.K.  Hardcover  0-7540-9679-3 (Chivers Large Print)
U.K.  Softcover  0-7540-9680-7 (Camden Large Print)

The text of this Large Print edition is unabridged.
Other aspects of the book may vary from the original edition.

Set in 16 pt. Plantin.

Printed in the United States on permanent paper.

**British Library Cataloguing-in-Publication Data available**

**Library of Congress Cataloging-in-Publication Data**

Isleib, Roberta.
    Six strokes under / Roberta Isleib.
      p. cm.
    ISBN 1-58724-664-3 (lg. print : sc : alk. paper)
    1. Women golfers — Fiction.   2. Psychiatrists — Crimes against — Fiction.   3. Large type books.   I. Title.
PS3609.S57S57 2004
    813'.6—dc22                           2004043065

For John,
who caddies for all my dreams

My warmest thanks go to:

LPGA staff Kathy Lawrence and Neal Reid, the staff and members of the Plantation Golf and Country Club, especially John Talbott; and Bunker and Divot, for making my own trip to Q-school a breeze.

The players and their mothers, including Jessica Popiel, Diane Irvin, and especially Kim O'Connor, for sharing stories of their real Q-school experience.

John, Molly, Andrew, and all of my extended family.

Fellow writers and editors Chris Falcone, Dale Peterson, Angelo Pompano, Dale Eddy, Katharine Weber, Sue Repko, Maureen Robb, Susan Cerulean, John Brady, and Joy Johannessen.

Friends and friendly readers Yvonne Sparling, Diane Burbank, Jane and Jack Novick, Lesley Siegel, Debbie Griswold, Susan Gilfillan, Carol Ballentine, Paula Fischer, Tim Boyd, Curt Fisher, Howard Blue, Jono Miller, and Don Gliha.

My friends at Business and Legal Reports, for making a forest's worth of draft copies.

RJ Julia's Bookstore and the First Congregational Church in Madison, for providing places to meet and talk about writing.

Paige Wheeler, for persisting. The IWWG

and Sheree Bykovsky, for helping me find her. Cindy Hwang for believing in the project.

All my pals at the MCC, for tolerating an endless parade of mediocre shots and sub-par language. *Caveat ludens.*

# Glossary

**Approach Shot:** a golf shot used to reach the green, generally demanding accuracy, rather than distance

**Back nine:** second half of the eighteen-hole golf course; usually holes ten through eighteen

**Birdie:** a score of one stroke fewer than par for the hole

**Bogey:** a score of one stroke over par for the hole; double bogey is two over par; triple bogey is three over

**Bunker:** a depression containing sand; also called a sand trap or simply a trap

**Caddie:** person designated or hired to carry the golfer's bag and advise him/her on golf course strategy

**Card:** status that allows the golfer to compete on the PGA or LPGA Tour

**Chip:** a short, lofted golf shot used to reach the green from a relatively close position

**Chunk:** to strike the ground inadvertently before hitting the ball; similar to chilidipping, dubbing, and hitting it fat

**Collar:** the fringe of grass surrounding the perimeter of the green

**Cup:** the plastic cylinder lining the inside of the hole; the hole itself

**Cut:** the point halfway through a tournament at which the number of competitors is reduced based on their cumulative scores

**Divot:** a gouge in the turf resulting from a golf shot; also, the chunk of turf that was gouged out

**Draw:** a golf shot that starts out straight and turns slightly left as it lands (for a right-hander); a draw generally provides more distance than a straight shot or a slice

**Drive:** the shot used to begin the hole from the tee box, often using the longest club, the driver

**Fairway:** the expanse of short grass between each hole's tee and putting green, excluding the rough and hazards

**Fat:** a shot struck behind the ball that results in a short, high trajectory

**Flag:** the pennant attached to a pole used to mark the location of the cup on the green; also known as the pin

**Front nine:** the first nine holes of a golf course

**Futures Tour:** a less prestigious and lucrative tour that grooms golfers for the LPGA Tour

**Gallery:** a group of fans gathered to watch golfers play

**Green:** the part of the golf course where the grass is cut shortest, only a putter may be used to advance the ball to the hole

**Hacker:** an amateur player, generally one who lacks proficiency; also called a duffer

**Hazard:** an obstacle that can hinder the progress of the ball toward the green; may include bodies of water, bunkers, marshy areas, etc.

**Hook:** a shot that starts out straight, then curves strongly to the left (right-handers)

**Irons:** golf clubs used to hit shorter shots than woods; golfers generally carry long and short irons, one (longest) through nine (shortest)

**Lag putt:** a long putt hit with the intention of leaving the ball a short (tap-in) distance from the hole

**Leaderboard:** display board on which top players in a tournament are listed

**Lie:** the position of the ball on the course

**Out of bounds:** a ball hit outside of the legal boundary of the golf course which results in a two-stroke penalty for the golfer; also called OB

**Par:** the number of strokes set as the standard for a hole, or for an entire course

**Pin:** the flagstick

**Pitch:** a short, lofted shot most often taken with a wedge

**Putt:** a stroke using a putter on the green intended to advance the ball towards the hole

**Qualifying school (Q-school):** a series of

rounds of golf played in the fall which produces a small number of top players who will be eligible to play on the LPGA Tour that year

**Rainmaker:** an unusually high shot

**Range:** a practice area

**Round:** eighteen holes of golf

**Rough:** the area of the golf course along the sides of the fairway that is not closely mown; also, the grass in the rough

**Shank:** a faulty golf shot hit off the shank or hosel of the club that generally travels sharply right

**Skull:** a short swing that hits the top half of the ball and results in a line-drive trajectory

**Slice:** a golf shot which starts out straight and curves to the right (for right-handers)

**Tee:** the area of the golf hole designated as the starting point, delineated by tee markers, behind which the golfer must set up

**Top:** to hit only the top portion of the golf ball, generally resulting in a ground ball

**Trap:** see bunker

**Two-putt:** taking two shots to get the ball in the cup after hitting the green; a hole's par assumes two putts as the norm

**Wedge:** a short iron used to approach the green

**Woods:** golf clubs with long shafts and rounded heads used for longer distance than irons; the longest-shafted club with the largest head used on the tee is called the driver

**Yardage book:** a booklet put together by golfers, caddies, or golf course management describing topography and distances on the course

# 1

The *South Carolina Sun News* lay on the kitchen table, folded open to the want ads. Mom had gone through the listings with a yellow highlighter. *Pastry chef, responsible for breakfast, desserts, and banquet production.* Me in a chef's toque? I'd never scrambled an egg without her one-on-one supervision. *Job coach for the disabled, experience in special ed and bilingual (Spanish) preferred.* I knew *hola* and *gracias. Telemarketing, business-to-business, hard selling required.* I couldn't sell Girl Scout cookies to my own grandparents. *Restaurant counter help, intelligent and upbeat.* Intelligent? Sometimes. Upbeat? Not so you could count on it.

Besides the astonishing lack of fit between me and her selections, Mom had overlooked the fact that I was flying to Sarasota in three days for the LPGA qualifying school, otherwise known as Q-school, a boot camp for wannabe professional golfers. The lesson plan, four days of mental and physical torment, determined who'd get a shot at becoming the next Nancy Lopez or Annika Sorenstam.

"I guess I don't understand you, Cassie," Mom said when I first broke the news. "You tell me your chances of making it onto the Tour are minuscule. Why pay three thousand dollars to put yourself through hell and then come home empty-handed?" Punctuated with a heavy sigh.

I love my mother. Honestly. Even on the days, and today was shaping up as another one of them, when I'd just as soon wring her neck as have a cup of coffee with her. I counted on weekly phone calls to my friend Laura for perspective when I thought I was going to blow.

"You don't have a clue what it's like to be without a mother," she told me from Connecticut. "She's trying to help. Be grateful she's there to love you, Cassie."

"I'll try."

Laura was eighteen when her mom's car careened off the road on a rainy night. The tree she hit compressed Mrs. Snow into a shape "not compatible with human life," according to the coroner's report. So on that score, Laura was right. As much as my own mother got on my nerves, yammering about how life was full of disappointments and who was I to think I was immune to them, I'd never had to face a Mother's Day or my birthday without her. Or any other occasion where mothers were an essential part of the equation.

"I'll be so glad to get out of Myrtle Beach," I said. "If I stayed with Mom and

Dave one more week, you'd have to fly down here and lock me up. It's not just Mom's want-ad fixation. Dave keeps telling me that playing golf is not work. And I need to get a real job and start acting like a grown-up. Every night he leaves applications from the outlet malls on the kitchen table."

I shifted into my imitation of my stepfather's Yankee-come-to-the-deep-South-lately growl. "Don't y'all give me this crap about finding yourself, sister. Trust me when I tell you my authentic self does not involve serving enough cholesterol every morning to choke the arteries of every golfer in the state. Though that isn't a bad idea."

"You've got the poor bastard nailed." Laura laughed. "I take it head breakfast cook is not his life's dream."

"He doesn't know how to dream. He hit a new low yesterday when he brought home an application from Hooters, home of fast food served by big boobs."

"Hey, don't knock waitressing. Your mom does it. I did it all through college. And Hooters's chicken wings rule."

"Have you seen what they make those girls wear? Skin-tight orange nylon shorts that can't begin to cover their cheeks. I bet you don't even fill out an application to work there, just write down your name and bra size in big block letters. Cassandra Burdette, thirty-six C."

"In your dreams, girl," Laura said through snorts of laughter. "Come to think of it, you probably don't have the right equipment for that position."

More laughter. Best friend or not, she was starting to seriously wear me out.

"Any word from Jack?" she asked.

"Nothing new. He's in Japan this week, so the time zones and the long-distance rates are killing us." I'd met Jack just before I left my caddie job on the PGA Tour. His rocky performance as a rookie golfer meant he was banished to the Asian Tour until his game picked up. Just thinking about him gave me a little physical jolt, a frisson, I think the Victorian ladies would have called it. Even though he split before our flirtation had time to catch fire, I had two dreams on the horizon now: the LPGA Tour and Jack Wolfe.

"Gotta run," I said. "I'm going over to the club to hit balls. I'll pick you up in Florida Monday afternoon. Call me on the cell phone if your flight's running late."

"Aye-aye, Captain."

Ha. Even if it looked like I was in charge, her carrying the bag and me swinging the clubs, I knew she'd have a lot to say. She always did.

I pulled off Route 17 into the driveway of Palm Lakes Golf Course, where my father had worked for twenty years as the assistant golf pro. Twenty years he waited for the head pro job to open up. At last it did. Then they offered it to someone from outside, a young guy who'd worked five years at a resort course in Florida.

"You can't take it personal, Chuck," the search committee chair told him. "We just felt we needed some new blood, some new ideas to keep up with all the competition coming in."

Dad did take it personal. How else could he have taken it? Half a working lifetime of "yes, ma'am, no, sir, let me get that bag for you, how'd you hit 'em, don't tell me you reached the third in two" and then they passed him by. From what I overheard in the fights with Mom before he split, he saw two choices. Either he could get the hell out and find someplace that could see his potential, or sink into the quagmire of bitterness and pessimism she called home.

From the outside, nothing much had changed since my father's working days. "The Grandpappy of Golf" the sign at the entrance still read. As I opened the trunk, a bag boy ran up and grabbed my clubs. He wore over-size green plaid knickers, a military-style jacket, and a tam-o'-shanter, kind of a cross between British colonial dragoon and leprechaun.

"Top o' the mornin', Miss Burdette! Let me get that bag for you!" The green pom-pom on his plaid cap bounced with each step as he trotted to the clubhouse ahead of me.

"You taking a little money on the side hawking Lucky Charms?" my older brother, Charlie, asked Dad the first time he saw the new uniforms.

"It may look like schlock to you," Dad said, "but it's our edge over the competition."

"Just don't let the NAACP play the tenth hole," Charlie said. That was my favorite spot on the course, where a black guy in a chef's hat and apron served chicken gumbo from a pot hanging over a wood fire next to the tee.

"We may not have the length or challenge of some of the other courses," Dad told Charlie, "but where else does Scarlett O'Hara meet Jack Nicklaus?"

Inside the pro shop, I walked past the black-and-white photograph of the club taken in 1965. Every person on staff posed on the front lawn, along with every piece of course maintenance equipment, including a 1963 Buick station wagon, a '62 Pontiac, and seven hand lawnmowers. The ladies wore Jackie Kennedy pillbox hats on their flip hairdos. My very young father had just been hired. He wore a Butch wax special and a huge grin.

Odell Washington rubbed my back while I waited for the assistant pro to bring me a bucket of golf balls. I leaned into his kneading fingers.

"Feeling okay today, sweetheart?" he asked.

Odell had worked alongside Dad for eighteen of Dad's twenty years. Being black and over fifty, he hadn't been at all surprised to be passed over for promotion when the head pro job came open. Then he ended up with the spot after all when the Florida hot shot absconded with the pro shop till at the end of his first season. Eight months ago, I'd come limping home from caddying on the PGA Tour with a serious case of post-traumatic stress syndrome, related to some rookie's errant drive landing between my eyes. Odell had hired me on the spot and insisted on sponsoring my trip to Q-school.

"Your dad gave me a shot. Now it's my turn with you," he'd said over my protests. "You can't argue with karma, sweetheart."

I gave Odell a quick hug when his assistant arrived with my balls. "Thanks for the massage. You're the best."

I carried the bucket out to the range and spilled the balls onto a patch of grass. I hit a few full wedge shots, then paused to watch the other golfers.

Most were men, middle-aged and paunchy. Their faces were charged with the excitement that comes at the beginning of an amateur's round on an expensive vacation course. I'd seen it every Wednesday, caddying for Mike Callahan during the professional-amateur rounds before the real tournaments began.

21

Most times, that excitement died over the five hours it took to play, killed off by too many balls lost in the marsh, too many putts yanked past the hole, too many approach shots dubbed into sand traps or water hazards or just plain out of bounds.

At the far end of the range, alone, stood a woman. She was different, not just interested in how far her drives bounced by the two-hundred-yard marker. Instead, she studied her target between shots, barely glancing at the trajectory of her balls once she hit them.

"She reminds me of you." I jumped, startled by the emergence of Odell just behind my bag. "Kaitlin Rupert. She was a few years behind you on the high school golf team. Maybe she has more natural talent than you, but I believe you've got the edge in drive." I glanced back down the range. The name sounded familiar, but I didn't recognize the girl.

"Hey, come with me," he said, grabbing my wrist. "Y'all should get acquainted. Y'all have a lot in common." He pulled me down the row of golfers until we stood behind her.

"Kaitlin Rupert, Cassie Burdette." I extended my hand. She laid hers limply in mine.

"Cassie's just come off a stint caddying on the PGA Tour. She looped for Mike Callahan through Q-school and his rookie year," Odell said.

"Interesting," said Kaitlin, turning back to

her bag. Not to her, I guess.

"Kaitlin's headed to Q-school next week, too. Maybe you could give her some tips on what she can expect," Odell said to me.

"I've already hired Butch Harmon for a consultation. That's Tiger's coach," Kaitlin said. "So I'm all set. Unless you think you have some tips he won't have thought of." She laughed, picked up a short iron, and resumed hitting pitch shots.

What a bitch.

Odell grabbed the back of my T-shirt and tugged me a couple of stations away. "I know she seems difficult, but she needs someone right now." His voice dropped to a conspiratorial whisper. "She's got family problems that could really get in her way."

Line up and join the damn club.

"You know her father," said Odell. "Peter Rupert. He was the football coach at the high school."

Everyone in Myrtle Beach knew Rupert. He'd been my brother Charlie's idol for the better part of his teenage years, much to Dad's chagrin.

"She needs a shoulder right now," said Odell, "or everything she's worked for will go down the toilet."

That sounded familiar, too. I poked at a range ball with the toe of my wedge.

"With your experience taking Mike through Q-school, you'd be a major asset."

Twenty feet from where we stood, I saw Kaitlin run her fingers through her curls. I bet she'd been born that way. Nothing out of a bottle could have produced the same golden shimmer. She took an easy practice swing and held the finish, showcasing long tanned legs and conical breasts with the dark outline of her nipples showing plainly through her shirt.

Barbie Goes to the Driving Range.

Nope, I didn't see how it would be possible to help her out. Matter of fact, I couldn't even be sure I'd give her directions to a gas station if her tank ran dry in a bad neighborhood. Never mind help her make the cut at Q-school.

I followed Odell back to where she stood. "So what do you think," he said, "can you help this young lady out?"

Man, I loved this guy, but he was a bird dog.

"No can do." I turned to face the girl and shrugged. "Sorry. I'm planning to try to qualify myself this year. Coaching you would be a conflict of interest."

"Then maybe y'all could just work together this week, kind of a Q-school support group." Odell looked totally pleased with his brainstorm. "Two hometown girls make good on the Tour. I can read the headline now."

Kaitlin swiveled her head back in my direction then posed gracefully against her leather bag. "You're going to Q-school? I can't recall seeing you on the Futures Tour."

"I didn't do the Futures Tour route. I was working here for Odell."

"You're going to Q-school without any professional competition under your belt?"

"I played in college. And like Odell told you, I've been caddying on the PGA Tour. I know how to get around a golf course."

"It's an entirely different experience when you're the one standing over those putts in this kind of competition. Until you've been through it over and over, six feet might as well be sixty yards."

I shrugged. She was probably right, but the snotty attitude galled me.

"You must have money to burn," she said. "Or maybe you're just out of your mind."

"Neither one," I said. "Just optimistic."

Just another optimistic asshole, I wished I'd had the nerve to say.

I walked back to my bag, hoping I looked confident, not mushy-kneed and queasy, the way I felt inside. I couldn't let myself dwell on the misgivings Kaitlin had stirred up. Or my own burning question, exactly the one she'd raised. Where the hell did I get off thinking I was going to make it on the LPGA Tour with no experience but a few college competitions and a year caddying?

The situation called for action. The kind of action I could get for a few bucks sitting at the bar of the Chili Dip Inn.

# 2

I stumbled out to the kitchen the next morning, grateful Dave had left too early to make rude comments on my bleary eyes and the tremor in my hands. Just another routine Wednesday night, closing down the bar with the other regular losers at Chili-Dippers. I poured the tepid dregs from Mr. Coffee into a mug that read, "World's Greatest Dad." My mother bought the cup the first year after she married Dave, then instructed me to wrap it up for him for Father's Day. We all three knew it was a sham, but Mom insisted on appearances, no matter what rotted just below the surface.

Mom had been at work on the newspaper with the highlighter again, this time in an article partway down the front page. I began to read.

HIGH SCHOOL COACH NAMED BY DAUGHTER IN REPRESSED MEMORY ABUSE CASE, said the headline.

Myrtle Beach High School football coach Peter Rupert has been arrested and charged with sexual abuse by his daughter, Kaitlin Rupert. Max Harding, attorney for

26

the defendant, refused to comment on the specific allegations made by Ms. Rupert. Said Harding, "I can only state that recovered memories of abuse have been one of the most controversial concepts in the field of psychology in the past decade. There have been many instances of overzealous psychotherapists implanting false memories in their patients. I cannot say whether this has occurred with Ms. Rupert, but I will state that my client has never abused her, sexually or otherwise." Harding also refused comment on alleged quotes from a member of his staff that Ms. Rupert was "participating in a modern-day witch-hunt" and "falling victim to the false memory syndrome epidemic."

Mom had used the yellow highlighter every time Max Harding's name appeared in the article. Shit.

A chorus of Mom's cuckoo clocks reminded me that I had promised Odell I'd open the shop at 6:30 a.m. Almost late already, I dropped the paper and hurried off to shower and dress.

While the hot shower water beat the knots in my back loose, I thought about Max Harding. I hoped I wouldn't run into him while he was in town. If I did run into him, I hoped he'd developed a receding hairline and a belly that lopped over the waist of his Sansabelt slacks. If he wasn't bald and fat, I hoped he would notice that I weighed the same as I did in high school, only now it was 110 pounds of toned muscle.

Then I wondered about Coach Rupert. Mom used to say he wrote the manual for living life on the edge. And the town never quite decided whether to canonize or crucify him, even the year he took the football team to the state championships. He wasn't objectively a handsome man, with a craggy face, piercing blue eyes, and a red mustache. The individual pieces worked okay, but taken together, his face resembled a Picasso more than a Rembrandt. He made up for it with the sheer volume of his muscles and the easy, warm way he had with girls of all ages.

After our Nighthawks won the state championship, Coach had a replica of the team mascot tattooed just above his left bicep. The ladies loved to roll his sleeve up, touching more of his skin than was absolutely necessary, then watch the bird's wings flap when he flexed that muscle. There were always rumors — Coach Rupert and somebody's mother or sister or daughter. None of it ever proven to be more than the fantasy of the women or the sour grapes of the men in the town, but enough material to keep the coffee shop chatter electrified for weeks at a time. And all the while, he'd been abusing his little golden daughter? Hard to believe. Really hard to believe.

My brother, Charlie, played running back that year we won the trophy. It wasn't long before Dad bailed out; I must have been thirteen. Every night at the dinner table, we'd hear words of wisdom from Charlie's god.

"Could you make me a couple of peanut butter and jelly sandwiches, Ma? Coach says too much red meat and salt will slow me down." That was after Mom served the pot roast with Lipton Soup gravy she had cooked every Sunday for every week we'd been alive.

"Coach says it's all in my vision. I just have to try to see the holes in the defense." That would be after Dad offered what he considered constructive observations on Charlie's performance during a game.

"I don't have time to fool around. Coach says football has to come first if we want the championship that badly." And that came after Dad asked him if he wanted to play handball, or hit a bucket of range balls, or join him in just about any activity you could name.

I think Dad recognized by then that his life's work consisted of giving lessons to tourists who weren't going to listen to him anyway, and that nothing would ever change as long as he stayed in South Carolina. Hearing Coach lifted up as the archangel of wisdom for teenage boys was finally more than he could stand.

"Go eat your fucking dinner at his house,

then!" he exploded one night. "Maybe he'll pay your goddamned college tuition, too."

Charlie tossed his napkin on the table and pushed in his chair. "He's two times the man you'll ever be," he said as he left.

I offered to go beat balls at the range with Dad, but he turned me down. I wanted to kill Charlie. Mom just cried.

I turned off the water and toweled off roughly, wishing I could rub out those old memories. I searched through my closet and found a pair of chinos with a faint press line, and a pink golf shirt. A white-and-tan-striped vest covered the coffee stain on the shirt. Then I clipped on a pair of gold earrings in the shape of golf balls and looked in the mirror. Professional, but just feminine enough, I hoped. I knew nothing in my wardrobe was going to raise me into Kaitlin's league. Charlie would have said I sold myself short. Not hard to do when the entire advertising world tells you you're dirt unless you're tall and blond, two attributes which did not apply to me.

I arrived at the club at 7:15, damp-haired and remorseful. Odell had already opened up the register.

"Never mind helping here," said Odell. "You need to get out to the range and get to work."

"I'm so sorry," I began. A shrill screaming interrupted my apology. We stepped out of the pro shop and saw two figures arguing at the end of the range. I picked up my bag and followed Odell down to where Kaitlin Rupert was screaming at an older woman. The woman was paper-doll thin and blond — the same silky-gold hair as Kaitlin's, but swept back neatly with a pair of expensive-looking tortoiseshell combs.

"Jesus, Mary, and Joseph," said Odell. "It's Margaret Rupert. What the hell is she doing here?"

Just as we arrived, Kaitlin gave her mother a quick shove. She stumbled back into the leather bag leaning against the adjoining bag stand, where she bobbled precariously until Odell grabbed her waist.

"Now, now, Margaret, Kaitlin," said Odell. "I'm sure we can work this out." Odell and two golfers who'd been hitting balls on the range fussed over Mrs. Rupert while she regained her balance and her composure.

"Go home and take a Valium, Mother," Kaitlin told her in a cold voice. "This is none of your affair. It's far too late for you to be worrying about this now." She brushed an imaginary wrinkle out of her yellow microfiber short shorts, pulled those golden curls into a loose ponytail, and turned toward the small crowd that had gathered around her.

"Show's over," she told us. "Mother's returning to her cage now."

I set my bag down on the wire stand twenty feet away from Kaitlin. As the by-standers dispersed, I glanced back over at her. My better judgment said KEEP OUT. But maybe Odell was right. We did have a lot in common, and both could use a friend. I flashed her a tentative smile.

"I suppose you read the paper this morning," she said. "Everyone else did."

"Only the headline," I lied. "I'm sorry for your troubles."

"Full of pompous quotes from the famous defense attorney Max Harding," she said. "I heard you and he were an item."

"That was over ten years ago," I said, squirming. "I wouldn't know him now if I tripped over him."

"He's a horse's ass," she said. "Even if my father had a decent case, which he doesn't, Attorney Harding would screw it up."

I shrugged. Max was real smart back when I knew him, but I sure wasn't going out on any limb defending him now, particularly not to her. I broke eye contact with her and peered into her golf bag. "Damn, that's some pretty fancy gear you have."

Kaitlin pulled her bag back out of my line of vision. "Deikon is sponsoring me this year. I'm trying some new stuff out for them, top of the line. Not out in the market yet."

"Like that golf ball Tiger was using," I said, laughing. "Now there was a public relations nightmare. All the hackers in America rushing in to buy a ball that only existed in Tiger's bag. Hey, those new clubs don't have the trampoline-effect faces, do they? You'd hate to be disqualified before you even got going."

The average golfer was always looking for the technical advantage that would increase the length of his drives — preferably something that wouldn't involve practice. Just lately, the United States Golf Association had decided that the newest technology, allowing golf balls to spring off the club face like a trampoline, was taking the whole trend too far.

"The clubs I use conform completely with every specification in the book," Kaitlin said, extracting a copy of the USGA "Rules of Golf" out of her pocket and shaking it in my face.

"Sorry. No offense intended." I backed away.

"Let me give you a little piece of advice. If you think you're good enough to compete professionally, I'd suggest you butt out of other people's business and spend that free time learning the rules." Then she glanced at my bag. "Still using Big Berthas? Well, I don't suppose the extra thirty yards I get off the tee amounts to much in the long run. Don't they say it's all in your short game, anyway?"

I was grateful to be leaving town soon. I could only pray our Q-school pairings would overlap as little as possible. There were other things I could pray for if I let my dark side take over. But even lapsed Presbyterians worry about going to Hell.

# 3

When I got home that afternoon, I called my friend Joe Lancaster. Joe was a psychologist who'd given up his practice with ordinary people to work with athletically talented, but equally nutty, professional golfers. He told me their problems might be different — like "my three-foot putts won't drop" instead of "my husband and I aren't communicating" — but the pain was all the same.

I described the snit Kaitlin had pitched at the range. "I don't get it," I said. "How can an adult behave that way in public with her own mother? She's not thirteen, for God's sake."

"I haven't met her, so it's not fair to guess," Joe said.

"When has that ever held you back?" I asked. "Go ahead. Start talking."

He laughed. "If you insist . . . sounds like borderline features."

"And in plain English that means . . ."

He laughed again. "She doesn't understand how to maintain a normal human connection that takes the other person into account. Could be she suffered some kind of psychological damage as a child. That's how you develop those borderline traits in the first place."

"You mean like incest?" I asked. "She's filing a suit against her own father. An article in this morning's paper said she's just now remembering that he abused her."

"Jesus," said Joe. "You have me taking wild guesses and you leave that tidbit out?"

"Yeah, but your wild guesses are always so juicy," I said, ignoring his outrage. "What do you know about repressed memories coming up in therapy?"

"Short version?" said Joe. "Controversy galore. A hornet's nest."

"What about the long version?" I usually didn't like to invite him down that path; it could turn into a tedious detour. He spent so much time listening to people, you could hardly get him to shut up when it was finally his turn to talk. But now I was really curious about Kaitlin.

"In actual practice, recovered memories of abuse are rare," he said. "Most people who suffered abuse remember some or all of it. I guess the official stand is that digging up forgotten memories is possible, but it's also possible to develop pseudomemories of events that did not occur."

"So you think you remember something, but it didn't really happen."

"Yes," said Joe. "And some shrinks who get involved in this area wish they hadn't —

36

we're talking harassment, court cases, public protests." He paused to take a breath. "So what's this girl's story?"

"She hasn't told me much directly," I said, thinking back over the interactions we'd had so far. "She was just short of vicious about my chances in Q-school. And my antiquated equipment. Then there was the scene with her mother. Still, I feel kind of sorry for her. And Odell thinks I could help."

"You want my free advice?" said Joe. "Stick to golf. Forget about the peer counseling. Patients who have this kind of history and are willing to get involved in that kind of controversy scream personality disorder. You could sink into a bog you'd never climb back out of."

Frankly, for a psychologist who made his living helping people, even people as difficult as Kaitlin, I thought his assessment was a little mean-spirited.

"I bet you're thinking I should be more compassionate," said Joe. "What's the girl like?"

"She's a looker," I said. "Blond hair, big boobs, the whole nine yards. You'd be drooling all over yourself." My turn to be mean-spirited.

"Give me a little credit here," he said.

"Credit for what? Have you forgotten Georgia so soon?" I hadn't forgotten Georgia — a blowsy, oversexed, lavishly perfumed, bleached-blond bombshell that he'd taken up with last summer to ease the transition away from his failing marriage. A little too much human frailty for a shrink to display, in my humble opinion. Especially since we'd had electricity crackling between us from the moment we met. Until Georgia showed up and blew the fuse in that circuit. Now, as far as I was concerned, Joe and me — we were just plain pals.

Joe interrupted my thoughts with a groan. "Okay, after I wiped the drool off my chin, what else would I notice about her?"

"Focus," I said. "She had the entire male population of the driving range sporting woodies and all she saw was her own swing path."

"Sporting woodies?"

"Sorry, I didn't mean to shock you," I said, laughing. "Let me put it another way. She seems to have the concentration it takes to make it big time. And her shots were nothing to sneeze about either. The swing path isn't what I'd call classic, but she hits the ball square and it goes a long ways. A lot longer than anything I could hit. To make things worse, she already has a sponsor and they've filled her bag with space-age technology. It's going to be hard to compete with that."

"Remember what I told you. You're not competing against one person in Q-school. Keep your focus on each shot and —"

"I know, I know," I said. "Play your own game."

Joe laughed. "I've gotten predictable."

"Gotta go, Doc," I said. "I'm off to see the wizard."

When I hadn't sprung right back from the accident last summer, Joe had diagnosed post-traumatic stress syndrome and suggested I get into psychotherapy. "Sure you could probably handle this alone," he'd said. "But you'll come out of it faster with some help. Take care of it early and the symptoms won't keep popping up at inconvenient times." Now he tried to walk the fine line between curiosity about my progress and respecting my privacy.

"Everything going okay with Dr. Baxter?" he asked.

"I'm thinking of stopping," I said. "I think I'm cured. Now I only have post-post-traumatic stress syndrome."

"Did you discuss this with him?" said Joe, his voice full of that I-know-better-than-you-that-you-are-about-to-screw-up tone.

"I'll be fine," I said. "Case closed. I'll see you next Tuesday."

"Good luck," said Joe. "Hit 'em straight."

I parked on the street outside Dr. Baxter's office and turned up the radio. I preferred to skate into Dr. Baxter's waiting room only a minute or so before my appointment. I knew if I got there late, we'd waste half the hour talking about the deep psychological ramifications of my tardiness, but on the other hand, I hated to get there too early and end up having to cool my heels with the losers waiting for his officemate, Dr. Bencher. Bencher looked normal enough — standard-issue close-cropped goatee, white button-down shirt with sleeves rolled up, sometimes a vest, sometimes a tie. All designed, I imagined, to give that professional yet rumpled and warm effect conducive to the spilling of guts.

But unlike Baxter and his merry band of high-functioning neurotics, Bencher seemed to specialize in the genuine crazies. God knows, maybe they thought I was wacko, too. But at least I didn't sit in the waiting area clanking through the bag of filthy cans I'd collected from the Dumpster outside the back door. Or wear a baseball cap with an Insane Clown Posse logo and rows of carpet tacks glued around the brim, pointy ends out.

I released the latch on the bucket seat of my Volvo and leaned back with my eyes closed to meditate to the sweet sounds of Patsy Cline. I had five minutes to fantasize about a steamy reunion with Jack Wolfe.

A siren interrupted Patsy's lament. Then I heard shouts in the parking lot outside Dr. Baxter's building. I got out of the car to investigate. Two men and a woman in business suits marched in front of the door waving placards and yelling. It wasn't the first time I'd had to wend my way through a receiving line of protesters — my shrink's suitemate seemed to gravitate to controversy.

"It's bad enough coming here at all," I'd told Dr. Baxter last time this happened. "But running a gauntlet of crackpots to get here . . ." I could only shake my head.

The businesspeople carried signs that read, "Manufactured Memories: Shattered Lives," "Charlatan Shrinks Stroll Down Pseudo-Memory Lane," and "Stick to Analysis, Skip the Fiction." A fourth protester wore faded jeans, three or four days' worth of whiskery stubble, and a black-and-red-checked hunter's shirt. He looked hot and just this side of losing it. He looked like he never should have left the back hills of Arkansas or West Virginia or wherever the hell he came from. His sign read, "Leviticus 18:22: You shall not lie with a male as with a woman. It is an abomination." Only God knew why this guy marched outside my shrink's office waving a sign that, by all appearances, hammered homosexuals.

One of Myrtle Beach's finest black-and-whites (tan-and-chromes, if you wanted to get technical) screeched up to the pickets. Two officers hopped out and began arguing with the protesters about how many paces away from the building they would have to stand. Too bad I had to go. This was obviously going to be a lot more exciting than anything Dr. Baxter and I could drum up.

"Tough neighborhood you live in," I said, pointing out the window to the police cars, as I took my seat in Dr. Baxter's inner sanctum.

"Um-hum," he said.

I could tell we weren't going to have much of a conversation if I stuck to that topic. So I talked about meeting Kaitlin and getting ready for Q-school.

"The weirdest thing," I told him, "is the way Mom's reacting. You'd think she'd be delirious with happiness that I'm finally going for my dream. Instead, all she can talk about is how could I do this to her, how could I get involved in something that will only remind her every day of how my father left her. Her latest maneuver is pretending I'm not going at all."

"In her mind, the feelings of rage and disappointment towards your father are still fresh," said Dr. Baxter. "They're like a touchstone for her. She goes back to them over and over. They're painful, but in a familiar way. Like touching your tongue to a rotten tooth." He leaned back in his chair and stroked his beard, a pose I thought he must have learned in shrink school. Something they pull out when they're moving in for the kill but don't want to alarm the prey. "You have other choices," he said. "How does it really feel to be going to qualifying school?"

"Okay," I said. "Fine."

He sighed. "Your mother stays stuck in her old feelings. You sometimes don't let yourself know what yours are."

"What does that mean?" I said. "I know what I feel. I just don't see the point of wallowing around in the past. You want me to break down and blubber about how scared I am. How's that going to help me?"

"You keep a distance from your feelings," said Dr. Baxter. "You're like a caddie to your own life — reading the wind, checking how the ball lies, studying the yardage book. You wait for someone else to hit the shot, rather than get involved."

I rolled my eyes. Like he had a clue about being a caddie. It was just as hard as playing golf, maybe harder. You had to carry the emotional weight of someone else's performance without having even a shred of real control over how the thing turned out. Let him spend one afternoon lugging Mike Callahan's bag around a golf course, trying to keep him from blowing sky high. Then he could tell me I wasn't involved.

"Q-school sounds like good news," said Dr. Baxter, interrupting my internal rampage. "You're putting yourself back in your life, not standing by watching on the sidelines."

I didn't say anything. I wasn't trying to be difficult or rude. But I still wasn't comfortable with this therapy thing, this constant stream of personal feedback, often way more than I wanted to hear, from someone I really hardly knew. And most annoying of all, he was usually right. In this case, though, I refused to jinx my chances by digging too far into the mixture of exhilaration and pure terror that flooded me when I thought about Q-school.

"What are you thinking?" he asked after a long silence.

"I'm wondering about repressed memories of sexual abuse. How accurate you think they are and what you'd say if a patient came in remembering something from years before."

His eyebrows drew together into one fuzzy gray line and he cleared his throat. "You've remembered something from your past," he said, his voice all delicate and tentative.

"Oh, God, no!" I said. "It's Kaitlin and her father. She's filed suit against him."

"This sounds important," said Dr. Baxter. "But our time is up. We'll talk more about this next Thursday."

Which seemed to be always the way with shrinks: either you had nothing to say and fifty long minutes to say it in, or you were on the verge of a major breakthrough but the next loony tune was banging on the waiting-room door.

Dr. Baxter ushered me out before I had time to remind him I wasn't coming next Thursday. Or to tell him that I wasn't at all sure I'd be back the one after that.

# 4

On my way down the exit hallway, I noticed that the double doors guarding Baxter's neighbor's office stood cracked open several inches. This was not up to Dr. Bencher's usual standard of security. Not that I blamed him for being careful. I, too, would have preferred to keep two steel-reinforced doors and a peephole between me and the sea of human flotsam that bobbed about in the safe harbor of his waiting room.

A muffled gurgling noise halted my beeline charge for the stairs. I heard the noise again — not so much gurgling this time as rasping, like someone who seriously could not breathe. I decided to go back and tell Baxter — let him check on Bencher.

But when I reached the waiting area, Baxter's door had been shut, and the heavy-set, miserable-looking woman who often followed my session no longer sat in the chair by the window. Damn. Now alerting Baxter to the weird noise would involve bursting into her reserved hour and reporting what would most likely turn out to be a figment of my presently overexcitable imagination. Then next session, we'd end up discussing sibling rivalry or not having gotten enough attention from my father in the process of growing up or some other equally absurd and embarrassing interpretation of my attempt to be helpful.

For the second time, I walked past Bencher's open doors. I heard a faint hiss, then more gurgling, slower this time. I turned back and knocked on the door. No answer. I peered around the door and into the doctor's office. An Impressionist print hung on the beige wall — a mother carrying a parasol, strolling through a hazy field of flowers with her child. Neutral colors, subtle subject, nothing that would agitate an already fragile psyche.

I stepped all the way into the room. The layout mirrored Baxter's office, but with the furnishings just half a step classier and more welcoming. Like in Baxter's inner sanctum, the office had a leather Eames chair for the doctor — comfortable enough, but not so plush that the occupant would be tempted to doze off. Bencher's patients had the choice of a flowered Victorian fainting couch or an upholstered rocker. I wondered whether he was a better shrink or just more generous with his decorating budget.

Then I was seized with an irresistible urge to try out the couch. I snickered. Goldilocks and the three shrinks. The pillow on the couch was covered with white paper — no sharing of head lice allowed. Just as the weight of my head began to crinkle the paper on the sofa, I spotted Bencher. He lay sprawled on his back, partly hidden by his rolltop desk. He had a hole punched in his neck. Although his body didn't move, his lips twitched. His eyes were wide and desperate. And the wound gurgled like some horrible, enormous baby's mouth as blood poured out onto the carpet.

I screamed. I leaped up and backed into the corridor yelling for help. Then I stepped back over Bencher's body and dialed 911. The police, who must have continued hassling the protesters during the length of my session, arrived quickly. Dr. Baxter was next, his fat, unhappy patient trailing behind him. The first officer on the scene interviewed me briefly, then grabbed Bencher's footstool, dragged it to a corner of the room, and pointed.

"Sit," said the officer, whose name tag identified him as Sergeant Dixon. "Don't touch anything."

I watched him speak with Baxter and his patient in the hallway. Then he returned to help cordon off the crime scene, while paramedics attended to the psychiatrist. As I sat, facing away from the doctor's body, my nostrils filled with a strong metallic odor. I knew it was his blood.

I remembered a technique Joe taught me for blocking out distracting or unpleasant thoughts on the golf course. "If your mind is

47

busy cataloging horizontal and vertical lines in your environment," he said, "it pushes the panic and negativity right out. Don't analyze the lines, just notice them." Bookshelves: vertical. Countertop: horizontal. Directory of South Carolina Psychiatric Services: horizontal. Pole lamp: vertical.

As I worked my way across the room, I noticed the disarray in the adjoining filing cubby. Manila folders were tossed in heaps on the floor and the drawers of the cabinets had been left dangling open. A small glass coffeepot lay shattered on the floor, its contents soaking into the folders. Without thinking, I walked over and began to blot the liquid up off the binders with a roll of paper towels I found on the counter.

"I said don't touch anything!" shouted Sergeant Dixon. I sat again. Now my teeth rattled — I felt cold and sick, any illusion of calm shattered. The paramedics covered the doctor's wound, fastened an oxygen mask around his graying face, and wrapped him in a shiny silver blanket.

"We're ready for you now, Miss Burdette," said a man dressed in a tweed jacket and corduroys. "I'm Detective Maloney."

"Is he going to live?" I asked. "I swear he was alive when I came in." I couldn't stop shaking. And I had developed that saliva-swallowing sensation you get just before you throw up.

"How did you happen to find the victim?"

"As I already told the fellow over there," I said, waving at Officer Dixon, "I was leaving Dr. Baxter's office when I saw both doors ajar and heard an odd sound."

"And you went in because . . . ?"

"Because this seemed strange. His doors are never open and I got worried about the noise."

"And you come here a lot?"

I knew where we were going with this — what kind of a kook was I, and just how far might I have carried my kookiness.

"Once a week," I said, trying to keep the irritation out of my voice. "Whether I need it or not." Dr. Baxter, looking naked without his armchair and notepad, flashed me a reassuring smile from across the room.

"How is he?" I asked, watching the paramedics as they loaded the doctor onto a gurney and carried him out. "He looks awful." In fact, he looked dead. I hoped my medically uninformed assessment was wrong.

"We won't know anything until they get him to the hospital," said the detective. "Did you know the doctor?"

"Only by sight."

"Did you see anyone leaving the area before you found the body?"

"No, I was busy talking with Dr. Baxter."

"Do you have any idea who might have wanted him dead?"

"No." I doubted he wanted to hear my unfounded opinions about the parade of weirdos I'd seen march through the waiting room each week. Or maybe he would, but then I'd rate a do-not-pass-go ride to the loony bin.

"You're free to leave now," said the detective. "But we'll need you to stay in the area over the next week in case we have further questions."

"That's not possible," I said, beginning to cry. "I'm leaving for qualifying school the day after tomorrow."

"It's a golf tournament," said Dr. Baxter, moving a few steps closer to where we stood. "She'll be back by next weekend. Maybe you could give the officers your cell phone number so they can call if you're needed?"

Finally, with Dr. Baxter's reassuring intervention, the police allowed me to go.

I headed directly to Chili-Dippers. Paul, the bartender, laid a napkin featuring kidney beans square-dancing with hot peppers on the bar in front of me, then set a draft Budweiser in a frosted mug on the napkin. All this before my butt had even settled onto the barstool. The perks of being promoted to a regular.

"I'll take a shot of tequila, too," I said. "Long, long day."

Just the sameness of the bar felt comforting. On the far wall hung pictures of every football team that ever came out of Myrtle Beach High. From 1970 on, Coach Rupert was in all of them, exhibiting a toothy grin you never saw on the ball field. The golf team portraits were posted high above the football teams. My father stood in the back row in the pictures from the sixties and seventies. Each year, his smile looked a little more strained, until he finally disappeared altogether — burned out on coaching. In the photos from my junior and senior years, I was the only girl, small and awkward among the crowd of gawky teenage boys.

Prom pictures had been tacked up to the right of the football teams — hundreds of them. I knew if I looked hard enough, I'd find the one of me and Max. Mom had fought me on the dress — clinging burgundy velvet with a scalloped décolletage that plunged halfway to my waist. She hand-sewed three inches of the gap shut to create a neckline she considered decent — and safe. Once we reached the dance, I clipped her stitches out in the girls' room with the tiny scissors on Max's Swiss Army knife.

Paul smiled as he delivered the shooter, then returned to the conversation he'd been involved with when I came in. I downed the tequila, took a long pull on the beer, and finally began to feel calm enough to consider the gruesome scene I'd just left.

Because they shared a waiting room, I figured

Dr. Baxter had to know Dr. Bencher pretty well. I wondered if they'd been friends. Did shrinks have real friends or were they too busy trying to psych each other out?

Then I wondered whether Bencher had been attacked while I was there. Or had he been lying in the suite next door the whole time I whined about my mother? I certainly hadn't heard a gunshot or any signs of a struggle. I tried to remember whether Dr. Baxter had seemed less attentive than usual. Hard to say. He didn't generally demonstrate what shrinks liked to call a "wide range of affect" during an hour with me. I counted it as a victory if I got him to laugh even once during a session.

As a rule, I tried to keep the idea of Baxter, the person, out of my mind. If I could think of him as a doctor, a professional without feelings, the gut-spilling felt more tolerable. But today we'd crossed a line. I felt grateful for his kind intervention with the police. I guessed I'd have to go back week after next, because now we'd gotten tangled up in a whole new way.

As I sipped my Bud, fragments of a conversation occurring down the bar came into focus.

"How was he killed?"

"Bullet right between the eyes," said a man at the bar, flicking a finger of ash from his cigarette onto the floor.

"Did you hear this, Cassie?" Paul called over to me. "The headshrinker involved in the Rupert sex abuse case was found murdered this afternoon. Who do they like for the shooting?" Paul asked his informant.

The smoker shrugged. "Too early to say, I guess."

"He was shot in the neck, not between the eyes," I said, sliding my beer down the bar to join the conversation. "Are they sure he's dead?"

The smoker nodded.

"Hot off the press," said Paul, his eyebrows raised at me. "What was his name?"

"Dr. Bencher. Gregory Bencher."

"How come you got the news flash on where he was shot?"

"He has an office on Seaview," I said. "I rode by there today and stopped when I saw all the commotion." No way was I going to admit that I'd seen the hubbub up close and personal because I was leaving my own shrink appointment.

"I know that guy," said Paul. "He has a way of mixing it up with clients that put him in the limelight. Hasn't he been testifying for the Harrington custody case?"

"Saw him on the five o'clock news just last week," said the smoker. "Both the parents sounded like they're fresh out of the asylum. I feel sorry for the kid, either way the thing turns out."

"This time, Bencher's made the spotlight for sure." Paul's tongue made a clucking sound as he wiped down the mahogany planks in front of him. "Five bucks says he's front page in the *Sun* tomorrow morning." He began to polish the copper edging along the bar.

"You knew Coach Rupert," said Paul to the man at the bar. "Do you think he did this or did Kaitlin make it up?"

The man blew a wide swath of smoke out of his nostrils and reached a meaty paw in my direction. "Lester Fortright. I knew your dad. Great guy, he was." He nodded toward the pictures of the high school golf team displayed behind my right shoulder.

I shook his hand and shrugged. One of the major drawbacks of coming back home: hearing my father, the ship-jumping rodent, described as a local hero.

"Coach Rupert had a lot of flaws," Lester continued. "A real bad temper, an awful high opinion of himself, and a tendency to scratch around henhouses where he had no business being. On the plus side, he was one hell of a fine coach."

"I'll never forget how he put the Rankin kid in at quarterback during the championship game," said Paul. "Everyone thought he'd gone and lost his mind. But Coach pulled it off — the kid came through for him."

"Besides all that, he wasn't a bad man, either," said Lester. "So I'd bet the long odds, she made it up. Hell if I know why, though."

"Maxie!" Paul hollered, interrupting Lester's theorizing. "Where've you been the last year, my friend? Come on in and take a load off, Counselor." A handsome man in wire-rimmed glasses, a gray suit, and a red power tie approached the bar. He had a slightly receding hairline and a triangle-shaped body — narrow waist and hips and strong shoulders that strained the center seam of his suit jacket.

I snatched up the laminated sandwich menu in front of me and buried my face in it. So. Max Harding was neither bald nor fat. Hunched down behind the menu, I listened to him order a beer and join the banter of the men lining the bar.

"What can you tell us about Bencher?" Paul asked. "Does this put a hole in your case, prime witness with a hole in his head and all?"

Max laughed, a deep baritone, bordering on bass, that I remembered just as clearly as if I'd told him a joke yesterday. "You know I can't tell you anything, Pauly. But we have lots of other witnesses. This has to hurt their case more than ours."

Sharlene, the waitress, approached me from behind and tapped my shoulder. "Do y'all

55

want to order something, darlin'? We have two specials tonight. Open-faced roast beef on toast with mashed potatoes and gravy or hash and poached." In spite of the name and the cocktail napkins, the food at Chili-Dippers was about as far from Mexican as you could stretch.

"I haven't decided," I whispered from behind the menu.

"I can't hear you, darlin'," she said, pushing the menu away from my face.

"The roast beef," I said, just wanting her to go away.

"Maxie, have you met Cassie Burdette? She's a caddie on the PGA Tour."

"Was a caddie," I said, lowering my shield in defeat. Max just stared.

I gestured to the bartender to bring me another round. "Nice to see you," I said to Max. As if we'd just exchanged pleasantries last week. As if it hadn't been ten years since he'd sweet-talked me into sleeping with him on the beach after the prom, with the help of a bottle of Boone's Farm Apple Wine and the pulsing rhythm of the Atlantic Ocean. Ten years since he'd barely spoken to me the following day or any of the days following that one.

"You two know each other?" asked Paul, replacing my empty glass with a full one.

"Myrtle Beach High," said Max, pointing to the prom pictures. "Classes of '90 and

'92." As if our only contact had been waving at each other across a corridor crowded with horny teenagers.

"He was the quarterback, you were the cheerleader?" said Paul.

"You got the first part right," I said.

"You look great, Cass," said Max. "How are you?"

"Great," I said, working to keep my voice cool and still. "I thought you'd moved to D.C."

"Uncle Doug made me an offer I couldn't refuse," he said. "So I moved back last week. They hung the shingle yesterday: Gill, McClellan, and Harding. Has a nice ring to it, don't you think?"

I swallowed the last inch of my beer, surprised it had gone down so fast. "Hit me again, Paul. So you turned out to be a big-shot lawyer."

"Hardly," he said. "Mom told me you were on the PGA Tour."

"Not anymore," I said, reaching for the third Budweiser. "I'm working over at the Grandpappy for now." Max's eyes widened.

"Where your Dad . . ."

"Yep. And Kaitlin Rupert's home base now, too. What's up with all that?"

"If you read the paper, you know the story. She says Coach molested her; he says not a chance. And I believe him. That's why I took the case."

"And now the headshrinker who brought this all out turns up dead. Sounds like trouble to me." This wasn't going so badly. Max and me actually having a conversation. "Buy you a beer?"

He glanced at his watch. Then a wave of red washed up his neck, flooded across his jawline, and bled into his cheeks. "Sorry. I'm meeting Brenda for dinner. I'm already late." He gathered his trench coat from the barstool and reached for his wallet. "Let me get this young lady's bill, too."

"Not in this lifetime," I said, in a voice so hard even the drunk three stools down from me looked up in surprise. Brenda was the cheerleader who'd replaced me a couple of months after Max shut me out. I'd heard from Mom she'd married Max five or so years ago — promoted to cheerleader for life. Let him buy her drinks. I would get blasted on my own tab, thank you very much.

I watched Max leave the bar. "Once an asshole, always an asshole," said a stocky man who slid into an open seat beside me. "Gary Rupert. You remember me, don't you? Katie's my baby sister. And don't worry, Brenda's still got the biggest ass Myrtle Beach High School ever saw. In more ways than one." He laughed loudly and pulled his stool closer to mine.

Jesus. It was beginning to feel like the set from *Cheers* in this bar tonight — everyone

I'd ever known was making a cameo appearance. I had no trouble remembering Gary. He'd asked me out several times after Max dumped me. With my sixteen-year-old heart broken, I wouldn't have gone out on a date even if my fantasy heartthrob Robert Redford had called. And Gary was no teenaged Robert Redford. Where Kaitlin had inherited the long-limbed, aristocratic features of her mother and the athleticism of her father, Gary had gotten the reverse — his mom's clumsiness and Coach's looks, only more squat and lumpy, and minus his father's charm. Maybe it was the beer and the tequila shooter I'd just swallowed, but it seemed like he'd improved on all those fronts over the intervening years.

Gary picked up my empty shot glass and sniffed it. "Bring us a couple more shots of tequila, Pauly. My friend Jose Cuervo, if he's available tonight."

"I'm sorry about your sister," I said. Which seemed entirely inadequate, given the circumstances, but the best I could come up with.

"I hear you've been working with Katie over at the Grandpappy," he said. "Can't you talk her out of this mess? It's tearing the family apart."

"I'm not working with her. We only met today," I said. "We're both spending time over there before we leave, but that's as close as it's going to get. Sorry."

"She's crazy," he said. "We can't figure out what's got into her. I'm the only one will talk to her anymore. It's breakin' Mama's heart. She's even joined a support group for wacked-out parents. They had pickets over there today at Bencher's office."

"Charlatan shrinks write shfiction," I said, noticing my words had started to slur.

He nodded. "I wouldn't be surprised to hear they were involved in the murder."

The second tequila shooter arrived at the same time as my open-faced roast beef sandwich. Although the mashed-potato-walled pool of congealing gravy made me queasy, I knew dinner was the smart choice. I'd suffer a whole lot more than heartburn tomorrow if I went with the tequila. I pushed the shot glass in Gary's direction.

"I'm over my limit. Thanks anyway."

# 5

Based on the front page of the *Sun*, Paul would be collecting five bucks from Lester tonight. Just as he'd predicted, Dr. Bencher headlined the morning edition.

> Outside Dr. Gregory Bencher's office yesterday, protesters picketed his participation in a sexual molestation case. Inside the office, an unidentified assailant shot the psychiatrist dead. Police sources have identified the motive as robbery, denying a connection between the protest and the murder. No suspects have been arrested in the case.

Robbery? I hadn't intended to go by the bar this evening, but I couldn't wait to hear the latest on this turn of events.

I rolled into the Palm Lakes parking lot at seven, grateful, in spite of a sour stomach and a pounding headache, that I'd found the good sense somewhere to turn down the second tequila. I was surprised to find the pro shop door still locked. Odell called out to me as soon as I stepped inside.

"I could use some help here," he said. His

voice sounded funny, tinny and strained. I traced it to the back office, where he sat with Kaitlin. She was slumped in a heap on the small sofa across from his desk. Odell was perched on the arm of the couch, patting her shoulder arrhythmically. She clutched a ragged golf towel in her right fist, which she used to blot the beads of blood that oozed from cuts along the inside of her left wrist.

"What happened?" I asked. If she'd tried to kill herself, I'd have to rate it a half-hearted attempt. "Should I call 911?"

"Too late for that," said Kaitlin. "That might have helped fifteen years ago."

Odell shot me a look loaded with worry, helplessness, and a touch of annoyance. "It's just a few scrapes on her arm," he said. "Nothing too deep. She's a little upset about her doctor being shot and all. I was hoping y'all could maybe talk while I open up the shop."

I didn't want to talk with her. I didn't need Joe Lancaster's warning to tell me that the best thing I could have done was to put a good distance between me and this girl. But I knew I owed Odell, going way back to those years after Dad split. All the peanut butter crackers and Pepsi he'd fed to me, and the dollars he paid me to shag balls out of the practice bunker when I was too sad to go home, and the five or six times he tried to talk to me about Dad leaving, even though I snapped each time that there was nothing left to say.

"Sure," I said to Odell. "Go on and open up."

At first, we sat without speaking. I balanced on the corner of Odell's desk and let my eyes wander over the bookshelves behind Kaitlin. Jack Nicklaus, *Golf My Way*. Al Geiberger, *Tempo. Harvey Penick's Little Red Book*. John Feinstein, *A Good Walk Spoiled*. And my personal favorite — Stephen Baker, *How to Play Golf in the Low 120s*. Cataloging Odell's collection was not why he'd left me in here, but I was at a loss for how to help Kaitlin. I was almost certain she'd made the cuts on her arm herself. I had no idea how to handle that. And I'd never mastered the skill needed to offer heartfelt condolences, never mind about a shrink who'd been murdered after persuading someone to file suit against her own father. Other possible topics of conversation seemed impossibly shallow, like golf, or even bigger minefields, like incest.

"I met your brother at Chili-Dippers last night," I finally blurted out.

"And he tried to talk you into asking me to drop the suit," she said. I shrugged. "I won't do it. Especially now that Dr. Bencher's dead. Someone tried to shut me up by killing Bencher, but it isn't going to work."

"You think he was murdered because of the lawsuit?"

"Maybe," she said. "Maybe it was those people Mother sicced on him — the False Memory Consociation. Fancy name for a bunch of cretins butting into business they know nothing about."

"You think they'd do something like that? While they're picketing right outside his door?"

"How the hell should I know what they would or wouldn't do," she said. "All I know is that he was the only one who believed me, and now he's dead."

"I'm sorry."

"Sure you're sorry," she said. "Everyone's sorry now. That doesn't help me live with it. Hearing his footsteps in the hall at night. All those games we played when I was little." Her voice had developed a girlish singsong quality. "Bouncing on his lap. A game for me. Masturbation for him."

The harsh thought crossed my mind that she was rehearsing lines for a court appearance. "You just forgot all this until now?" My question brought the cold tone back.

"It happens to a lot of us women," she said. "Even in families that seem picture-perfect on the outside." She looked at me hard. "In your shoes, with your history, I'd take a look in my own mirror. I doubt you'll find the risen Christ among the men in your family. And don't overlook your precious Maximilian Harding. He's no different than the rest of them." She stood up, flung the bloody rag into the trash can, and marched out of the office, leaving me no time to smooth things over.

"I have nothing to do with Max," I called out after her. Silence.

Nice work, Cassandra. If golf doesn't pan out, you've got a real future in the helping professions.

Ten minutes later, unable to tolerate further procrastination, I followed Kaitlin back into the pro shop. News crews from Channel 14, Channel 8, and Channel 2 had arranged themselves in a circle, covered wagon–style, outside the door. Technicians had wrapped wires around the wrought-iron hitching posts in front of the door, and halogen spotlights rested on the chowder pot and the cannon. The area was lit up like a ballfield at night. Four anchorpeople shouted questions at Kaitlin. I let myself out the back door and slunk around the adjacent building, past the locker rooms, to eavesdrop.

"Can you tell us something about the details of the sexual abuse?" asked one anchor, her face composed into a mask of concern in distinct contrast to her intrusive questions. "Did you remember this in the process of psychotherapy or had it come up before you contacted Dr. Bencher?"

"Did your doctor make suggestions that your father had abused you?"

"Do you have any ideas about who murdered Dr. Bencher? Did he have any enemies that you were aware of?"

"How will Bencher's death affect the lawsuit against your father?"

In spite of my instinctive dislike for this girl, I felt a rush of sympathy. The bright lights of the cameras washed her features out to shadows. With her eyes wide and her mouth open in confusion, she looked young and lost. Even so, I had to believe she would lash out at anyone who had the misguided urge to try to help her get her bearings.

Now there was a conflict a good shrink could seize upon. Unless, of course, your shrink was lying in the morgue with a bullet hole in his carotid artery.

I jumped in alarm when Odell tapped me on the shoulder. "Your junior clinic golfers are here," he said. "I'd suggest you start early and get them away from this zoo." I nodded, ashamed to be caught snooping.

I developed a hunch early on in the session that the seven kids Odell had me working with had been sprung from an expensive reform school just that morning. For the next hour, I was too busy to worry any more about either Kaitlin's dilemma or my own whopping failure as peer counselor.

"Swing it like a baseball bat," I told Angela, a chunky girl with pigtails and a broad band of freckles across her nose. "Slow it down at the top just long enough that a bird could sit and rest for a minute on your club. Then let her rip." Angela coiled up and belted a shot out past the fifty-yard marker. "Good girl," I said. "Now you're getting the hang of it!"

I left her to separate James and Joshua, twins with a death wish who were using their nine-irons to conduct a sword fight. They weren't bad kids, I had to remind myself, just a little swollen with overprivilege and dangerous to themselves and others with a golf club in hand.

Two hours later, the mothers and nannies, wearing color-coordinated shorts sets, big hair, and strappy platform sandals, arrived to pick up their charges and transport them to the next lesson. Tennis, karate, swimming, and, because it was still the South, etiquette. God forbid they should be allowed to spend time on their own — who knew what trouble they might find. I moved down the range, picking up the clubs the children had left scattered on the Astroturf mats. Dad would never have allowed Charlie to treat his equipment with such carelessness.

"Those are the tools of your trade," he told him a hundred times, as he supervised Charlie cleaning the grooves and then wiping down the grips. By the time I was old enough to play, Dad had lost interest in teaching, beaten down by my brother's persistent and petulant

rejection, too tired to notice that I now followed his instructions exactly.

I stashed the children's equipment in the
pro shop and returned to the range with my
own clubs. Kaitlin had surfaced from her im-
promptu press conference and parked herself
two stations down from me. A tall, athletic
man in magazine-perfect golf attire stood
with his arm draped around her. He had the
Deikon logo written across the bill of his
baseball cap, on both the sleeve and the
pocket of his golf shirt, and painted down
the entire length of his bag. Based on what
Laura would have called an idiot's educated
guess, I assumed this must be her Deikon
rep.

"I shouldn't even be showing you this
one," I heard him say. "Strictly experimental.
I can't wait to see how you make it sing."

Gag me with a spoon.

He offered Kaitlin a driver, a long,
slender club with an enormous copper head
and silvery-blue shaft. I strained to make out
his now-whispered words. I thought I heard
"Ball Hog," "Tee Warrior," and "Fairway
Bruiser." Kaitlin laughed, shrugged off his
hand, and accepted the club he offered. He
stood behind her, arms folded, and watched
as she clobbered a ball out into the field,
well past any reasonable range where the
drive of my dreams would have landed.

"Wow!" he said, pretending that the force

of her swing had knocked him to the ground. She helped him to his feet, giggling, and brushed invisible debris off his backside with more meticulousness than the brief interaction with Astroturf seemed to merit. If I squinted hard enough, I could still make out the tic-tac-toe pattern of the cuts on her left arm. Hard to believe this was the same girl I'd seen crumpled up in Odell's office only a couple hours earlier. It seemed almost like theater. She had to know I was watching.

I hit a few shots with my short irons, working on the precise placement of my fingers on the club shaft. "Close the zipper and keep the hot dog in the bun" was how I described it to the kids this morning. I'd stoop to anything it took to bring the excruciating difficulty of the game down to their level. Or my own. Next I worked on keeping the tempo I'd tried to teach Angela. But my mind couldn't let go of the length of Kaitlin's drives. Or the sight of her running her hands over the Deikon rep's buttocks. From the wash of envy that followed both events, I guessed the long dry spell without a real boyfriend was beginning to wear me down. My few static-filled, long-distance phone conversations with Jack left a lot of needs unsatisfied.

I replaced the clubs in my bag. I'd have plenty of time to practice at the range in Florida. Besides that, if I didn't know how to swing a golf club by now, hitting a few more dozen balls at Palm Lakes sure wasn't going to help me survive Q-school.

"I'm going home to pack," I told Odell. "My plane leaves early."

"Good luck, sweetheart," he said. "I know you can do it. We're all behind you." All part of the problem, I thought. Too damned many people behind me, all leaning hard. Members of the country club and even some visiting tourists that Odell had persuaded to back me with their bucks.

"She's goin' to be a star," I'd heard him tell them. "You'll see her on TV when she's playin' on the LPGA Tour, and you'll be able to say, That's Cassandra Burdette. I helped get her there."

More likely, That's Cassandra Burdette, working the cash register at the pro shop. When the hell is she going to pay back that money she owes me from when she flunked out at Q-school?

# 6

I pulled into the driveway behind Dave's pickup, surprised I didn't see him in the yard. After he finished his breakfast shift at Littles' By the Beach, you could usually count on finding him fussing over his domain: polishing the truck, sweeping pine straw off the roof of the house, or pulling interloping Spanish moss off the live oak that screened him from the neighbors on the left. This was a side of Dave I had to admire. Lord knows, hell, we all knew, he'd made a colossal mistake when he refused to sell out so they could build condos on our lot. Now ours was the only one-family home on the block. But damned if Dave let it bother him. He treated the property like it was a Rockefeller mansion, not an asbestos-shingled ranch in the middle of a tacky tourist zone.

I waved at Mrs. Driggers, who lived in the duplex next door and made our business her own. She could have played back the details of any fight the four families within her immediate jurisdiction had ever had. "Hey there, Cassie. You've got comp'ny," she said. She pointed at the unfamiliar Oldsmobile Ninety-eight Classic that was parked behind Mom's rusty Escort.

Just inside, I heard voices from the direction of the living room. A misnomer, if there ever was one. With its white velveteen furniture, artificial flowers with real potpourri scent, and pale blue carpet, this room was not used for living, only to embalm the rare guest. Coach Rupert sat wedged on the sofa between Mom and Dave. Dave had flipped up the foot rest on his section of the Barcalounger couch, causing Coach to have to hold his weight shifted toward Mom in order to avoid sinking into Dave's lap.

"Damn shame they let Darren Walker go," said Dave, ignoring my arrival. "The Raiders could have made it all the way this year with him at wide receiver, don't you think, Coach?" Mom had that fluttery, anxious look that I knew would translate later into an extra gin and tonic. Coach lumbered to his feet and held out his hand to me.

"Good to see you," he said. "I always had a soft spot in my heart for the Burdette family. Charlie was one of my top players ever."

"Leiner, goddammit," said Dave. "This is the Leiner family now."

Coach grunted. He looked bad, his skin blotchy and loose. Whether from stress, age, or booze, I didn't know. I wondered whether the Nighthawk tattoo on his bicep had sagged as much as the flesh on his neck and jowls.

He turned to face me, his pupils wide and glistening. "Odell talked me into coming to see you," he said. "He thought maybe you could help me out with Kaitlin."

I frowned. It had to be obvious by now, even to Odell, who liked to think the best about everyone until absolutely proven wrong, that I had no connection with that girl. She wouldn't take a tip from me about where to buy a good sandwich.

"I really don't think I can help —"

"I want you to know, I never touched my baby," said Coach, before I could finish my sentence. His voice broke. "I'm so proud of her." Now he looked at Dave. "You know how it is with a daughter. She's the bright light in your life. You'd do anything for her. You'd never hurt her." He sat down hard, dropped his head in his hands, and let out what sounded to be a strangled sob.

My mind raced in a million directions. I doubted Dave could relate to anything Coach said. An expression of disgust flooded his face as soon as Coach mentioned "touch" and "baby." I flashed briefly on the memory of my own father. I doubted he could have related to Coach's misery, either — a man who'd left his daughter at a time when she needed him most. I pushed my thoughts away from Dad, and back toward Coach Rupert. I recalled a game we used to play as teenagers: Truth or Dare. Truth: Did you ever fondle your daughter?

Mom broke the painful silence. "I'm sure everything will work out just fine," she said, patting his knee awkwardly. My mother, master of the meaningless platitude.

"She needs help," said Coach Rupert. "And not from the likes of that asshole who screwed her up. I would have killed the bastard myself, if someone else hadn't beat me to it. She was fine before that. High-strung, yes. If anything, I should have paid more attention to her, not less."

"Leave it in God's hands," said Mom, still patting his knee. This was a new one on me. Mom didn't like to leave anything in anybody's hands, God included.

"That's why I came," said Coach. "Cassandra, I need your help. If only you could try and talk to her." He turned again to Dave. "We all have regrets about how we raised our kids. We should have done this, if only we'd given them that."

He looked at Dave for confirmation. Dave's face was flat. No regrets there, I guessed. Not an introspective molecule flickered in that guy's body. Not a glimmer of fatherly feelings, either. Dr. Baxter liked to point out how hard I was on him, how hard he tried to fill Dad's shoes right after he walked out on us, but I couldn't see it. Maybe wouldn't see it. I couldn't get past how he bullied Mom. Or how he seemed to like tearing down and stomping on any dream someone had that was bigger than his own shoelace-narrow worldview.

I stood up. "I'll try, Coach. I can't promise anything." No point in telling him how badly my few conversations with Kaitlin had already gone. Also no point in telling him I didn't know whose story to believe, and didn't even really want to know the truth. Any way it turned out, it seemed like it had to come to an ugly end.

" 'Preciate it," Coach said as he struggled out of the sagging couch cushions. "And good luck in Florida. Just don't try to outhit Kaitlin. She's bigger than life on the tee." He winked, shook hands with me and Dave, kissed Mom on the cheek, and left. Just what I needed, another reminder about Kaitlin's superior length off the tee box.

"Get me a beer," Dave told Mom. "That guy makes me sick."

"He said he didn't do anything," said Mom.

"Just get me the damn beer."

Before I could escape to my room, the doorbell rang again. "From the halls of Montezuma . . ." sang the chimes — one of the first changes Dave instituted after he bought out Dad's share of the house and moved in.

"Show some respect. You owe your freedom to the men of the United States

Marine Corps," he liked to tell me whenever we disagreed about anything. As if his years ladling out stew to the recruits at some North Carolina military base had anything to do with earning respect from me.

Mom ushered Detective Maloney into the living room.

"If you don't mind," he said, looking at Mom and Dave, "I'd like to speak to Miss Burdette alone." They left the room, Mom moving slowly and watching back over her shoulder, her forehead furrowed with worry.

"Chief thinks we need you to stay in the area until we get a better handle on the Bencher case," he said. A day that had already been plenty bad enough was now taking a turn for the worse. My lips and tongue felt thick and heavy. For a minute, I had trouble even getting my mouth to form words.

"Please," I said. "This is my only shot, Detective. Please don't take it away. I promise I'll stay in close touch. It's only six days." He thought for several minutes, then gave a small nod.

"I'm going to give you the phone number for Arthur Pate at the Sarasota County sheriff's office. Call him as soon as you get in. He can make sure we get a hold of you if we need to." I nodded. "My ass is on the line here, Cassandra. It's not protocol to allow anyone connected to a murder case to leave the state in the middle of the investigation."

"Maybe you don't believe me," I said, "but I didn't do it. I didn't even know the guy." He shrugged. I guessed he'd heard that one before. "Thanks for letting me go."

The detective grimaced as he stood to leave. "One more thing," he said. He paused, then smiled. "Hit 'em straight. We could use a gal from Myrtle Beach on the Tour. Show 'em we don't just make golf courses, we know how to play 'em, too."

I thanked him again and showed him to the door. Mom reappeared the minute it slammed shut. From the syrupy sound of her voice, I knew she hadn't wasted any time hitting the gin bottle.

"What is it, Cassie? What's wrong?"

"Nothing to worry over, Mom. He just had a couple of questions about the doctor who was killed. He had the office next to Dr. Baxter and they wondered if I'd seen anything funny." Mom didn't like to acknowledge the existence of shrinks, never mind being reminded that her own daughter talked to one.

"I never should have let you play golf. It's brought nothing but trouble to our lives." This was a discussion that could only lead to an unpleasant dead end, one we'd visited frequently over the last several years.

"I have to pack now, Mom."

Her trembly voice followed me down the hall. "By the way, that nice Max Harding called this afternoon. I wrote the message down for you." I came back out of my room and took the scrap of paper she offered. The message was printed in her neat block letters.

SORRY ABOUT RUNNING OFF LAST NIGHT. CAN WE GET TOGETHER WHEN YOU GET BACK IN TOWN? Mom had underlined "sorry" and "get together" with her yellow highlighter.

"He left numbers for his office and his car phones," said Mom. "He was such a sweet boy. He sounded like he really wanted to see you."

"He's married, Mother," I said. I wadded the note up and shoved it in my pocket. "I'm going to pack."

Cashbox the cat was stretched across the end of the bed, obscuring everything but the *C* and the *e* in the *Cassie* that was embroidered in loopy script on the pink gingham bedspread. My collection of stuffed cats lined the shelves above the bed: Mothball, Fuzzy Wuzzy, Wuzzy Fuzzy, Licorice, Tangerine, and Queenie. All of them neatly mended in spite of their dyed rabbit-fur coverings worn shabby and thin with age. My golf trophies were pushed to the back of the shelf, the taller ones poking up like dandelions through the carpet of fake fur.

Mom preferred to keep this room, like my relationship with her, firmly planted in the era when I was still ten years old. Well before

I'd really gotten involved in what she called devil golf, before Charlie had pushed her away, and even before Dad had run off with Maureen. Maureen of the neon spandex and buns so tight she could send Morse code signals just by squeezing the muscles in her ass. I rubbed Cashbox behind the ears until he rumbled with satisfaction.

I lay down next to the cat and picked up the golf club I kept beside the bed. It was a Ben Hogan blade nine-iron, part of the hand-me-down set my father let me fool around with once I turned eight. I fit my fingers into the training grip I'd glued onto the end of the shaft, and flexed the club. I always thought more clearly with my hands in the proper overlapping position.

What had life really been like in the Rupert household? According to Kaitlin, Coach's so-called love for her had gone well past acceptable fatherly affection. His story, which couldn't have been more different, seemed a whole lot easier to believe. Was he capable of shooting the man who'd put those ideas in her head? Where was the fine line between loving a child too much and not nearly enough? In my case, Odell insisted that the reason my father stopped calling was because having just a little contact with me hurt more than having none at all. But all I felt was the gaping emptiness of his absence and the rage of my mother's blame. The phone rang downstairs, interrupting my gloomy ruminations.

"It's for you, dear," Mom called up the stairs. "It's Joe somebody."

"Hey, Doc," I said, picking up my pink Princess extension. "You won't even believe what's going on here." I told him about Dr. Bencher's murder, the scratches on Kaitlin's wrist, the visit from her father, and Detective Maloney's insistence that I keep in contact with the sheriff in Florida.

"So let me get this right," said Joe. "You think the guy was alive when you came into the office?"

"I'm no doctor," I said. "But honest to God, it looked like his lips were moving. And the sucking noises . . . it was horrible."

"I can't believe they think you killed him," said Joe. "Maybe they figure you saw something that could help solve the case, coming in so soon after he was shot."

"Like what? The murderer leaving? That seems too obvious."

"Were Bencher's lips just twitching or do you think he was trying to tell you something?"

"If he was, we sure weren't speaking the same language. He was well on his way to another world when I found him."

"What about the papers you tried to clean up? What was written on them?"

By now, Joe's questions were reviving the

scene in my mind in sickening detail. "I can't think about this anymore. It's making me want to barf. Honestly, I didn't see anything, except a gruesome display that's going to provide the material for a lot of future nightmares."

"Sorry," said Joe. "We'll drop it. So then Kaitlin cut herself the next morning — that fits perfectly with my borderline diagnosis."

"The weirdest thing is how easily she seems to be able to shake all that off — one minute she's in the pits of despair, the next she's publicly feeling up this hunk out on the range. Maybe she's got a split personality."

"Probably not," said Joe. "Just a real good way of shutting off her feelings. You could take a half page from her in that department. Forget all this and focus on your golf."

"Hah. Easier said than done. I can't wait for you to get to Venice. I need professional help. You, my friend, are just the man for the job."

"'That's why I called," said Joe. I didn't like the note of sheepishness that had crept into his voice. "I'm not going to be able to get there until later in the week. Three guys withdrew from the PGA championship — that puts Mike in. I feel like I really need to be there with him. I'll try to get over to Venice on Thursday, Thursday night at the latest."

"Shit," I said. "Thursday is likely to be too late. You know the cut's on Wednesday."

"You know what to do, Cassie," he said. "And Laura will be there with you. I'm thinking it might even work out better if I'm not around — too many cooks spoiling the broth and all that."

"Fine," I said. "That's just great. Tell Mike to hit 'em straight. I'll see you later."

"Come on, Cassie . . ." I heard the pleading in his voice as I slammed down the phone.

# 7

The plane circled over Sarasota and slid to a smooth landing. I collected my duffle bag and golf clubs from the baggage claim area without incident. The Ben Hogan nine-iron I carried with me on board — everything else could be replaced, but I'd freak if I lost my lucky nine. While I waited in line to register for a Rent-a-Wreck, I dialed into my cell phone to retrieve three new voice mail messages. With any luck, one would be from Jack.

The first was from Joe, firm but at the same time apologetic. "I know you're disappointed. But you'll understand and forgive me when you think this through," he said. Always the optimist. "This is a big deal for Mike. My being there could really make the difference —" I hit the delete button. He couldn't really believe this wasn't a big deal for me, too.

The second message was Sheriff Pate. I try not to make a habit of judging people by either their voice or their appearance — what God gave a man shouldn't be held against him. Even so, this guy's gravelly bark rated him one, with Katie Couric at ten, in terms of friendly first impressions.

"Pate here. I'll look for you at the Plantation

this afternoon. Stick around until I find you."

The third message was Joe again. "I didn't get a chance to tell you that I've put in a couple calls to some friends about Bencher. I'll let you know what I hear. And remember what we've been talking about — don't worry about how you're playing on the practice rounds, you're just getting a mental picture of the layouts —" I punched delete. Son-of-a-rotten-bitch.

I knew Mike's first appearance in a major championship was a pivotal moment in his career. He could either handle the pressure well and set the table for even better performances in future majors, or choke, and color upcoming events in a negative way that would be difficult to override. You saw it over and over with golfers on the Tour. If they played well in one event, their confidence mounted and they tended to do well again the following year. Same with a big collapse — deep in some primitive part of the brain, the failure got connected with the tournament or golf course where it had occurred, making future wins there a lot less likely.

I also knew that since last summer, Mike had grown to rely on Joe. He hadn't said much about it, but I'd seen how Joe helped him get a grip on his nerves, and how that translated to his improved putting. If Joe could keep him from blowing up, no contest

84

— anyone would rate that as more important than holding my hand through the Q-school practice rounds.

The bare-bones facts about Q-school were brutal. Hardly any of the girls who tried made it through to the LPGA Tour on their first attempt. From what I'd heard, you were supposed to learn a lot your first time out, maybe realize that with a little more work you belonged in this elite company. Then you'd come back the next year, maybe with a better putting stroke or nerves of titanium rather than linguini.

But there would be no second chances for me. I'd allowed myself one shot. The stakes were too damn high. No way would I accept handouts from Odell and my other backers for a second chance at humiliation. Besides which, the girls who returned over and over didn't have Mom and Dave nagging in the background about how it was time to just grow up and get a real job. I needed every advantage I could muster to give this try all I had. So with Joe bailing out, I felt as low as I could remember feeling since Mike told me he'd found another caddie and I wasn't welcome back. I tended to take rejection hard, another of Dr. Baxter's favorite refrains.

"Outside your conscious awareness," he'd told me more than once, "when someone important to you leaves, your mind will make the automatic connection to your father. You may feel more distressed than the current situation really warrants. You'll need to work hard to separate out the two circumstances."

So, Baxter would have had me say, Joe wasn't abandoning me, merely arriving a day or two late. It felt a damn lot worse than that. I wished Laura could have come down earlier. I knew I should be grateful she was coming at all — lots of the girls competing wouldn't have a caddie. And unless I managed the unlikely coup of finishing in what little prize money the LPGA offered, Laura's compensation for the week would be zero. Ten percent of nothing was still nothing, no matter what accounting procedures you used. She was already paying her own expenses to Q-school — I could hardly ask her to give up the proceeds from a weekend of lucrative golf lessons in August, the Connecticut high season, as well.

I pulled my rented Pontiac out onto Interstate 75. Even if I'd been set down blindfolded, I would have known instantly I was in South Florida. No mistaking the flat, flat landscape and shimmering heat. Not to mention my brand of haute cuisine at every rest stop — Waffle House and Cracker Barrel — homestyle Southern cooking that the rest of the country was just beginning to discover. I loved it here. After four years of college at UF, I called this crazy, mixed-up state loaded with retirees, itinerant wanderers, and rabid environmentalists my second home.

Forty-five minutes down the road, I arrived in Venice and at the Starlight Motel, recommended by the volunteers running Q-school and insisted on by Odell. "The week will be hard enough without spending the nights in some fleabag," he told me. "You pick some nice place and send the bill to me."

The lobby was big on "faux" — faux green marble floor, faux Impressionist paintings behind the desk, and a big island of faux palms decorated with cafe lights in the middle of the space. Even the desk clerk, with false eyelashes and Mary Kay foundation applied by trowel, seemed a little unreal. A young woman carrying her clubs arrived in the lobby just after I approached the counter. She and her mother were dressed in matching Liz Claiborne golf outfits. I watched them as the clerk processed my reservation.

"Look, Becky, they have a stamp machine right there," her mother said. The older woman pointed to a dispenser near the breakfast nook in the corner. "You can get that postcard to Daddy into the mail today." Why the hell would she be sending postcards from Q-school?

"Dear Daddy, Having a great time, wish you were here. Love, Becky"? Too weird.

I knew from the pit in my stomach that I felt bad about the mother thing too. Not that

I'd want my own mother here this week. What a disaster that would be. But I wished I had the kind of mother I could have traveled with. Without Joe or Laura, I felt really alone. And the girl's mother had only served to grind that in.

I checked into my room: two queen beds, a kitchenette, a fold-out couch — more than enough room for me, and Laura, when she arrived. I stashed my duffle in the closet and the nine-iron under the bed and went downstairs to investigate the other features of the motel. The charms of the swimming pool were limited — it wasn't much bigger than a one-car garage and fronted directly on the Interstate off-ramp. I used my room key to get into the exercise area — not much happening there, either. Three aerobics machines lined the far wall: a wobbly stationary bike, a stairstepper powered by genuine Atlas shocks, and a treadmill with a prominent "out of order" sign. The rest of the room contained one Nautilus knock-off and a hodgepodge of free weights. Jogging it would be.

The black vinyl seat of my rented car singed my thighs during the entire five-mile ride to the golf course. Finally, a large banner marked the entrance to the club: "Plantation Golf and Country Club Welcomes LPGA Qualifying School, August 17–21. Spectators Welcome!" The last two words in particular gave me the willies. As Mike's caddie, I'd grown used to crowds watching every move we made. But this time, I'd be the one hitting the ball. I crossed a small wooden bridge over a dyed-blue pond and walked until I saw a hand-lettered sign identifying the LPGA office. With my gut doing cartwheels, I could tell the competition was finally beginning to feel real.

"I'm here to register for Q-school?" My voice veered off into a question mark, sounding small and scared.

A short, stout senior citizen with thick glasses and a friendly smile greeted me. "I'm Bunker," she said. "And this is Divot." She pointed to a petite woman behind the desk. "You need to check in over there. We're in charge of all the volunteers. Let us know if we can help you in any way this week." Divot nodded vigorously. Little people named Bunker and Divot? I wondered if I'd walked into golf's version of *The Wizard of Oz* — I braced myself in case they burst into song. Or began a soft-shoe with their partners, Fairway and Chip Shot.

When no song and dance developed, I thanked the ladies and stepped in line behind two Asian women. One was in tears, the other argued in broken English for an exception to be made for her friend's lost application.

"That's why we spell it out on the form," said the woman behind the desk. She was dressed like a golfer — white polo shirt, khakis, sensible shoes, and a short hairstyle that would stand up to a brutal travel schedule and a parade of golf visors. She pointed to the paper in front of her and began to read aloud. " *'Late or incomplete entry not acceptable,'* " she said. " 'Deadline for entry means time of receipt at LPGA Headquarters. Entries should be submitted early to allow ample time for delay or error in transmission.' " The Asian player continued to sob. "I'm sorry," said the woman. "If the application turns up, you'll be able to play in the California tournament." Add *brisk* and *firm* to the list of adjectives that described her.

I was shaking when I approached the desk. "Cassandra Burdette." I offered her my sweating hand.

"Alice MacPherson," said the woman. The crushing handshake confirmed my first impression: no nonsense tolerated. Alice inclined her head in the direction of the weeping girl. "You feel bad about that, but there are rules." I nodded. "You're all set," she said, after pulling my record out of a stack of papers on her desk. "Here are the times we have available for practice rounds. For tournament play on Tuesday and Wednesday, you'll have one round on the Panther course, one on the Bobcat. Both rounds after the cut will be played on the Bobcat. So I'd suggest you try them both.

The informational meeting for all players is Monday, eight in the morning. Attendance is not optional." I nodded. "Mandatory, in other words. Don't miss it." I nodded again and scheduled two practice rounds, one on each of the courses I'd be playing. Alice handed me a fat packet of materials.

"Read through this," she said. "Welcome guide, list of nonconforming drivers, rules of play, yardage books for both courses. Pairings for the first round will be posted Monday. Good luck. Let us know if you need anything."

I shook her hand again, my mouth bent into a weak smile. I stopped outside the office to peruse the players' bulletin board. Someone had tacked up the list of nonconforming equipment and a copy of the local rules of play. I also noticed a hand-written sign announcing a get-together the next night at "Joanne and Nicki's" condo. "Come for a time of fellowship and friend-ship. You will find what you need, if you follow in the way of our Lord," the notice read.

I needed something all right, a way to get out of my own head — and maybe into someone else's brain. But I doubted that either Alice MacPherson or even Jesus himself could help me with that. Second best would be to get to the range and work on grooving my swing — the only place I might get relief from the thoughts swirling in my mind.

"Leave enough time to get acquainted with both courses, but not so much you get stale or panicky," Joe Lancaster had told me. Good advice, but way too late, at least in the panicky department.

The practice range was supplied with Titleist balls, scuffless and sharp white — better quality than most of the balls the customers at Palm Lakes used. I leaned my clubs against the bag stand and stretched. Hard to believe I was really here. Another piece of advice from Joe Lancaster came to mind.

"Try to stay away from thinking about the big picture," he'd said. "Your mind can run on a thousand tracks, but your body can only reasonably handle one shot at a time. So, when I ask what you're thinking, I don't want to hear, 'How am I going to beat all these girls who are better prepared than me and have more experience and who will probably kick my ass and ruin my dream of competing on the Ladies Professional Golf Tour?' Okay?"

I'd laughed hard when he put it that way a couple of weeks ago. Today, that run-on thought was as real as the grass in front of me, and not the least bit funny. I couldn't stop thinking about the Asian girl, whose chances for qualifying this week had been torpedoed by the U.S. Mail. Or maybe, to give the mail service the benefit of the doubt, some office clerk had screwed up and misplaced her application. Ouch. Or, suppose the girl's ambivalence about competing had subconsciously sabotaged her to the point where she "accidentally" threw the thing out herself. I laughed. I'd obviously spent too damn much time lately in the presence of headshrinkers.

I pulled out my wedge and set up to hit short pitch shots to a red flag fifty yards out in the range. I wasn't going to make the cut as a long ball hitter, if Kaitlin was representative of the other players in the field. I'd have to depend on accurate approach shots and lots of putts dropping. After shanking two balls out to the right, I put the wedge away and retreated to easy swings with my nine-wood. It was hard to hit a bad shot with a club that forgave almost anything.

"Your backswing looks a little flat."

Some poor chump getting last-minute advice, I thought. Let's hope it helps.

"Miz Burdette, in my experience, with a backswing that flat, you're goin' to tend to a big banana slice." Now I recognized the gravelly voice.

"You must be Sheriff Pate," I said, offering my hand to a short, very sweaty man, whose uniform barely stretched over the expansive girth of his stomach. His shirt buttons had to work harder here than I thought their manufacturer had intended.

"Let me see your club," said the sheriff. "I had the same problem last year. I'll show you how I fixed it."

I didn't want to give him my club. It was a five-hundred-dollar titanium wood, with a graphite shaft and a custom Winn Contour grip. Three weeks of my paycheck at Palm Lakes had gone to pay for it. Even worse than lending him the club would be listening to his advice. It astonished me how the worst golfers considered themselves experts when it came to telling someone else what was wrong with her game. I sure didn't need a head full of Sheriff Pate's silly tips as I teed off on Tuesday. But I was in no position to quibble. I passed him the nine-wood.

"You're taking it away like this," he said, demonstrating an ugly baseball swing. "You want to hold it out here, so you don't end up comin' outside in. That's where you get your slice." I nodded. He took a couple of big cuts with my club, ugly and fast. "Let's try her out." The ball he hit barely cleared the grass, starting out right and curving almost ninety degrees before it hit the ground and bounced to a halt.

The sheriff scowled and inspected the club head. "I hope you didn't pay too much for this. The balance is all off. But you get the general idea."

"Hard to hit them straight with a girl's

club." I hoped I could suppress a powerful urge to laugh in his face.

"So. You're the little gal they think offed that headshrinker." He handed me my club.

"No." I wiped the sheriff's sweat off the grip of the nine-wood. "I'm the one who found him after he'd been shot."

"You don't 'specially look like a cold-blooded killer." He hitched his trousers up until they almost covered the stretch of stomach and undershirt that had escaped while he swung.

"I didn't —"

"Maybe a crime of passion," said the sheriff. "Yeah, that looks like more your style. Say you asked the doctor out for a drink and he says he's married. Then you don't want to take no for an answer so you push harder and he still says no. So you shoot 'im. Maybe you didn't think it out ahead of time, you're just hot-blooded, that's all." His eyes swept over my entire body, stopping to linger on my chest and just below my waist. "Or maybe he didn't say no. Those doctors all have couches in their offices, don't they? Just waiting for the pretty girls. Then he felt bad later about acting unprofessional and called off the whole thing. And then you shot 'im."

"I did not know the man." I spoke the words slowly, as if to a very young child or a mentally retarded person, trying to hold the fury and fear out of my voice.

He continued on as if I'd said nothing. "We know it couldn't have been a professional job. No hired gun worth his salt is gonna shoot some guy in the throat. Too messy, first of all. Second, might not really finish the job. Guy could talk or signal something on his way out. Know what I'm sayin'?"

What was he saying? It was hard to tell from his demeanor whether he considered me a serious suspect or just enjoyed playing with me, knowing he had me trapped. "I guess maybe I don't know what you mean," I said.

"I mean, if you didn't shoot 'im, chances are, the fellow that did thinks you know who did it. Get what I'm sayin' now?"

"I'm in trouble either way," I said. "Either I killed a man, or else the guy who did might be looking for me. Might think I know more than I do."

He nodded. "I'm sayin' watch your back, darlin'."

"Do you think this will get wrapped up soon?"

"We're tryin', little gal." Then he winked. "What kind of driver you hittin'?"

"I don't use a driver," I said. "I tee off with a three-wood."

"That so. Hope you get that shank thing worked out, then. You're going to need one hell of a short game." He grinned and walked away.

# 8

I packed up and left the range as soon as Sheriff Pate's squad car pulled away. I planned to stop at the Publix supermarket I'd passed on the way to the club, buy a few staples to stock my kitchenette, and retreat to the motel. From there, my plan consisted of blotting out my mounting anxiety with bad TV sitcoms and a six-pack of Busch beer.

I browsed the frozen food section in Publix and selected black bean burritos, well within my budget at three for a dollar. Then I moved to the produce section for a few bananas. Becky, of the postcard-to-Daddy fame, was there with her mother, who pushed a shopping cart loaded with strawberries, yams, melons, and broccoli. Sure, rub it in. Mommy was going to serve home-cooked meals all week so Becky didn't get gas or otherwise feel uncomfortable as she stood over her important putts. I glanced down at the frozen lumps in my carry basket, then abandoned them in front of the beer cooler and checked out with just the Busch. Screw the budget, microwaving frozen burritos would be too depressing.

More than anything, I wished for the familiarity of Chili-Dippers. Maybe the regulars I hung with were a peculiar bunch of misfits, maybe some of them even further out than odd. But sitting on the fourth barstool from the end would feel more like home right now than anyplace else I could name. I drove by a branch of the chain restaurant Chili's. That would have to do. The name was close enough, and I knew I could get comfort food, even if it wasn't hush puppies and Calabash seafood. In the bar, I took the fourth seat from the entrance to the kitchen. When my Corona arrived, I squeezed in a wedge of lime and sat back to watch the other customers.

A crowd of blue-hairs who'd taken advantage of the early bird special was leaving, replaced by young couples starting their Saturday night fun with a Chili's happy hour. A waitress dressed in jeans and a red golf shirt presented herself next to me. "Hi, my name is Cindi! I'll be taking care of you tonight."

Damn, that sounded good. Though I knew she didn't mean taking care of what I really needed — reassurance that I belonged here and that everything would turn out just fine. Instead, I consoled myself by ordering fried chicken and mashed potatoes with cream gravy — heavy on fat and carbohydrates. It might not make any coach's list for a desirable training meal, but it was the closest I could get to South Carolina low-country cuisine.

I watched Cindi work the room. She was

adorable — her appeal centered mostly in the smile, the dimples, and a heartfelt solicitousness that seemed wasted at Chili's. I doubted she had a single thought about golf or murder on her mind, and she was the happier for it. If I bombed out this week, maybe Chili's was hiring. Realistically, though, I lacked the dimples and, more importantly, the sincere and sunny concern for the well-being of random customers.

Halfway into my second Corona, I felt a tap on my shoulder. "Penny for your thoughts, Cassie. You're looking very serious tonight. As well as lovely, I cannot help but add," said Gary Rupert. It took me just a moment to recognize him, then I felt a rush of relief and gratitude for a familiar face. Any familiar face.

"You startled me," I said. "I didn't expect to see anyone I knew in here. Have a seat. You're down here to watch Kaitlin?"

"I'm her caddie," said Gary. "I thought you knew that."

"Lucky her," I said. "You don't see my brother out here with me." I felt disloyal even mentioning Charlie. He supported me the best he could, considering his own pressure-cooker career as junior partner in a big D.C. law firm. "How'd you get the time off?"

"At the moment, I've got all the time in the world," he said. "I made the mistake of signing on with a dot-com last year. They did a great selling job — I was going to make a million before I hit thirty-five. Instead, they hit the skids and I'm on the street."

"Sore subject, I guess. But good timing for Kaitlin."

We chatted about our respective trips down and places we'd found to stay. The Ruperts had rented a condo on the Bobcat's eighteenth fairway — "Kaitlin wanted to be close in," Gary explained. He looked hard at me. "How are you holding up?"

I sighed. "Rough day."

"Practice didn't go well?"

"There's that, though I hardly got any in, really. The worst is this business about Bencher's murder." I told him about my meeting with Sheriff Pate.

"So he thinks the murderer might believe you know something about how Bencher was killed?" I nodded. "Like what?"

"Like maybe Bencher said something identifying his attacker before he died and I heard him. That's what my shrink friend Joe Lancaster thinks, too."

"Did he say something?"

I shrugged. "I don't think so. It was just a bunch of horrible gasps and gurgles as far as I could tell. And I've explained all that to the police several times."

"Maybe Pate was just blowing smoke up your ass, enjoyed seeing you squirm." He half-patted, half-rubbed my knee.

"Quite possible," I said. "The more rattled I felt, the more cheerful he seemed."

"Was there anything else unusual about Bencher's office? Besides a dying headshrinker, I mean."

I chuckled and thought back to the scene. "It was a mess — papers strewn everywhere. I caught hell when I started to clean things up. I know it was dumb. It was strictly instinct."

"Or your mother's excellent training," said Gary. "So did you see anything there?"

I shrugged again. "I don't think so." I laughed. "Maybe if they put me through hypnosis, all this important subconscious stuff would come out. On the other hand, could be you'd just hear gibberish about how Mom didn't play classical music when she was pregnant with me or some other stupid psychobabble."

"Couple of beers here," Gary called to the bartender. "The police seem eager to relate this problem to Kaitlin's lawsuit. But from everything I've heard, Bencher was like a heat-seeking missile when it came to controversy."

"That's what my friend Joe says," I told Gary. "He promised he'd ask around the shrink circles and see what dirt he could turn up."

"Sounds awfully distracting, this bullshit. Let me know if I can help." He patted my knee again and smiled. "Kaitlin's not really so bad, you know," he added. "She's just mega-insecure. In her mind, everyone's a threat. Especially a woman as talented and attractive as you."

His hand brushed a little farther up my thigh, maybe accidental, maybe not. In any case, the combination of alcohol, Gary's concern and compliments, and the feel of his touch on my leg was surprisingly pleasant. I tried to think why I'd been so definite about refusing a date with him ten years ago. Just a dumb, shallow teenager, I decided. Drawing conclusions based on how clear someone's complexion was or how many touchdowns they scored. Attributes which didn't mean too much at this stage of life. Then I decided that if he touched my leg again, even farther up the thigh, I would not remove his hand.

Kaitlin's arrival at the bar truncated any further development. She had her Deikon rep in tow, radiating an odd combination of testosterone and bonhomie.

"I hope I'm not interrupting something," she said. The unpleasant curl of her lip suggested the opposite.

"Hi, sis," said Gary. "I'd just about given up on you. I'm starving. Have you met Walter Moore, Cassie?"

"Yo." My hand disappeared briefly into the Deikon equipment hunk's fleshy palm.

"Want to join us for dinner?" said Gary.

One quick look at the expression on Kaitlin's face made it clear just how unwelcome I would be at the Rupert dinner party. "I'll stay where I am, thanks. I'm sure my order's just about ready to come up," I said. "How'd you make out today, Kaitlin? Hit 'em straight?" That said just for the annoyance value of making her acknowledge my presence.

"Just fine."

"It's common courtesy to ask, 'And you?'" Gary said.

"And you?" she said, her voice telegraphing controlled disdain.

"I've got a small case of the shanks," I said. "Nothing that should affect your appetite, though. Have a good dinner." If I was lucky, my mention of the forbidden s-word would worm its way into Kaitlin's superstitious golfer's psyche.

Gary patted my back and followed his sister, Walter the hunk, and perky Cindi into the dining room. I dug into the food the bartender deposited in front of me, eager now to clean my plate and return to the solitude of my room. Sooner I could get to sleep, sooner I'd have the chance to put all this out of my mind.

Three women I thought I recognized from the golf course walked by me on their way into the restaurant. "Are you here for Q-school?" asked the last one through. "You look familiar."

"Cassie Burdette." I offered her my hand. "I think we met a couple years ago at the

NCAA tournament in Alabama."

"Mary Morrison," the girl said. "And these are Adele Simpson and Eve Darling. We noticed you having a little chat with our favorite golfer."

"Best thing you can do there is ignore the bitch," said Eve.

"Sounds like you all know her pretty well," I said, laughing.

"Futures Tour," said Mary. "She's a legend in her own mind. Come on, bring your plate and your beer and sit with us."

After ordering their drinks and dinner, the three women began to describe their experiences with Kaitlin.

"To put it bluntly," began Adele, "she's insufferable."

"Don't you guys live in the same town?" asked Eve. "You're not distant relations or anything?"

"Oh, please," I said. "Spare me that. Unfortunately, we do both come from Myrtle Beach. And I wouldn't mind having her talent off the tee, but any similarity stops there."

Mary laughed. "She hasn't made a lot of friends out on Futures. If she wins, she's unbearable. When she loses, she's worse."

"The only things she's really interested in talking about are her golf game and this false memory business," said Adele. "We're people, too. Even if you don't want to be best friends, you could at least make a little conversation. How're you doing? Where're you from? Are you married or happy?" I laughed, thinking of Gary insisting that Kaitlin ask about my day.

"It's worse than that," said Eve. "She's mean. Things don't go her way, she lashes out at whoever's in her path."

"And don't forget calling people on obscure rules in the USGA book. She's called girls on teeing up ahead of the markers, using tees as ball-markers, the two-ball rule, you name it. She's never heard of giving the benefit of the doubt," added Adele.

"The low point was a match play tournament when Kaitlin's opponent chipped in for bird and Kaitlin insisted she replay the shot because she was away," said Eve. "By the letter of the law, she was correct, but the spirit was mean. It really took the heart out of the girl she was playing."

"She's always correct," said Mary. "But what gets to you is the steady drip, drip, drip of her self-righteousness. Most of us avoid her like the plague."

"Except for Julie," corrected Eve.

"Who's Julie?" I asked.

"It's a long story," said Mary. "Short version, Julie Atwater seems to be Kaitlin's new best friend. Long version, we think Kaitlin talked her into accusing her own father of incest a couple of months ago."

"I'm confused," I said. "Kaitlin got Julie involved with this stuff several months ago? I thought she just filed the suit against Coach Rupert last week?"

"The lawsuit is new," said Eve, "but the accusations against her father are not."

"Next thing we knew," said Mary, "Julie's wondering if she's a lesbian. You'll probably see her dad this week. He's been picketing every stop we've made for the last couple months. He's got the girls in the Bible study group in a tizzy over this, too. Julie used to hang with the Bible thumpers; now the group doesn't speak to her at all."

"Is her father that Leviticus guy?" I asked.

"You know this dude?"

"I saw him marching outside Kaitlin's shrink's office last week in Myrtle Beach." It occurred to me that these girls might wonder why I was that familiar with a shrink complex. "It was big news in the Myrtle Beach paper," I added quickly. "First Kaitlin filed her lawsuit and then the psychiatrist was murdered. I couldn't figure out why a Bible thumper was picketing there. So he blames that psychiatrist for his daughter's problems?"

"From what I heard, Kaitlin set Julie up for a consultation with her doctor. That's when the trouble started."

"What a mess." I sighed, more than ready to change the subject. "Have any of you played the courses yet?"

"The Panther's a bitch," said Adele. "I really hope I get it over with the first day."

"The good news is you only have to play it once," said Eve.

"Yeah, but once around the Panther's Claw is plenty."

As I finished my beer, the girls joked about their practice round earlier in the day. I suddenly felt exhausted. Some girls liked to socialize the whole time they were here at Q-school, distract themselves from what otherwise might feel like unbearable pressure. I was glad to have made the acquaintance of some friendly faces, but at the same time, I felt desperate to get off by myself and regroup. I hoped for an inspirational and sexy phone message from Jack Wolfe. I also wanted to talk to Joe. I just wasn't sure I was quite ready to forgive his defection.

"I'm going to hit the hay," I said, standing and sliding a twenty-dollar bill onto the table. "I'm beat."

"Sure you don't want to go clubbing with us?" Eve demonstrated an abbreviated funky chicken.

"Thanks anyway, big date tomorrow. My first encounter with the Panther."

I made my way back through the bar, which was now crowded, noisy, and smoky. I caught sight of Gary Rupert sitting at a stool on the far side of the room, but I'd had enough conversation for one night with him as well. It wasn't until I was buckling the seat belt in my rental car that it occurred to me how familiar the man talking with him looked. Something about the broad shoulders and slightly thinning hair.

I drove back to my motel, wishing I could get Sheriff Pate's warning out of my mind. Even worrying about double bogeys on the four holes that comprised the Panther's Claw would be preferable to imagining the possibility of being stalked for information I did not possess. I thought back over the evening. I decided to put any feelings about Gary, sexual or otherwise, on hold. His sweet defense of Kaitlin reminded me of my own brother, Charlie. Charlie would stick up for me no matter what the circumstances. In this case, Gary had to be off the mark. From all that my dinner companions reported, Kaitlin didn't have much going that could be sincerely defended. In fact, I didn't have to stretch far to picture her, in my place, in the ugly scenario Sheriff Pate had described — a crime of passion gone sour. Disappointment twisted into murder. For what it was worth, I'd run that by Pate tomorrow.

# 9

Finally, my turn on the tee had come. I smelled the sharp scent of the newly cut Bermuda grass. A morning mist made visibility zero more than fifty yards down the fairway. Not that it mattered. My three-wood had squirted short and crooked, barely out of sight. Then Kaitlin's drive whistled three hundred yards straight down the middle. The spectators who lined the first hole cheered. "Rupert! Rupert!" Their bloody, pulsing lips mirrored my memory of the dying Dr. Bencher.

I dragged myself awake and lay breathing hard in a tangle of sweat-dampened sheets. I got up and stumbled halfway to the minifridge before I remembered that yesterday's shopping expedition had yielded only a six-pack of Busch. The beer might dull the shooting anxiety that nightmare had left behind, but I knew it would also blow the rest of the day. I flicked on the TV and did my stretching and calisthenics, waiting for the complimentary continental breakfast buffet to open up downstairs.

At 6:30, I bought a copy of the *Herald-Tribune* in the lobby. I planned to shroud myself in the paper and fend off potential chitchat with traveling salesmen about the latest tip from *Golf Digest* on how to get out of a sand bunker. I loaded my tray with orange juice from concentrate, anemic-looking coffee, corn flakes, and a chocolate-covered donut that had seen fresher days. Becky's mom was probably whipping up a whites-only, veggie omelet and a fresh fruit salad while Becky lounged in bed watching cartoons.

I skimmed a small article on the front page of the *Tribune:* LPGA SECTIONAL QUALIFIER RETURNS TO PLANTATION GOLF AND COUNTRY CLUB. The writer described how the future stars of the LPGA generally scrapped their way through Q-school and onto the professional golf Tour right here in Venice, Florida. It certainly wasn't news, but the facts in black and white caused my heart to rev up in what had to be an unwholesome way. At the end of the article, the reporter interviewed the club manager about the unusually strong presence of protesting pickets at Futures Tour venues over the last half year.

"This is a sporting event, not a political debate or a circus. We will absolutely not tolerate any disruption of that kind at this tournament," insisted Manager Jones. "These people have been put on notice."

Kaitlin's Deikon dude appeared next to me

with his tray of breakfast food.

"Yo. Mind if I join you? It's Lassie, isn't it?"

"Cassie," I said. I knew I needed a haircut, but really, a collie? Jesus, this guy was a dope. And I did mind if he joined me, but with his buns already hitting the wrought-iron café chair across from me, I saw no gracious way out. So I folded up the paper and pulled my tray back to make room for him at the table. "And you're Wally."

"Walter," he corrected me. "Wally makes me sound too much like a pet walrus."

I laughed politely. "And you must get all the bad jokes about *Where's Waldo.*"

"That I do." We chewed for several minutes in silence.

"So, who've you landed for equipment sponsors?" he said.

"No one yet," I said, perking up a bit. Could he be feeling me out to make an offer? Maybe some good would come out of this intrusion after all. "So far, there's not been an awful lot worth representing." Damn, that sounded too negative. "The best is yet to come," I added quickly. "I'm on the comeback trail."

"It's a dog-eat-dog world," he said. "At this level, you have to have something really special going for you — like Kaitlin does — to get yourself noticed." I nodded, trying not to take too much offense. After all, I hadn't been playing on the Futures Tour, and he would have had no opportunity to see my talents otherwise. "But lots of my competition are here this week, looking for just the right future star to show off their up-and-coming-gear. You girls aren't the only ones having to fight for a living." He grinned. "So don't be discouraged. You could get discovered."

"We'll see." I wiped my chin with my napkin. "Tell me about the Tee Warrior-slash-Ball Hog."

His face crinkled up in an expression of horrified disbelief. "How do you know about that?"

"I was on the next tee at the Grandpappy range when you were showing the club to Kaitlin," I said. "She sure did make it sing." I tried to rein in my mocking tone.

The tension in his face relaxed. "She's really something, isn't she? I want to get her down to headquarters so the technical guys can measure her club head speed and the torque she puts on the shaft. As far as I'm concerned, she's got the template for a nearly perfect swing." He laughed. "Perfect body, too, but don't tell her I said that. She'll get the PC police after me." I waited for him to comment about how he'd like to measure the torque she put on *his* shaft, too.

He grinned as if reading my mind. Peculiar twitching movements had begun to march up the side of his neck and into his jawline.

This guy seemed clearly head-over-heels in love, but laced with an Oil Can Boyd kind of just-about-tipped-over-the-edge intensity.

"But, hey, listen, that club, the Ball Hog or whatever we end up calling it, it's not out yet," Walter said, dropping his voice to a low rumble. "I'm not supposed to be using it for demo. My ass would be grass. So do me a favor and keep it under your hat, okay?" I nodded. "Hey, have a fantastic day," he said, cramming the last half of a bran muffin into his mouth. "I got places to do and things to be."

"Catch you later then, dude," I said. I watched him lunge out of the delicate chair and jam the contents of his tray into the trash. *Hunk* was the only way to describe him — muscles that made every Deikon logo on his clothing quiver. But Lord, what a moron.

Back in the motel room, I dialed into my cell phone voice mail. Joe had left the first message the night before. "I hope you're not still ticked off. I'm at Sawgrass. Mike's a mess. I'm trying to hold him together, but it may take every bottle of Elmer's glue and roll of Scotch tape they have in Ponte Vedra. His new caddie doesn't have your magic touch. I'll get over as soon as I can, but it could be Thursday. Call me tonight. By the way, before he was killed, Bencher was up to his eyebrows fighting the False Memory outfit. They had him targeted for harassment. He had hired a big-name lawyer and was set to testify against one of their founders next month. Turns out the guy lives in Sarasota — Will Turner. I'll look him up when I get over there. Stay cool. I'm thinking of you."

Mike could eat his heart out. I didn't want to wish him ill, but I had to admit a small measure of satisfaction that the new caddie wasn't doing the job I had for nine months. I deleted Joe's words and moved on to Sheriff Pate.

"We need to talk. If I don't catch you on the course, call this afternoon." He didn't even bother to leave his name. Another moron, as far as I was concerned. Only this one I couldn't afford to alienate.

I warmed up briefly at the driving range, then drove my cart toward the first tee of the Panther course. The club grounds seemed a lot busier than yesterday, the practice areas bursting with lady golfers and their caddies. I noted an astonishing array of body types: tall and willowy, short and chunky, narrow shoulders, Atlas shoulders, flat butts, huge asses that spread across more than one zip code.

In my previous life on the PGA Tour, I had been a rare woman in a man's world. There were advantages to that — like the absence of cat-scratching, back-biting, hormonally driven emotional roller coasters, such as the ride Kaitlin Rupert appeared to be on. On

114

the other hand, the guys tended to skate on the surface of their feelings, relying on communal beer drinking, dirty jokes, and stories about the largesse of golf groupies to carry their friendships. I had orbited the outside perimeter, peering in — not a man, not a player, and certainly not included in the caddies' inner circle.

"Interesting career selection," Dr. Baxter had said after I described my life on the Tour. "You felt quite isolated, but at the same time, special. We should explore what went into your choice." According to him, you couldn't just stumble into something — everything you did or said had some deeper meaning. Hah!

Two Asian women introduced themselves to me on the path to the tee. Sachiko was blocky and masculine. Hiroko was so delicate I couldn't imagine she had the strength to swing a full-length driver. Neither one spoke much English. I was able to make out that they were Japanese, had spent the last year competing on the Asian Tour but had not met Jack Wolfe, and not much else. Hiroko introduced me to her mother, who was even smaller than her daughter. She carried an enormous silver umbrella to shade herself from the Florida August sun. She was dressed in exquisite golf clothing, down to white anklets with pink pom-poms and spiked Lady Fairway silver saddle shoes. Perhaps she was poised to take her daughter's place in the event of an emergency.

Divot, one of the volunteer Munchkins I'd met yesterday, greeted us on the first tee.

"How are you girls doing?" she asked.

"Great," I said. "We haven't hit a single ball yet, so no chance to get into trouble." The Japanese women laughed.

"You may find the greens a bit fast," said Divot. "An underground water pipe burst two days ago. Our irrigation system is out of commission until they get the replacement part from Miami. We're dreadfully sorry for any inconvenience."

As we set off down the first fairway, there was little sign of the tension that I knew would dominate the first round of the tournament. Like the other girls, I could repeat any shot that didn't meet my standards. Today I was under no obligation to accept balls hooked out of bounds, putts missed on either side of a hole, skulled chips, balls in the water, or any other missteps with ugly consequences. I added my own descriptive notes to the LPGA yardage book, hoping Laura would be able to decipher my scrawl. I was pretty confident their measurements and drawings would be accurate. But the difference between pretty confident and dead sure could mean the difference between a career on the Tour and one teaching the basics of the golf swing to ungrateful preadolescents.

In my humble opinion, other than putting, the Panther's Claw presented hurdles more psychological than physical. In fact, the whole course was straightforward. Under the best of circumstances, it suited my game just fine. All I had to do was drive the ball straight, hit consistent medium and short irons, and drop the putts. Hah!

Other than four three-putts, I limited my damages to one brush with disaster, a triple bogey on the par-four twelfth hole. The hole required a straight drive, then a blind shot over trees and marsh to the green. Under ordinary conditions, this would present no great challenge. But after I'd blocked my tee shot right, my attempt at a miracle wedge buried the ball so deep in the woods a trained bird dog couldn't have found it. I told myself I'd learned some things. And that's what practice rounds were for.

We finished the round and headed back to the clubhouse. If anything, Divot had understated the speed of the greens. As we passed the pit dug alongside the seventeenth hole that contained the broken water pipe, I prayed the missing part would arrive soon. Mastering greens that ran like billiard tables during this already difficult week seemed too much to ask.

Protesters with placards, a confusion of players and volunteers, and a handful of police officers crowded the area outside the LPGA office. Sheriff Pate and several of his cohorts barked out orders instructing the individuals with picket signs to clear the premises. I recognized Leviticus, who carried the same Bible verse I'd seen in Myrtle Beach. He probably hadn't seen a shower stall or Laundromat since then either. The other protesters were strangers. This time the signs read: "Whatever Happened to 'Honor Thy Father'?" and "Mythical Memories Cause Real Pain." I had to assume their presence was related to Kaitlin's suit. It was hard to see how she could concentrate on golf with that much ruckus around her.

I skirted around the crowd, delivered the cart to the maintenance area and my bag to my car trunk, and headed back to the putting green. Maybe if I sank a hundred short ones this afternoon, I could avoid a full-blown panic over a must-have putt during Tuesday's or Wednesday's round.

After half an hour, I started to get a rhythm going. I felt comfortable with my left-hand low grip, which I'd revamped just a month ago, and developed an eye for the subtle breaks in the green. I focused on Joe Lancaster's putting credo: Visualize the relaxation flowing down my arms and into the putter. Putter and arms are one.

"Miz Burdette, do you have a minute?" said the gravelly voice of Sheriff Pate. Polite of him to put it that way, but I knew chatting with him wasn't really a choice. I picked up my balls and followed him to the scanty shade of a palm tree.

The sheriff looked frazzled and hot. His shirttails had come loose from his pants, and a wide band of dark sweat striped the length of his back. "Let's return, if we may, to the scene of Dr. Bencher's office," he said. "Explain again why you were there." I repeated what I'd told the first police officer on the scene, then Detective Maloney, then Pate himself, just yesterday.

"I understand you were visiting with the doctor next door," said Pate. "What I want to understand is why."

"It was my regular appointment," I said. "I generally see Dr. Baxter on Thursdays."

The sheriff looked pained. "That's restating the obvious, darlin'. I know you were there for an appointment, but why? Why do you need to talk to a shrink? Is it a situation similar to Miz Rupert's? Problems with Daddy? Sometimes you girls ask for trouble, dressing like you were going out to work the streets." Again, his eyes ran over the contours of my body.

I was speechless. No way in hell was I going to discuss my personal issues with Sheriff Pate. I had a handful of close friends who knew the bare facts about my meetings with Baxter, and this moron was as far from landing on that short list as anyone could get. A groundswell of anger tightened the muscles in my throat as the full impact of his words sank in. Even if a girl, Kaitlin included, wore clothes that would have sold well in a red-light district, it was unfair and downright disgusting to assume she had a set of round heels. So how did I continue talking with Pate, appearing cooperative, without telling him any of my personal stuff or leaking the rage that threatened to choke me?

"I know you'll understand that my business with Dr. Baxter was strictly personal," I said in a low voice. "And not related to Kaitlin at all."

"You're not helping, darlin'." He reached over and took the putter from my hand. "You're an old-fashioned gal, huh? Personally, I favor the Odyssey Triforce 2. You have toe-heel weighting on this antique?"

"Am I a suspect in Bencher's murder?" I asked. I ignored his question about my putter. Opening the door to putting tips from Pate could very well torch my opening round before I teed up the first ball. "Maybe I should call Detective Maloney and get this straightened out," I said.

"We're not charging you with anything yet," said Pate quickly. "Now walk me through what you saw in that office."

I sighed. I could feel and smell the perspiration dampening a wide circle under the arms of my golf shirt. I breathed in deeply and focused on the horizontal lines of the clubhouse across the street. When I felt calm enough to speak, I repeated the story of finding Bencher lying behind his desk. In spite of Pate's barrage of questions about what I might have seen or heard, I had nothing new to add.

"It's been nice talkin' to you. I'll see you tomorrow," said Pate, returning my putter. He left me under the palm, angry and wilted.

# 10

By the time I reached my motel room, I'd moved through stages of outrage, despair, disgust, fear, and queasiness. Enough angst already, time for action. The week was sufficiently bad without some bozo ratcheting up the stakes with his own personal vendetta against female golfers from South Carolina. Truth: Sheriff Pate had it in for me. Dare: Could I persuade anyone else in law enforcement to see it that way? I placed a call to the number on Detective Maloney's business card.

"Maloney."

"Hi, Detective. It's Cassandra Burdette."

"Hitting 'em straight?" he asked.

"So far so good," I said, encouraged by his friendly tone. "But I'm having trouble with the Sarasota Sheriff's Department. Am I a suspect in Bencher's murder? I can't figure out why Pate's bugging me every day."

The coziness evaporated from Detective Maloney's voice. "I warned you that you would have to stay in close touch with Pate," he said. "Those were the conditions under which we allowed you to leave the state."

"I know that," I said. "But you didn't say

he would be harassing me. How's the case really coming?"

"No suspects arrested," he said. "That's all I can tell you. Do you want to file a formal complaint against Pate?"

I considered this. Pate was plenty mean already. Filing a complaint would be like poking a sleepy rattlesnake with a nine-iron.

"No. Thanks anyway." Thanks for nothing, I thought as I hung up. Then I decided to call Joe. I'd nursed my grudge long enough. Now I needed his advice.

"You've reached the voice mail of Dr. Joe Lancaster. I can't take your call right now, but leave your name and number and I'll be happy to get back to you. Meanwhile, keep your head down and have fun out there!"

I left a message asking him to call and then stretched out on the bed to think. I pictured Joe out on the practice green with Mike, where I should have been. Where Joe should have been with me. Where I *would* have been, Joe or no Joe, were it not for Pate's annoying interruption. From all appearances, the police had not made much progress in solving the murder. Either Pate still thought I had reason to kill Bencher, or he believed I had seen or heard something that would identify the actual killer. Or he got a buzz on by throwing his status around and knocking me off balance. Regardless of the reason, I was sick of our little conversations. I saw one way to get that ape off my back: look into the Bencher situation myself. Joe wouldn't approve of this plan, but he hadn't had to sit through two miserable sessions with Pate, with more tête-à-têtes looming the rest of the week.

I pulled out the phone book and looked up Will Turner, the head honcho of the False Memory Consocation. In bold caps, his listing read: DR. WILLIAM TURNER, THERAPEUTIC CONSULTANT. Then a smaller line underneath: "Specializing in Post-Pseudo Traumatic Actualization." Whatever the hell that was. From the little Joe had told me, I knew damn well this guy was no doctor. At best, maybe he held a Ph.D. in some obscure academic field. Even with the constraint of a two-line listing, he managed to sound like a master of doublespeak, not to mention a fruitcake. I scribbled his number on a pad provided by the Starlight Motel. I'd call tomorrow during office hours and see if they could work me in.

Next stop: Bible study. I hated to pretend an interest in religious fellowship that wasn't genuine, but I didn't know where else to turn. I hoped I could learn something about Julie Atwater's friendship with Kaitlin and her subsequent consultation with Dr. Bencher. How would I squeeze that out of the Bible study group? I had to trust a plan would come to me later.

I swung through Burger King's drive-thru window and wolfed down a Whopper and large fries on my way back to the Plantation Country Club. Power eating at its finest. I found Joanne and Nicki's golfside condo, number 714, without difficulty. Wiping the last bit of mayo off my face with my sleeve, I composed it into what I hoped was a pious expression.

"I'm here for the get-together I saw posted on the bulletin board," I said to the girl who answered the door. "Cassie Burdette."

"Please come in. Welcome. I'm Nicki." Before I could react, she folded me into a tight bear hug. Then she showed me into the living room and introduced the four other women gathered there. They seemed normal enough, if shaded a bit in the direction of cloyingly warm. I scolded myself for unnecessary cynicism.

At first, the conversation centered on golf. We all agreed that the Panther greens verged on the edge of suicidally fast, and that the volunteers were sweet, the sandhill cranes aggressive, and the fairways in excellent condition. If any of these girls lacked confidence or harbored other unpleasant feelings about the week ahead, they showed no sign of it. Nicki went to the small kitchen and returned with a plate of Oreos and a pitcher of grape juice.

"Let's get started," said Joanne, a plump,

dark-haired girl with an eerie resemblance to Rosie O'Donnell. "Our scripture reading tonight is from Romans, chapter one, verses eighteen to thirty-two." She opened her Bible and read a passage about the many faces of ungodliness, homosexuality prominent among them. It didn't look like it was going to be difficult to steer the subject in the direction I needed it to go. Joanne finished reading and prayed that we could all live as Paul had instructed us to do. Then she and Nicki went through the Bible verses line by line, explaining how we were to apply them to our lives.

"As I see it, Paul condemned the Greeks for a lifestyle of debauchery and self-satisfaction. He expected them, and us by extension, to live a God-centered life instead. Any questions?" Joanne inquired. The group sat silent and smiling.

I took my second plunge of the evening. "I know I have a lot to learn," I said. "I'm a part-time Presbyterian with barely a leaf-through familiarity with the Bible." Two of the other students giggled. "But you seem to be saying that we should interpret what you've read to us quite literally."

Nicki and Joanne exchanged glances. "It's the word of God," said Nicki, holding her hands out in an expression of heavenly acceptance. Joanne clutched the Bible to her chest and bobbed her head in support.

"I don't mean to cause offense," I said,

trying for a tone of earnest confusion. "But says who? I mean, how do you know that?"

"The men who appear in the Bible were called by God to record what he wanted said and done," said Joanne, in a brook-no-questions tone.

I asked one anyway. "What if the meaning of a passage is unclear?"

"If there is any ambiguity, we must take the clearest interpretation, the plainest meaning. In the case of today's reading, for example, God is telling us that homosexuality is wrong." The student sitting across from me stiffened noticeably.

"Why would God have created people with different kinds of sexual feelings if some of them were wrong?" I asked. As uncomfortable as I was beginning to feel pushing this line of questioning, I didn't want to leave without getting the information I'd come for.

Joanne sighed and reached for a cookie. "God didn't make them that way, Cassie. They have chosen to walk a path of sin." She twisted off the top of the Oreo and nibbled at the white cream center.

"And how does one get off the path of sin and back into righteousness?" I asked. On the way over, I'd actually considered masquerading as a confused homosexual. Everyone knew there were players on the Tour with nontraditional lifestyles, just like in every other walk of life. However, I was not at all sure that the information I could glean would be worth the sacrifice of offering myself up to the study group as a repentant sinner. I didn't care one way or the other whether a golfer was homosexual, bisexual, heterosexual, or asexual. But I did not want to begin a potential life on the LPGA Tour with an awkward reputation. I'd seen the press and the public devour those women often enough to know it was a path I'd prefer to avoid.

The group leaders rose from their seats and came to sit on the couch on either side of me. "You are doing the right thing," said Nicki. "We'll help you."

"I didn't mean me. . . ."

Joanne put her arm around my shoulder and squeezed hard. I could smell the icing on her breath as she whispered to me. "The first step is to confess your sins before the Lord. You must not give in to the devil's temptation."

"I wasn't talking about my issues," I said. "I'm worried about a friend who seems to have started down this path. She's changed a lot recently." I hesitated. "She has family problems."

"Ah," said Joanne. "A friend who has been misled by the smooth words of the devil. Could it be Julie Atwater?" I lowered my eyes, then nodded.

"Satan circulates among us on this earth," said Nicki sternly. "Sometimes he takes the form of a woman. Julie met the devil and was persuaded to follow his ways." I figured she had to be talking about Kaitlin. Who did have a bit of the devil in her, as far as I was concerned.

"Wasn't that Julie's father I saw marching today at the club?" I asked.

"The Lord told Mr. Atwater he must seek to destroy the devil wherever he finds him," said Joanne. "Whether that be in his own daughter or wherever he chooses to make his presence known. Mr. Atwater is a true soldier of the Lord." Her admiration of what appeared to me to be unreasoned fanaticism raised a warning crop of goose bumps on my chest and arms.

To my enormous relief, the meeting broke up shortly after this discussion. I thanked the girls for their hospitality and comfort and bolted from the condo. The moon had risen during the meeting and now cast long, serrated shadows from the coconut palms onto the eighteenth hole. I walked out onto the fairway and willed myself to forget about anything but the upcoming competition. But the stories of Kaitlin and Julie kept returning to my mind. I wondered about the memories of molestation they reported. Had these ideas just sprung unfounded into their minds? Or had Dr. Bencher planted them there? Were they completely factual, totally untrue, or some confused combination of fact and fantasy?

I stopped at the one-hundred-yard marker and looked toward the green, imagining this was where my final-round tee shot had landed. I pictured my drive coming to rest just enough left of center to take the pond on the right out of play, without catching the fairway bunker. Then I visualized myself hitting a perfect, soft wedge, which approached the green with the slightest draw, landed softly on the collar, and then rolled to within two feet of the cup. I heard the excited clapping and conversation of the spectators. I bounded up to the green, pulled the pin from the cup, and pantomimed sinking the putt.

"Center cut," said a voice in the darkness. "Well struck." I recognized Gary Rupert's deep voice, and felt embarrassed that he had caught me playing charades.

"Gary? What are you doing out here?"

"We're staying over in that building." He pointed to the condos closest to where we stood. "I saw a phantom golfer on the green and came out to check. I'm delighted to see that it's you. But isn't it a bit dark for practice?"

"It sounds silly," I said, choosing not to reveal my study group encounter. "I'm steadying the nerves with a little creative visualization by moonlight."

"How about a nerve-steadying nightcap?" he asked. "It would only take a minute to run inside and get a beer." I nodded. A beer sounded great, just one, to help me unwind. The combination of building anticipation for the tournament and my clumsy detective work had hardened my back and shoulder muscles into stony knots.

Gary returned in several minutes with two Rolling Rocks. We sat down with our backs against the bark of a live oak and drank. The moon gleaming through wisps of Spanish moss made a checkerboard of shadows on his face, softening the sharp contour of his nose and smoothing the roughness in his skin. We chatted about the day, the golf courses, the thunderstorms predicted for the following afternoon. By the time I'd finished my beer, the tightness had begun to ebb from my neck muscles. Gary took the empty bottle from my hand, then leaned over and kissed me. He broke away as quickly as he'd leaned in.

"I'm glad we got that over with. It was ten years overdue," he said. "But maybe we can talk more back in Myrtle. You've got enough going on already this week. Have a good night, pal. Good luck tomorrow." He stood up, collected both empties, and walked back in the direction of his condo.

What in the hell was all that about? I wondered, as I stumped back to my car. Now I'd developed a pounding headache, as well as new knots in every muscle above my waist. Gary was right: a romantic interlude had no place in a week already too full. And he didn't know the half of what I was into. So why in the bloody hell had he even brought it up?

# 11

When I stepped out of the shower, I heard both the alarms I'd set the night before buzzing. Then the phone rang with my backup wake-up call. Alice MacPherson had put the fear of God into me two days earlier: I wasn't taking any chances about missing the mandatory eight o'clock players' meeting.

Gary Rupert had me steamed. As Kaitlin's on-again, off-again caddie, he had to know the dangers of introducing chaos into the fragile mind of a golfer right before a tournament. Unless he found me so irresistible he could not hold himself back. Hah! Anyway, if he was so overcome with desire, what was the deal with the one snowflake-light kiss, then scram routine? More likely, Kaitlin was using him as her secret weapon — she'd commissioned him to rattle the competition so we would deteriorate and knock ourselves out of the contest. In which case, Gary would have several very busy nights, necking, even briefly, with over a hundred girls.

I listened to my new phone messages before leaving the motel. The first was from Mom. I remembered, with the usual surge of guilt, that I hadn't called her since arriving in Florida.

No greeting, just a tremulous voice. "Max Harding came into the restaurant for lunch yesterday. He's so handsome. He asked how the week was going for you. I told him he would have to call you himself, because even though I'm your mother I would certainly have no idea. Love you." And she hung up. The second message was not much better.

"This is Pate. I'm busy at the office today and can't get out to the club. Stop by the sheriff's department when you're finished this afternoon. Take 41 toward downtown Venice, turn at State Road 776, we're on the left." Great, just what I needed, a command appearance from the grand buffoon. I left the motel in a nasty funk.

I grabbed a banana and a cheese Danish as I entered the dining area at the country club, then found a seat at a table with Mary Morrison and Eve Darling. Mary pointed out Julie Atwater, who chatted with Kaitlin several tables in front of us. I would not have guessed from Julie's perfectly made up face and cheerful façade that she had a major feud going on with her dad and the Bible study group. Not to even mention inner conflict.

The deputy commissioner of the LPGA started the meeting off by introducing Alice and the other LPGA staff in attendance, then the head honcho of the Plantation Country Club. We clapped politely for each of them.

"There will be two waves of tee times on

both courses tomorrow and Wednesday, at seven-thirty and eleven a.m.," the commissioner explained. "As you know, a random draw will determine your pairings. After Wednesday, half the field will be cut, with the remaining golfers arranged in threesomes according to their cumulative scores." The dreaded cut. Slamming the trunk, the players on the PGA Tour called it. Over the last year, Mike and I had gotten very familiar with the concept. Nothing else could bleed the air out of a dream quite so fast.

"You must be physically inside the roped area around the tee at your group's starting time. Otherwise, you will be assessed a two-stroke penalty. When you physically leave the roped area around the scoring tent, your card is ours. You will not be allowed to return to sign the card or change a score at that point." All the girls competing in the tournament were familiar with these rules. Still, even on the professional Tour, it was amazing how many top players had disqualified themselves with some dumb blunder over the course of their careers.

"We have a relatively small field this year," the commissioner continued. "Slow play will not be tolerated." I noticed Mary rolling her eyes in Kaitlin's direction. "You have lots of running room, so move smartly. If you see an official in a rules cart, you can assume you are being timed. Any player who shoots eighty-eight or higher will be automatically withdrawn from the tournament." I didn't even want to think about that hideous possibility. Eighty-eight might sound acceptable to an eighteen handicapper in the qualifying round of her club championship, but oh, my God, what a humiliating way to end the Q-school experience.

"Just a couple more friendly reminders," said the commissioner. "Each threesome will be assigned two carts. At no time may you and your caddie ride in the cart together during the play of a hole. However, both of you may ride from the green to the next tee. Second, volunteers with radios will be posted on holes three, six, nine, twelve, fifteen, and eighteen. They can call a rules official for you if needed. Please, ladies, remember that it's a bad idea to accept rulings from spectators." The players around me laughed. That seemed an obvious and gratuitous reminder, but I knew how common sense could completely evaporate in tense tournament conditions.

"Third, a list of nonconforming equipment is posted on the bulletin board. The use of one of these drivers in USGA competitions is the grounds for disqualification. Finally, your practice balls are provided courtesy of Titleist. They'll be donated to junior girls' golf programs after this week. They're very nice balls, but please don't take them home. We get very upset if they disappear into your bag." The girls at my table laughed again.

"Only thirty of you will go on to the final round of the LPGA Q-school. As far as we're concerned, you're all winners. Play your best and good luck." The tears that sprang to my eyes surprised me. It was really happening. I was no longer lying home on that gingham bedspread, looking at the posters of Nancy Lopez and Freddie Couples holding their trophies, dreaming that one day I'd be there, too. This was my chance: I promised myself to enjoy every minute of it. Okay, at least some of them, I bargained.

Before heading over to the Bobcat course, I called Dr. Turner's office. His receptionist was delighted to offer me an appointment the same afternoon at five p.m. She was probably afraid she wouldn't get a paycheck this month if she didn't book a few more suckers into his schedule. I'd have time to pick Laura up at the airport and still make my pseudo-session with Turner.

"May I ask your chief complaint?" the receptionist said. "You certainly aren't required to tell me this on the phone, but it does help the doctor prepare for you."

I vacillated for a moment about how much to say. I already regretted having given my real name. "I'd rather not. . . . I'm not really comfortable. . . ."

"Oh, I'm so sorry," she said, her voice trembling with concern. "But don't worry.

You've done just right. He's very good with that problem." She said *that problem* in the same tone I'd heard TV announcers use when they talked about feminine hygiene products. I wondered what she thought my problem was. I wondered how much it would cost me to get Laura to pose for an hour as the possibly traumatized Cassandra Burdette.

I hung up and hurried over to pick up a cart for my 9:15 practice round. At the tournament office, I learned I had been assigned to play with Jessica Anderson and Julie Atwater. This was good news and bad. Maybe I'd have the chance to casually inquire about her problems with her father — if it were possible to casually inquire about such problems. On the other hand, the golf course had to be my primary focus. If all went well, I'd be playing three rounds on the Bobcat course this week, and I needed to feel comfortable and prepared. I lugged my bag to the cart barn and spotted my playing partners.

"I'm Cassie," I said, reaching out to shake hands. Julie was a big-boned girl with big boobs and wide hips. She wore a turquoise straw hat and pearls, and a fine sheen of sweat on her forehead. Her shirt gapped open between buttons just enough to show a flash of purple lace as she returned my handshake.

"Howdy," she said. "Good luck today. I guess we'll be sharing a cart."

"Great to meet you," said Jessica, stepping

up next to Julie. She was dwarfed beside Julie, small and slight with a big smile and quick, birdlike hand movements. "That's my dad, Harvey." A balding, middle-aged man with a prominent potbelly, thin legs, and knobby knees waved to us from Jessica's golf cart. I hoped he wouldn't slow play down by having a heart attack on the course tomorrow. Pure sour grapes, I scolded myself. So my own father hadn't expressed the slightest interest in caddying, probably wasn't even aware I was competing at Q-school. Buck up. It could be worse. He could be Leviticus.

"Aren't you from Myrtle Beach?" asked Julie on the ride over to the first tee. I nodded. "Kaitlin's mentioned you."

"I don't like the sound of that," I said. "Whatever she said, puh-leeze give me the benefit of the doubt."

"It's not that bad," she said with a smile that struck me as sincere. "She doesn't have me brainwashed or anything." She pointed to the players in front of us reaching the first green. "Looks like we're good to go here."

I watched as the other two players hit their drives, Jessica's long and straight, Julie's a wicked slice that dribbled into a bunker on the right side of the fairway.

"Damn it," she said. "I must be swinging over the top."

I hit a pop-up fly straight down the middle, though barely past the hundred-and-fifty-yard marker. I joined Julie in the cart for the ride to my ball. Next I skimmed a seven-iron low and ugly down the fairway. Julie stepped on the gas when I'd barely sat down and we lurched toward the green. Once there, Jessica sank a three-footer for birdie and slapped hands with her father. Julie and I both three-putted for bogeys.

"Number two's a beast," I heard Jessica tell her father as she got into the cart. "With my draw, I'm either in the mounds or the trap. The approach to the green's even worse."

"You gotta love it, though, honey," said her father, replacing her putter in the bag. "Just being here — what a dream come true." She hugged him before he trotted off toward the next hole. It was going to take every bit of mental toughness I owned to finish this round without feeling pathetic.

Julie patted me on the back. "You'll be fine once you settle down into a rhythm."

The rhythm would have to wait. All three of the players in front of us knocked their approach shots into the pond to the right of the green, promising at least a short delay. Julie and I chatted about her year on the Futures Tour and her disastrous experience at Q-school last year.

"You already look a hundred times more comfortable than I did," she said. "I never broke eighty either day."

"Yikes," I said. We watched the girls ahead

of us fish multiple balls out of the water. Given the friendly tone of Julie's comments so far, I decided to blunder ahead. "This must be a hard time for you," I offered. "All the extra pressure with your dad, on top of just being here."

"It is."

"I don't know if you heard this, but I'm the one who found Dr. Bencher last week."

"You're joking." Now her face looked genuinely shocked. "That must have been horrible."

"It was. This is awkward, but I hoped you'd talk to me about your experience with him. The sheriff's office seems to think that I'm somehow involved."

"Get out! They don't think you killed him?"

I shrugged. "Either that, or I know something that I don't realize I know about who the murderer was."

"I'll help if I can," said Julie. "What do you need?"

"Tell me whatever you feel comfortable saying. I guess my biggest question is who would have wanted the guy dead?"

"Since you're asking me, I assume my father has already come to your mind," said Julie. "I wouldn't have pictured him as a killer, but one never knows. I've found a lot out about him in the past year, all of it news and none of it good."

I got out of the cart to stretch. "Bencher helped you figure some stuff out?"

"I only saw the doctor once," said Julie. She wiped the perspiration off her forehead with her golf towel, then waved it in the direction of the clubhouse. "Those idiots with placards want you to believe that there's no such thing as an honest memory. Evil and persuasive shrinks plant thoughts into the weak shells of the women who come for help. In my case, Bencher barely said a word. It was like all this garbage had been bubbling inside me and it took fifty minutes of spewing it out in his office to figure out what I'd been thinking and feeling. You know what I mean?"

"I think so. Just having someone listen sometimes helps you put words to what's in the back of your mind."

Julie nodded. "I knew for a long time that there was something wrong with my relationship with my father. Some of the things he did . . ." She looked first as though she might cry, then she pulled her lips into a thin line and narrowed her eyes. "But I didn't want to see this too clearly — who wants to think their father is a lech?"

"Obviously, I don't know you very well, but you seem so different from him."

"He and Mom split up when I was eight so I've seen very little of him since then. Trust me, there was a good reason Mom

141

dumped him. The better question is why she married him in the first place."

"So Bencher didn't suggest he'd abused you?"

"No. The only thing he commented on specifically was how my father had hurt me emotionally. Dr. Bencher was quite clear about that."

I glanced up toward the green. Two of the three players ahead had dropped their balls outside the hazard and were preparing to chip on. "Do you mind saying how?"

"He said a good father should start out as the sun in his daughter's life. Then, to allow her to grow into a woman, he has to step back and give her room to connect with other men. He moves from sun to moon." Her laugh was harsh and mirthless. "My father scored oh for two."

"He said all that in the first hour?" She nodded. I'd droned on for what seemed like months before Baxter offered any comments on the trouble I had with my father.

"You don't have to answer this," I said, "but what about . . . ?" I stopped, unsure whether I'd offend her if I said the word lesbian.

"Aha," she said. "You've stumbled across rumors about my sexuality. My conversion." I shrugged. "Rumors that my interest in men is dead have been greatly exaggerated." She laughed. "Not that it's anyone's business, but talking to Bencher about my father this way

142

raised a lot of questions all around. It will be a long time before I have them all sorted out."

"I can understand that," I said. And I could. My own father hadn't done badly on Bencher's first criterion. But then he hadn't just stepped back, he'd taken a nosedive off the face of the earth. He certainly wouldn't qualify as a moon, probably not even a distant planet.

We stopped talking to hit our second shots. Julie's ball went left this time. I hit a screaming worm-burner, so low it nearly took out two sandhill cranes preening on the mounds, before it skipped into the pond.

"I think I need to concentrate on what I'm doing here," said Julie. "That's pretty much all I know to say anyway."

I knew she was right — I, too, should have been paying attention to the landscape of the golf course, getting familiar with quirks and challenges that I'd be facing in the tournament later. Joe would have had my head for my lack of focus.

We finished the remainder of the round without further conversation, other than "nice shot" or, following a number of my unfortunate skirmishes with the water, the woods, and the rough, "tough luck." Nothing seemed to be working. I pulled out the note card listing swing thoughts I'd worked on with Joe and Odell back at the Palm Lakes driving range. These short phrases were to be used to help clear messages from mind to body that interfered with a smooth swing.

"Don't get too technical," Joe had told me. "Your body knows very well what to do. Your mind has to let go, get out of the way, and let your body do its job."

Whispering "Let it go" produced a snap hook out of bounds on five. Using "Let it flow," I popped two balls in the water on six. By the time we reached the eighteenth green, where Gary had watched me pantomime my putt last night, I was more over par than I even wanted to count.

"Lucky thing you got that out of your system," said Jessica. "Good luck tomorrow, girls."

I turned in my cart and prepared to head north to Pate's office and the airport. My cell phone vibrated, letting me know I'd received a message while out on the golf course.

"Cassie, it's Jack. Sorry I missed you. The time difference is killing me. Good luck tomorrow, Gorgeous, and don't let anyone tell you Budweiser isn't in your training regimen. Have one on me. Let me know how it's going. Take care."

I whistled all the way to Sarasota.

# 12

The sheriff's department was a cream-colored, stucco building with a Spanish-style tile roof, both neater and friendlier-looking than its ambassador, Sheriff Pate. I parked and rolled out into the blanket-heavy heat of the afternoon.

"I'm here to see Sheriff Pate," I said to the girl at the desk.

She laughed. "*Sheriff* Pate? I'll tell him you're here." What the hell was so funny? Given Pate's grumpy disposition, I wasn't surprised that the girl didn't offer me coffee or even a seat. This office seemed unconcerned with public relations. Ten minutes later, Pate arrived and ushered me into a windowless gray room that I could imagine worked well for pressuring reluctant suspects into confessing.

"Big day tomorrow?"

"Yes."

"How'd the round go today?"

"Fine, thanks." I sure as hell wasn't going to discuss my golf problems with this bozo.

"Any new thoughts about Bencher?"

"Honest to God, Sheriff Pate," I said. "I'm doing my best to forget about Bencher. I told you everything I possibly knew. I even made up a few extra details just to make you happy." I could see he didn't find my little joke at all funny.

"This is serious, Miz Burdette. A man's been killed here."

"I'm well aware of that, sir. You may remember that I found him."

"Then until we solve the case and determine that you in fact were not involved, I'd suggest you do your best to cooperate."

"I'm trying." I didn't want to cry in front of Pate, but it was going to take all the willpower I had to hold back the frustrated tears.

"I'll look for you over at the Plantation tomorrow," he said. "They may need some extra protection if the protests continue." He sighed as if it were a great burden to have so much responsibility.

"That's it? I'm free to go?" Pate nodded. I left the building, again infuriated and confused by the man's interrogation. Today, I couldn't discern any real reason for him to have asked me in.

I felt better the instant I saw the round face and sturdy fireplug shape of Laura Snow getting off the plane. She insisted her size was a by-product of her combination Eastern European peasant and Choctaw heritage, and that it brought many advantages — not the least being a low center of gravity, useful for weathering windstorms and balancing golf swings. In addition, Laura brimmed with optimism and common sense. At the moment, I needed both.

"Before we get dinner," I said after extracting myself from her vise grip hug, "we have one quick stop to make. A five o'clock appointment with Dr. William Turner."

"Who the hell is Dr. Turner?" asked Laura, laughing. "Don't tell me you can't last a whole week without seeing a shrink?"

"It's been tough here," I pretended to whine. "Without you or Joe."

"No, really," said Laura. "Who is this Turner and why is he delaying my dinner?"

"I'll tell you the whole story over a beer later," I said. "But in a nutshell, this guy is a big wheel in the False Memory Consociation. Joe told me about him. So I made an appointment."

"Joe told you to see him? What do you plan to discuss?" Her worried tone told me this wasn't going to go over easily.

"Joe didn't send me to see him, he just mentioned that his office is here in Sarasota. I'm thinking of telling him I'm an incest victim."

"Are you nuts? You're here to play golf —"

I cut her off before she could work herself into a full-blown rant. "I wouldn't get involved with this if the pork-rind blowhard who calls himself the sheriff wasn't pressuring me. He doesn't have the slightest idea how to solve a murder case, so he just shakes me down every chance he gets, just hoping some random piece of crucial evidence will drop out." I guided the Pontiac off Route 41 into a strip mall that housed a pet store, a deli, and several sorry-looking professional offices.

"How are you going to pull this off?"

"I have no idea," I admitted. "Will you go in for me?" Her scowl did not require a verbal translation. "I'll try not to be long."

Dr. Turner's waiting room was plainer than the one shared by Baxter and Bencher. Metal chairs with thin, blue vinyl cushions lined the walls. A faded travel poster featuring the Eiffel Tower hung above the secretary's desk. If I had to wait long, there wouldn't be much to distract me from counting the fast thumping of my heartbeats.

"I'm here to see Dr. Turner. I'm Cassandra Burdette," I told the receptionist.

"He's tied up with some unexpected business. You can have a seat over there." She flipped her long blond braid over her shoulder and waved at the metal seats in the corner of the room. I sat and paged through the latest issue of *My Self* magazine. While I read "Cheapo Beauty Buys That Will Take Ten Years Off Your Face," the secretary painted her nails purple. During "The Single Best Diet for Your Abs," she lined her eyelids with silver and applied three coats of mascara. I couldn't help staring as she began dabbing at her cleavage with cotton balls dipped in two separate colors of liquid foundation.

"It's the new thing," she explained when she caught me gawking. "The shadows fool the eye into thinking there's more there than is actually the case."

I smiled. To me it appeared that her gifts in that department were bountiful to begin with. Through the connecting office door, I heard voices raised in heated conversation. The secretary lifted her shoulders in an apologetic shrug, outlined her lips in magenta, then filled them in with glossy pink. When I could no longer stand sitting still, I got up and began to pantomime my putting stroke.

"Are you here for that golf tournament?" the secretary asked.

"Yes," I said. "Qualifying school."

"Gosh, that must be so exciting. I'm Jeanine. I love golf. I never miss the Players' Championship in Ponte Vedra. I was so excited when I heard the PGA Championship was going to be held there this year, too! I tried to get time off this week to go, but Dr. Turner's swamped." She pursed her perfect pink lips into a pout. I would not have pegged her as a golf fanatic. Nor did she look particularly busy.

"I caddied for one of the rookies last year," I told her. "He's playing over there this week.

149

His first major. Mike Callahan."

"That must have been so exciting," she said. "Do you know Rick Justice? He's my favorite. I know everyone is gaga over Tiger Woods. But I just love that Rick. He's adorable with that little turned-up nose and sweet smile. I cried when I heard the speech he gave at the British Open."

I nodded. Everyone remembered that speech. It had been sweet, completely from the heart.

"You must know all those guys, then. Did you realize he's on the list of the country's most eligible bachelors? Do you have any idea how I could meet him?"

I could picture Laura warning me that I needed to mind my own business in order to concentrate on my tournament. So I started to give Jeanine my standard spiel about players' privacy. Then it occurred to me we might strike a useful trade.

"Yes, I know lots of the guy golfers. I know Rick." Which was almost technically true. We had nodded at each other when Mike warmed up next to him before last year's Kemper Open. Rick went on to win the tournament, while we packed up early, having missed the cut by ten shots. "He's just as sweet as he looks on TV."

"Could you arrange for me to meet him? Oh, my God, it would be a dream come true!"

"I can't promise too much, but I could certainly call over and get you a grounds pass to the tournament for the weekend. Maybe Mike would introduce you after the round is finished on Saturday. The guys aren't always in the most social mood, though. A lot depends on how the day went." I knew damn well I was leading her on. Mike Callahan would no more consent to playing matchmaker than put on a pair of culottes and tee off on the women's Tour. Though he definitely had the legs for it.

"Oh, wait 'til my girlfriends hear about this! They'll be absolutely green. Let me give you my home phone so you can tell me what you were able to set up." Distributing her still-tacky nails carefully around a purple pen, she wrote out her name and number in looping script and offered it to me. "Oh, my God, what do you think I should wear?"

"As you can see," I said, gesturing to my baggy khaki shorts and navy blue golf shirt, "I'm not part of the fashion vanguard. I choose clothes strictly for comfort and the size of their pockets. And I really can't speak for Rick's taste."

"Oh, he definitely dresses preppie. Haven't you seen him in the Polo ads? He looks so cute with his hair slicked back!"

I laughed. "I know you'll come up with something nice. That magazine" — I pointed to where I'd been sitting — "says the trend is to show skin, but not necessarily cleavage. I guess bare breasts are considered cliché this year. So what does that leave? Halter tops? Short shorts?" I hated to egg her on with sleazy suggestions, but if you wanted to stand out from the pack of golf groupies in the gallery, there was an awful lot of competition.

"Oh, my God, how could I ever repay you?"

"Well, maybe you could help me with something. I came to talk to Dr. Turner about the False Memory Consociation. I need to get some information about what's going on in the Rupert case."

"Oh, so you're not a patient."

"No." I wondered how far the goodwill I'd built up with her over the prospect of meeting Rick Justice could take me. I decided to chance a plunge. "But I'm actually thinking of telling him that I am."

She nibbled at her lower lip. "You'll definitely get more out of him that way. He's one weird doctor. I can't wait to get out of this job. Don't tell him this, but I've got applications in everywhere."

"Weird how?"

"He's always fighting with someone. And either on top of the world or in a really bad mood. This office isn't big enough to stay away from him when he's like that."

"I hate to sound dumb, but I really don't understand what all this false memory stuff is about."

She dropped her voice to a whisper. "He's never really been willing to discuss the organization with me in detail. He says I don't need to know other people's private business. But I think he's spent a lot of time lately hunting down and recruiting parents who've been accused of abuse by their kids. He wants them to fight the counselors who do this kind of work. And he's more aggressive than he ever used to be."

"Lawsuits, you mean?"

"That's all I know about." Her raised eyebrows suggested there had to be more. "All I can say is that if Will Turner goes down, he'll take everyone he can with him." She made a zipping motion across her lips.

I glanced at my watch. It was now 5:30. "Damn, I have a friend waiting out in the car."

"I'll call him and see how much longer he'll be," said Jeanine. She dialed the intercom into Turner's office and had a brief conversation. "He's so sorry. He's just about ready to wrap things up." I heard two doors slam from inside Turner's office.

"Let me give you my cell phone number in case you think of anything else." I handed her a scrap torn off the paper she'd given me. "And I'll call you about the tournament this weekend."

"Miss Burdette?" A tall man with a thin mustache peered out of the office. He wore gray polyester slacks, pilled around the pockets and the seat, and a white short-sleeved shirt so thin I could see the outline of his muscle T-shirt underneath, along with a crop of bushy black chest hair. Definitely a candidate for the fashion "don'ts" column of *My Self* magazine.

"I'm Dr. Turner. Please come in. You can go home now, Jeanine," he said to the secretary. He frowned. "I thought I told you to leave at five." Jeanine scraped the beauty products off her desk into the top drawer and scurried out of the room.

Turner's inner office was as plain as the waiting area. Metal filing cabinets covered one wall; bookshelves piled with masses of papers lined the other side. The desk was crowded with a computer, fax machine, scanner, and more stacks of papers and files. Nothing at all on the walls.

"Have a seat," he said, indicating twins of the metal chairs I'd seen in the outer office. "Sorry about the wait. Sorry about the mess. We just moved in a couple of weeks ago and I haven't got things sorted out." His forehead wrinkled in concentration. "Miss Peters said you wished to discuss a possible family problem with me. Tell me about that."

"I've been in counseling." My voice came out in a squeak. "When I told my mother some of the things I'd been remembering, she begged me to come to talk to you before anything else. . . . Before I confronted my father." Now my voice shook with what I hoped was a reasonable imitation of genuine distress. It didn't take much effort. After Jeanine's description of Turner, this charade had begun to feel seriously dicey.

"Your mother sounds very smart," said Dr. Turner, leaning forward in his chair. "I'm glad you decided to talk to me first. Can you tell me what you've been remembering?"

"I'm really not comfortable going into it," I said. "No offense, but I don't know you at all. If you don't mind, could you talk about what you do first? How you go about helping someone in my situation?"

"Of course," he said, beaming reassurance. "In our research, we've learned that sometimes people remember things about their past that didn't actually happen."

"How do you know that?"

"We've done experiments," he said. "Of course we can't experiment with actual abuse. We wouldn't want to do that and it wouldn't be ethical. But we have implanted false memories in subjects — incidents that we know for a fact did not occur. For example, we may suggest that a person had gotten lost in a shopping mall, separated from their parents as a child. The subjects become convinced these episodes happened, just as if family members had been telling stories about the incident for years."

"No one implanted anything in me," I said.

"We think the same thing can happen in the course of counseling," said Dr. Turner. "Sometimes therapists and counselors tell their clients that their psychological symptoms exist because of hidden abuse in their family. In fact, the abuse never happened. Unfortunately, as you can imagine, the family relationships suffer very badly under this kind of strain."

"Why would my counselor tell me there'd been incest if there wasn't any?" I asked.

Dr. Turner shook his head sadly. "Lots of reasons. Sometimes it's just naïveté, sometimes people are incompetent, sometimes it's zealotry, or greed."

"Sometimes they must be right," I said.

"Of course. But let me be perfectly blunt with you, Cassandra, trauma therapy means a long recovery. And a long recovery means a steady income."

"You mean he told me that those things happened to keep me coming to my sessions?" I opened my eyes wide in what I hoped looked like shocked disbelief. Which wasn't difficult — I *was* shocked. Did shrinks really keep their customers coming just for the income? What about Baxter? Was the frequency of my appointments based on the projected level of his retirement fund?

"It's possible," said Dr. Turner. I had to remind myself that we weren't talking about

Dr. Baxter here. We were trashing a made-up shrink, a hypothetical man without scruples who'd taken advantage of a vulnerable and confused young woman. "I could help more if you'd be willing to describe what your treatment has been like. Did your counselor use memory recovery techniques?"

"He didn't call it that," I said. "What does that mean?"

"There are a number of techniques which allow these people to suggest or implant memories that did not really occur. Hypnosis, massage therapy to uncover body memories, sodium amytyl injections, to name a few." The sneer in his voice was unmistakable.

"I guess I had hypnosis. My counselor said he would take me back to those years so I could remember things I'd forgotten. I don't know what to think. I'm so confused." Now would have been a good time to squeeze a few tears out or at least a few distressed whimpers, but I was afraid Dr. Turner's bullshit detector was a lot more sophisticated than that of the girls in the Bible study group.

"Look over this checklist." He handed me a pamphlet. "It was designed to help people determine whether their therapists are doing honest work with them. See what you think, then we can talk some more."

"Maybe I'd feel more comfortable telling you about the memories in another appointment," I said. "I'm just not up to it today."

"It's certainly not my intention to talk you out of something that really happened," said Turner. The volume of his voice went up a few decibels. "But I am interested in protecting you from an ill-intentioned and unprofessional counselor. Truth is, there are therapists out there who destroy lives with their dogmatism and greed." He took a deep breath. When he resumed speaking, his voice had dropped back to a normal volume. "Sometimes it helps to take the glass half-empty, half-full approach."

"I'm sorry?"

"Let me give you an example. I'm not asking for details now, but did you have any good times with your father? Close your eyes and think about a birthday party that you remember when your father was present."

I shut my eyes. Memories of my tenth birthday came to my mind, the only party I could remember my father attending. Long before the advent of hiring clowns or other expensive party entertainment, Mom had planned a scavenger hunt in our neighborhood. My father came home early from his duties at the Grandpappy and took my friends around looking for the list of souvenirs she'd provided. By the end of the afternoon, all twelve of my guests were in love with him. They adored his knock-knock jokes, his terrible but energetic imitation of Elvis singing

"(Let Me Be Your) Teddy Bear," and the way he had of listening to you like what you said was the most important thing he'd ever heard. That was the day Mom christened him "Mr. Fun." I felt real tears running down my cheeks.

Dr. Turner looked satisfied. "I can see you understand what I mean. Sometimes therapists forget to look at the whole picture. He's told you your glass is half empty. Maybe it's half full. No parents are perfect, Cassandra. But most of us struggle to do our best. You may need to look for the silver lining."

"I was about ready to come in there after you," said Laura, when I located her in the tropical fish department of the pet store at the end of the strip mall. "You look like hell. Let's go get a drink and some real food. I got a recommendation for a French place in Venice. My treat — it's a good-luck splurge." I was happy to turn the reins over to her.

Over a crabmeat imperial crêpe, spinach soufflé, and a glass of Chardonnay, I updated Laura on the events surrounding Kaitlin's lawsuit and Bencher's murder, including my visits to the Bible study group and Dr. Turner.

"Jeanine said that Turner's organization has been very active lately. She says he's ruthless."

Laura rolled her eyes. "Mind if I ask a few questions here?" I knew she'd ask them even if I did mind.

"What was in the folders you saw on Bencher's floor?"

"I don't know. I didn't have the time or the wherewithal to read them," I said.

"Okay. What was on the floor around the folders?"

"Nothing important, as far as I could tell. Shards of glass from the broken coffeepot."

"Did you see or hear anyone in the office or out in the hallway after you found Bencher?"

"No."

"My point is, you don't know anything, Cassie. You've got yourself all wound up thinking someone is after you for information, when you don't have any. You just got damned unlucky stumbling into that scene. You had nothing to do with it."

"I know that," I said. "It's Pate that keeps bringing all this stuff up."

"Pate's an ass," said Laura. "I can tell that without even laying an eyeball on him. From what you've told me, there's no one threatening you except for him. And he's wreaking havoc on what is already your tenuous grip on mental stability."

"Thanks a lot, pal."

"Listen. Q-school starts tomorrow. You've got to drop the cloak-and-dagger routine and let the cops do their work. You're a mallard in the rain, Cassie, a mallard in the rain."

"Excuse me?"

160

"Water off a duck's back, babe. Take in Sheriff Pate's nonsense like water off a duck's back."

She paid the check and led me back to the Starlight Motel for a Laura Snow–imposed early curfew.

# 13

Finally it was here: my first day of School, with a knee-knocking capital *S*. When I pulled into the club in the near darkness at 6:30, the range was deserted. Now, with the first streaks of sun lighting up the golf course like a carpet of emeralds, every centimeter of the practice area was filled. And no light-hearted chitchat today. I heard only the crack of balls whistling out into the range and the quiet murmur of caddies coaching their golfers. Laura had roared off on a quick tour of our first hurdle — the Bobcat course — with my notes and the LPGA yardage book in hand.

As Mike's caddie on the PGA Tour, I'd loved this moment in a golf tournament most of all. Not one shot had been officially struck, so in theory, anything was possible. There was no discouraging high round from yesterday to overcome, no muffed shot from the last hole to forget, not even a fantastic finish to live up to. None of the confidence-crushing history of previous rounds. There was only hope, promise, and enthusiasm for the round ahead.

I hit about a hundred balls out into the

range, running through my clubs from wedge to three-wood. The results, though unspectacular, were respectable in a reassuring and familiar way. Finally satisfied, I cleaned the grooves on the clubs and wiped down the grips, humming Patsy Cline's "Someday You'll Want Me to Want You." Patsy never gave up on love, though you could tell she knew what heartbreak felt like firsthand.

"How's it look out there?" I asked Laura when she returned.

"Manageable," she said. "How'd your warm-up go?"

"Good. I just need to chip and putt."

"You've got the time, baby," she said. "Five hours, to be exact." We'd argued about getting over to the golf club so early. With a one o'clock starting time, she had strongly suggested I hang around the motel, maybe exercise or watch a couple of talk shows so I wouldn't get too jazzed up waiting to tee off. I'd told her no way was she going without me.

By ten o'clock, I had to admit she was right. I'd visited the bathroom so many times, I caused a rumor about a virulent strain of the stomach flu. I'd been to the driving range twice more, with declining results for each successive excursion. Tom Reilly, the LPGA public relations coordinator and a captive audience, stationed by his laptop in the tournament office, was my new best bud. He now knew more than he'd ever wanted about the Burdette family tree and my junior golf experiences.

Finally, I'd memorized Walter Moore's slick sales approach to the women warming up at the range: what Deikon manufacturing and I can do for your financial and golfing future. I noticed he only selected six or seven of the bigger hitters for his pitch. Girls who'd make his clubs look good if they made it onto the Tour using his equipment. Girls who'd make any clubs look good, anywhere.

"Cassie, how are you?" I stopped my pacing, astonished to see Max Harding in front of me.

"What the hell are you doing here?"

"Here at the tournament? Business. Here with you? I've been wanting to talk to you since I ran into you the other night at Chili-Dippers."

"This is a lousy time to talk. I'm teeing off in forty-five minutes."

He nodded. "I know. Sorry. Maybe I can catch up with you later. Hey, good luck. I know you're going to be great." I watched him walk all the way back to the clubhouse. He filled out the yellow Cutter and Buck golf shirt just as well as he had the business suit I saw him in last week. I returned to the putting green for one last session.

"Putter and I are one," I muttered. I jabbed at a practice Titleist ball. It went screaming past the hole I was shooting for.

"Let's go," said Laura. "Ten minutes to blastoff."

We met our playing partners waiting on the path leading up to the first tee. I introduced Laura to Julie Atwater. I wasn't sure whether it would help or hinder to share a cart and play with her again today, not that I had any say about it. On the bright side, she'd be familiar, and familiar was good. On the dark side, we'd both played lousy yesterday — just seeing her here brought that springing clearly to mind. I knew we'd stay away from discussions about her possibly confused sexuality or my problems with finding dead bodies. That could only help my focus.

Our third contestant, Heather Boyle, had brought her fiancé as caddie and her mother as gallery. The mother was elfin-sized, with painted eyebrows and lids, spiked hair, and pixie sparkles on her cheeks. The boyfriend looked more like a banker than a caddie — blond and solid, the kind of solid that would turn on him fast as he edged closer to middle age. All three seemed pleasant, but distant, just focused on Heather. As we waited for the threesome in front of us to hit their first drives of the day, Gary Rupert approached the tee.

"Hope the day goes well for you, Cassie," he said. He moved close enough to rub my shoulders. Which reminded me for a minute of Odell Washington. And felt damned good, I had to admit.

"I don't think you've met Laura Snow," I said. "She'll be piecing me together this week. Laura, this is Gary Rupert, Kaitlin's brother." He stopped his massage long enough to shake her hand.

"Take good care of her," said Gary. "She's got a bright future." He trotted back down the path toward the tenth hole, where I knew Kaitlin would be teeing off in twenty minutes. He passed Julie polishing her balls at the ball washer without a word or a smile.

"I don't like that guy," Julie said, as she reached our cart and threw her putter in her bag.

"It's time, ladies," called the starter.

"Get your butt onto the tee box," said Laura. "You've been waiting here seven hours and you're going to disqualify yourself by standing around like a bonehead outside the ropes?"

Julie and Heather laughed at her scolding. We compared the brand of balls we were playing and the identifying marks we'd drawn on them — a smiley face for Heather, a big, black JA on Julie's, and two blue slashes under the Slazenger cat logo for me. Receiving a two-stroke penalty for hitting the wrong ball would be a demoralizing mistake. Then Heather leaned over, balanced her ball on the tee, and stood back to squint down the fairway.

"Say a prayer that it goes straight," whispered

Heather's mother. Heather swung, producing a low, straight ball that skimmed the center of the fairway and rolled up the hill and out of sight.

"Nice ball," said Julie, taking her place on the tee. Her drive leaned right and skidded into the fairway bunker she'd found the day before.

"Next on the tee, Cassandra Burdette from Myrtle Beach, South Carolina." My legs felt wobbly and my arms like overcooked Ramen noodles. Laura smiled reassurance. The other girls were smiling, too. More, I assumed, from the relief of getting off the tee themselves than for my benefit.

I waggled my three-wood and stared down the fairway. "You can do it," I whispered. "Let it go." I coiled up and launched an adrenaline-powered drive that landed just short of where Heather's ball had come to rest.

"Good start," said Laura, as I hopped into the cart and roared by with Julie. When we reached my ball, I chose a seven-iron without hesitation and hit it to the back of the green. A triumph — a birdie try on the first hole. Never mind that the putt was unsinkable by anyone outside of Tiger Woods. I leaned over against the cart to stretch my calf muscles while the others hit their second shots.

"Do you have something going with that Gary?" Laura asked, breathing hard from her jog up the fairway.

The blood rushing to my face felt hot.

"What do you mean?"

"You know what I mean," she said. "The little public massage. The 'she's got a bright future' routine. Does that guy have the hots for you?"

"That's Kaitlin's brother," I said, not addressing her question. "I know him from high school and we've talked some about the tournament and the mess she's in."

Laura shrugged. "Just checking, pal. It's a little hard to keep up with you and your guys. Remind me later to tell you my theory about you and men."

"It's not fair to leave me hanging," I said. She laughed, took the putter from my bag, and walked toward the green.

I putted first, my approach having skidded off the back of the green, sixty feet from the front pin placement.

"Just get it to the hole," said Laura. "Right edge."

I sent the putt across the entire length of the green. It passed the cup and dove back off the putting surface onto the far-side collar. "I got it there," I said grimly. Two putts later, I carded a bogey and we headed on to the second hole, a par four lined with a water hazard along the right side.

"The second shot's blind," I told Laura. "The whole fairway slopes right. It's not an easy hole. And the green's even trickier."

"Fairway first," she said. "Then we aim for

the center of the green. We'll worry about the putt when we get there."

In spite of a cement truck passing by in the backswing of my drive, and a weed-whacker starting up during my approach, I hit two serviceable shots and produced my second birdie try. This time, I would not underestimate the speed of the green, I assured myself. Three putts later, Heather wrote another bogey on my card.

"No problem," Laura told me. "You got caught up in worrying about the speed and forgot about the line. You're getting the hang of them. We're doing great."

We crossed the road to the third hole, a par three with water on the left, condos on the right. The group in front of us had just arrived on the green.

"Looks like it could be a long day," said Heather.

"We've got the time," said her fiancé. Easy for him to be cheerful: Heather had shown no flaws in her game so far.

"What's Max Harding doing down here?" asked Laura as we waited.

"He said business."

"He's Coach Rupert's lawyer now?" I nodded. "Why would that bring him here?" I shrugged.

"These girls are so slow our clothes will be out of style by the time we finish the round," said Heather.

"Don't sweat the small stuff," said her fiancé. I wondered if they'd spend a lifetime of marriage speaking in cliches.

By the time the girls ahead finally cleared the green, I felt even tighter than I had on the first tee. I popped my drive up short of the green.

"At least it's not wet," said Laura. "And chipping's your game."

*Was* my game, I thought, after chunking the shot fifteen yards short of the flag. I banged my ball up the hill. Instead of curving gently to the left and dropping into the cup as I'd predicted, the putt held its line and hung out six inches from the hole.

"Tough break," said Laura. "You made a good run at it."

I stomped off to the fourth tee. Heather teed off with another screaming drive and Julie followed closely on her heels.

I could feel the gears churning in my brain. There are two kinds of golfers out there, those who play by understanding mechanics and those who play by feel. The mechanical players, like Nick Faldo, are always tinkering with their swing. They want to know precisely where the toe of the club should point at each position on the backswing. They've spent hours with slow-motion videotapes and full-length mirrors getting their swings just right. I wasn't in this camp.

I liked to understand the golf swing along

170

with the best of them, but when it came to working around the greens, I was strictly a feel player. I just seemed to have an easy knack for reading the contours and knowing what speed would get the ball to the hole. Maybe it came from having grown up around a golf course. The point was, this was where I thought I'd really make up for other weaknesses. Length off the tee, for one glaring example.

But today, my so-called feel had evaporated, leaving me alone with shortish tee shots and even shorter on confidence. I knew that pairings in a tournament could have a big effect on a golfer's state of mind. If you got stuck with a girl who was off her game, it was hard not to be poisoned by her choppy rhythm or foul mood. On the other hand, a girl playing in zone, and it looked like Heather was headed that way today, could carry a struggling golfer right along with her. I sure hoped this would happen with me.

I stood up on the tee box and manufactured a weak slice, which rolled to the right, almost dribbling into the pond that ran along the length of the hole.

"Forget about it," said Laura. "Everyone's got to lay up on this hole — you'll just have a five-iron in your hand instead of an eight."

As she'd predicted, all three of us laid up in front of the pond that guarded the green, then hit third shots on. The Plantation had some pretty vistas, but this green was not among the most picturesque it had to offer. It was lined by crackerbox ranch homes crowded with the flotsam of vacation living: above-ground pools, swing sets, buzzing lawn mowers, and, to top it off today, a frantically barking dog on a too-short leash.

"Say a prayer that it goes in," said Heather's mother as her daughter stood over her putt. God was going to be awfully busy this afternoon, watching over each of Heather's shots. She sank the birdie putt and walked off the green into her fiancé's embrace.

I, without the benevolent intervention of either a mother or a higher power, pulled my birdie putt left. "Shit!" I said, not so softly. "We might as well be playing putt-putt golf in a trailer park. There's no way I can concentrate with that racket going on."

Laura nodded. "Let me know if I can help," she said.

"You can muzzle that freaking mutt," I said. "Now that would be helpful."

We made the turn with me four over par, not a good omen even by Laura's ever-optimistic standards.

"The hell with a training regimen," I said. "I need a big, fat hot dog, maybe two. Mustard, sauerkraut, and onions. And if they sold Budweiser, I'd buy one of those too."

"What training regimen?" Laura laughed. We ordered hot dogs and chips and stuffed them down while we waited for the tenth tee to clear.

# 14

With the pressure relieved for the moment, I had time to notice that the puffy clouds that had filled the sky earlier this morning were turning dark gray. The starter informed us that the weather channel had promised 100 percent humidity. I felt every percentage point.

"Pray the rain holds off until we finish the round," said Heather's mother. By now, I couldn't have said which was more annoying — her mind-numbing commentary or the relentless squeak, squeak, squeak of her tennis shoes trailing behind us on every shot.

"New nine," said Laura. "Fairways and greens, then we'll worry about putts."

Maybe it was the nitrites in the hot dog, maybe I was just too tired to remain as tightly wrapped as I had been on the first nine holes. But my swing felt less foreign, and the ball stayed within the range I'd come to call "straight." After a near-miss putt on thirteen, I'd made two pars, one birdie, and only one bogey. No one liked a bogey on a par five, but at least I'd managed to scrape along without any penalty shots. Overall, holding steady. Then, an enormous crack of thunder clapped overhead, followed by one prolonged horn blast coming from the direction of the distant clubhouse.

"That's the warning siren! We've got to take shelter," said Heather's fiancé. "They said not to hit another shot after play is suspended." We all piled on the golf carts and rode to the shelter attached to the rest room to wait out the storm. Heather and her entourage began to discuss the merits of her new putting stroke.

"What's your beef with Gary Rupert?" I asked Julie, preferring to make conversation about anything other than golf.

"He's arrogant," she said. "He hit on me last month. Since I turned him down, he acts like we've never spoken. I hate that kind of guy — everything, including common decency, revolves around whether you worship their sex appeal."

I didn't say anything. Truth was, Gary had been nothing but charming as far as I was concerned. I could empathize with the "hit on" experience, but from my perspective, it was rather exciting.

Two more cartloads of golfers and their caddies streamed into the shelter, drenched from the sudden downpour. A tall woman with a long, narrow face and very dark eyebrows was shrieking at her caddie. "Damn it to hell, I know the goddamn rules. I played on the damn Tour for two years. Do you think I'd risk my damn career doing something that stupid?"

"I think she was trying to be helpful," the caddie offered.

"Calling in the rules official to chastise us? You call that helpful?" The tall woman poked a finger in her caddie's chest. "I'm warning you," she said. "Keep that bitch away from me or you're likely to find golf cart tire tread marks across her forehead." She stomped out from under the shelter into the driving rain and crossed the cart path to stand under a firecracker bush. Aptly chosen, I thought.

I glanced again at her caddie. He had a shoulder-length blond ponytail and blond mustache, and he'd dressed all in white, including a white straw cowboy hat. He looked like he belonged in some location more exotic than a Florida golf course. I suspected that's where he wished he was.

"What happened?" Julie asked him.

"Kaitlin Rupert turned us in for riding together on the cart," said the caddie.

"Did you get a penalty?"

"We had to argue like hell to convince the guy I'd only been standing on the cart while it was stopped at the tee. He let us off with a warning. Next time he catches us, it'll cost us two strokes. Believe me, there are lots of other ways she could add two strokes to her score. We don't need that one." He dipped his head in the tall golfer's direction. "I guess

175

I'd better go try to calm her down. Not sure that's even possible."

"That's Kaitlin," said Julie, watching the caddie dash through the rain to the firecracker bush. "She's always scanning the horizon to see who might be inching ahead of her. And then wondering how she could knock them back. She's got her nose in everyone else's business like a dog tracking a hot trail."

"Then how are you two friends?" I asked.

Julie shrugged. "For whatever reason, she helped me out when I needed it. Still, I wouldn't describe us as friends. I feel sorry for her. She has no clue how she comes off and how she pushes people away."

"It shouldn't take a brain surgeon to figure that out," said Laura.

"She needs kindness, too," said Julie, her voice quiet. "Jesus didn't only befriend people who were easy to get along with."

The hour we spent waiting out the thunderstorm improved no one's game, including mine. Even Heather, with heaven and her mother watching over her, hit her tee shot out of bounds on fourteen and took a double bogey. I had managed a birdie on the par-three fifteenth, but lost that advantage with three-putts for bogeys on the final two holes. A big, fat seventy-seven: five strokes over par for the course and nowhere close to the score of my dreams.

"Not that I had that much to work with after the front nine," I said to Laura as we walked off the eighteenth green. "What's a couple more three-putts if you're not going to make the cut anyway."

"That's a lousy attitude," said Laura. I checked over and countersigned my card, then turned it in to the scorer's tent. Kaitlin and Gary were arriving from the ninth hole as we left. Out of Kaitlin's line of sight, Gary saluted me with a smile and a thumbs-up.

"I heard you shot the second lowest score today, Miss Rupert," a bystander said. "I'm with Golfnews Online. Could I have a few words with you when you finish here?"

"Let's hang around a minute," said Laura. "I want to hear this."

"How was it out there?" the reporter asked when Kaitlin emerged from the tent.

"I had a fantastic day," she said. "I played great. I hit greens; my putter was hot so I made some birdies. It was more fun than I could have imagined."

"There had to be a lot of pressure out on the course today. How did you keep your focus?"

"I just hit every shot as though this was my last day ever playing golf," said Kaitlin. "That way, everything else just dropped away." She patted Gary's forearm. "And my caddie was awesome."

"Don Sandos from the *Herald-Tribune*,"

called out another reporter. Her royal golfing highness flashed a gracious smile in his direction. "We've heard a rumor that the False Memory Consociation is planning to contribute to your father's defense against your lawsuit. Would you care to comment?" Kaitlin's smile faded. Her shoulders tightened and she drew a slow breath.

"My father can spend as much as he likes. Run up the national debt, for all I care. Throwing money around will not change the facts. Will you excuse me, please? I'm in a tournament here." She huffed off toward the scoreboard. Gary trotted behind her, her enormous green plaid bag banging his calves as he ran.

"That must be why Max Harding's in town," I whispered to Laura. "Maybe they're upping the pressure on her when she's vulnerable, hoping she'll drop the lawsuit."

"Would Rupert do that to his own daughter in the middle of Q-school?" Laura said.

I shrugged. "There's an awful lot at stake on both sides."

We trailed Kaitlin back to the clubhouse, where a small crowd had gathered. Most were players who'd finished earlier in the day and waited anxiously for the news of the afternoon rounds. Julie's disheveled father stood in the background with his Leviticus sign, guarded by Sheriff Pate.

"Repent and the Lord will have mercy!" he shouted in our direction.

"Stand back," ordered Sheriff Pate. "Step aside."

"One Kings, fourteen: twenty-four," shouted Julie's father, thrusting his sign toward Kaitlin. "And there were also perverted persons in the land."

"He's not altogether wrong about that," I whispered to Laura.

"I can't even believe he's related to Julie," she whispered back. "She seems so normal."

We made a wide circle around Julie's father and approached the scoreboard that dominated the west side of the clubhouse. The scores from the morning had already been posted. The low round, sixty-seven, belonged to So Won Lee.

"Now there's a score you could sleep like a baby on," I said to Laura.

"Haven't you ever heard the expression 'sleeping on the lead'?" she asked. "It's a different kind of pressure, but pressure all the same. Most players I've seen shoot a super-low score like that blew up in the next round."

Kaitlin and Gary Rupert watched as her name was inscribed in Black Magic marker under the number sixty-eight, just below So Won Lee's sixty-seven. She accepted the congratulations of a cluster of players, then swept off toward the locker room. With the help of Laura's not so gentle persuasion, I dragged myself back to the putting green. There were demons to slay — I had to put today behind me, taking from it only what I could use profitably in tomorrow's round.

"I'm thinking about changing my grip back over to the right hand down," I told Laura.

"I don't think you need to change anything," she said. "Your stroke looks terrific. Let's just work on tempo." We putted for half an hour — first, long lag putts, then dozens of short no-brainers that could turn into knee-knockers under the high-beam pressure of the tournament.

"I need a break," I said. We stretched out on a bench in the shade. "You were going to tell me your theory about me and men."

"It's no big deal," she said. "I was just thinking about what a hard time you've had choosing a driver this year. You try them for such a short time, you don't give yourself the chance to know if one really suits your game. Maybe it's the same thing with you and guys."

"I change drivers because my tee shots stink," I said.

"You could probably use any one of those clubs, if you stayed with it long enough to get used to it. You have the skills, it's what's in your head that trips you up."

"If I can't hit a driver any farther than I do the three-wood, there's no advantage to carrying one. One-fourteenth of my club allotment is wasted — I'd rather have a third wedge. Using a driver I can't handle only gets me into trouble."

Laura smirked. "Like I was saying about your guys . . ."

"You know what? I'm not paying you to analyze my psychological issues. I'm paying you to carry the damned bag. Or, in this case, the damned putter, since the bag is riding on a cart."

"I hadn't noticed you cutting any paychecks at all," said Laura.

Her cell phone rang.

"Hello?" She listened to an excited female voice on the other end of the line. "Let me see what Cassie thinks," she said, then placed her palm over the mouthpiece. "It's my aunt Barbara. She wants to know if I'll come down to Boca Grande and spend the night with her. I said I'd have to talk with you. If you need me here tonight, I'll wait to visit until the tournament's over."

At this moment, space between me and Laura felt like a gift. As badly as I'd wanted to have her here, the intimacy of her commentary had begun to feel abrasive and maddening. "You should go," I said. "She doesn't get the chance to see you much. I'll be fine. I'm just going to get to bed early and rest up for tomorrow."

"Sure you don't mind?"

I nodded vigorously. As she concluded her conversation with her aunt, loud voices drifted over from the driving range. I turned and saw Kaitlin screaming at Walter Moore.

"I thought we had an exclusive deal here," she said. Her complexion had flushed to a mottled red and a hank of hair had sprung loose from her usually perfect ponytail.

"I said we would sponsor you. I never said you would be the only one that we sponsored."

"She's Oriental, for God's sake," said Kaitlin. "You think that's going to sell golf clubs?" Now her voice verged on hysterical.

"She hits the ball longer than any woman I've ever seen. You included. That's what sells golf clubs," said Walter. "And just for your information, Oriental is for rugs. Asian is for people." He stalked away, leaving her fuming alone on the range.

"Tut, tut," murmured Laura. "A lovers' spat."

"Go, Walter," I said. "I wouldn't have believed he had that much backbone in him."

"Afternoon, ladies," said the gravelly voice of Sheriff Pate. The bench creaked as he lowered his bulk down next to Laura. He sighed and mopped his forehead with a graying handkerchief. "I thought the thunderstorm would cool things off."

"I'm Laura Snow. You must be Sheriff Pate." She shook his hand. "You guys had your hands full out there today."

"You're tellin' me," he said, puffing up at her recognition of his importance.

"Any progress on the Bencher case?"

Pate snorted. "They've decided they like one of his wacko patients for the murder. The guy showed up at the Myrtle Beach station and confessed. He had a bloody rag with him he claims he used to try to stop the doctor's bleeding after he shot him. Voices told him Bencher needed ventilation in his neck."

"I guess we won't need to have any more of our chats, then," I said. "I'll miss them so." Laura pinched me.

"Personally, I think the guy's a crackpot who made that up for some extra attention," said the sheriff, staring at me. "I doubt we've seen the last of each other, Miss Burdette." He hoisted himself up off the bench, arranged his clothing over his stomach, and walked away.

"Nice going, Cass," exclaimed Laura. "It's not a good move to aggravate the law."

"He deserves it," I said fighting back my irritation. "I'm going to get some dinner and get to bed. If I don't know how to putt by now, it's all history anyway."

I was relieved to have the evening alone. Both of us were way too crabby to stay the night together in a small space without danger of a serious squabble. At this point, my own personality quirks were all I could handle.

# 15

Laura left me at the Cracker Barrel, happily gorging myself on meat loaf, fried okra, and biscuits dogpaddling in sausage gravy. I didn't feel tired by the time I returned to the room, though I knew I should follow my own advice about getting to bed early. I'd hate to run out of steam halfway through tomorrow's round. I washed up and got into bed with the thriller I'd brought with me. After I'd read the first chapter three times, I gave up and turned out the light.

Against my will, my mind began to run over my performance today, lingering painfully on the bogey putts on one, two, three, five, thirteen, seventeen, and eighteen. Anyway you looked at it, seventy-seven could not be considered an LPGA-quality performance. Then my mind shifted seamlessly to the Panther course. I began to review all the ways I could get into trouble, especially on the holes comprising the Panther's Claw.

Cut it out, I told myself. Think about something else, anything else.

Next subject. It annoyed me that my friends felt so free to analyze my problems getting committed to a man. Laura herself was no paragon of mental health when it came to this issue. As far as I could tell, she hadn't gone on a date since we'd graduated from Florida. Which put her damned close to her freshness expiration date. Even so, she seemed completely unself-conscious about her dedication to her dad. What would Bencher have made of that?

"When Mom died, it was just me and Dad," she told me a couple months ago. "He stuck with me through the worst time in my life. So I'm sticking with him until he doesn't need me around anymore. It may sound queer or screwed up, but that's the way it is. There'll be plenty of time later to think about finding a guy I want to marry and spend the rest of my life with."

Truth was, I couldn't really picture myself ever getting married. Though, as Dr. Baxter had pointed out, I did have a certain one-day-my-prince-will-come mentality. I couldn't help myself, raised as I had been on bride and groom paper dolls and Barbie and Ken. My grandmother sewed my Barbie a formal wedding gown from white satin and scraps of Belgian lace. Over and over, I played rehearsal dinner and then society wedding. Sick.

"Run while you still can, Ken," my father used to tell the boy doll before Barbie minced down the aisle.

"That's not funny," Mom would say.

"I didn't mean it as a joke," said Dad.

Making the mental leap from general neurosis to old flames, I thought about running into Max Harding. He had, as they say about old wines, aged extremely well. Not that he wasn't fine in those early days. For a couple of months during my sophomore year, I'd been the envy of the female population of the high school. I'd overheard girls gossiping in the hallways about why he'd chosen me — a small, gawky, shy, tomboy golfer — instead of one of the popular and glamorous cheerleaders who'd have killed to take my place. All of which meant I had a long way to fall when he dumped me without explanation. If I was willing to dig around, I could still feel the deep well of shame and hurt I'd locked away ten years ago.

But I wasn't willing, so back to the facts. What was he really doing at Q-school? It seemed unlikely that Kaitlin's lawsuit would have brought him down to Florida, unless he had business with the False Memory Consociation. It occurred to me that the guy I'd seen talking to Gary Rupert in the bar the other night looked a great deal like Max. Then I remembered my mother's phone message about Max coming into the restaurant for lunch. It made no sense that he would be in Florida on Saturday, Myrtle Beach on Sunday, then back in Florida today.

But speaking of Gary, what was up with that? If Laura was right and we had something going, I had no idea what it was. I wished Jack Wolfe were here. I knew part of the problem was just plain loneliness. In the end, having a boyfriend seven thousand miles away was about as much use as having no one at all. Besides which, Jack would know exactly how it felt to be in my position. He'd been through his own Q-school nightmare last year. And he had a way of taking things so easily.

"You're tense, Cassie. Go ahead and have a beer," I imagined him saying. In honor of Jack, and bowing to my spinning brain, I got up and cracked open the second-to-last can of Busch. Halfway through the last can, the phone rang.

"Cassie, it's Joe. I hope I'm not waking you up. How are you? How was the day?"

"Not great," I admitted. "Call me the bogey queen. I shot a big, fat seventy-seven."

"Hmmm," said Joe. "Tough day. Tell me the good parts."

I described the two birdies on the back nine. "My problem is putting. And the bad news is, I'm playing on the Panther tomorrow. Its greens are much faster because of the broken sprinkler system."

"Did you spend some time on the putting green after you played?"

"Duh," I said. "With Laura cracking the whip? Of course I did."

He laughed.

"How's Mike doing?" I asked.

"I think I'm on the verge of being fired," said Joe. "He's like a munitions storage facility. The smallest spark and the whole thing may blow."

"Sounds familiar." I'd felt like that myself today. And the experience was giving me a lot more empathy for Mike's roller-coaster moods — I'd come to know them well while carrying his bag. Now I realized there was no way someone else, no matter how well-meaning she was, could understand this kind of pressure secondhand.

"Have a plan for tomorrow?" Joe asked. "How will you calm yourself down?"

"I'm drinking a beer," I said. "It's the best I can do on short notice."

"I'm not so sure that's a good move, Cass."

"Jack would say you should do what you always do before a round of golf. If you usually have a few drinks or a big meal, go for it. You shouldn't make changes in your routine that will distract you from your mental preparation."

For a moment, Joe was silent. "I don't know that Jack's the expert on preparing for a big match."

"At least he's a player," I said. "He's not one of those guys that stands around telling other people how to do it."

"Fine," said Joe. "But he barely earned a dime on the Tour, and as a reward, he got himself banished halfway around the world." I heard him breathe in sharply. "I'm sorry. I didn't call to fight with you. I only wanted to wish you well." His voice was very formal now.

I matched his tone. "Thank you. I'd better get some rest."

I lay back down and turned out the light. I reviewed the conversation with Joe, then caromed back to the seven three-putts, then back to Joe. Things were out of control if I was even picking fights with him — a paragon of unflappability. There was no way I would sleep now. I got up, threw on my jeans and a T-shirt, and walked to the nearby convenience store to buy more beer.

As I got off the elevator, I heard the phone ringing through the door of my room. I struggled to slide the card key into the lock, ran inside, and grabbed the phone. With all fingers and toes crossed, I hoped it would be Jack.

"Cassie? It's Max Harding. I'm sorry to call you so late." I was silent. Shocked, actually. Almost as if I'd conjured him up again, just by thinking about him. "Um, your mom gave me your phone number. I know it was bad timing to try to talk to you earlier today. I wanted to apologize to you for that. And for high school."

"For high school?" Jesus, wasn't he about ten years too late? His hoarse breathing filled the receiver.

"Gosh, this is harder than I thought it would be. I'd really like to do this in person. Could I come by for a few minutes and talk to you? I feel terrible about what's happened."

"I don't think so. Jesus, Max. Give it a rest. That was ten years ago. It's late and I'm tired. What could we possibly have to say to each other?"

"Please, Cassie," he said. "Just a couple of minutes. I know I've behaved like a first-class ass. Please let me explain." I thought for a minute. It was a stretch to imagine that anything good could come of having him over. A late-night chat with Max Harding would not fit into anybody's idea of a training regimen.

"Sorry. I have to be up early. Let's just leave it alone."

"I'm begging you. I really want to make this right." The pleading tone in his voice melted my resolve.

"I'll give you ten minutes."

While I waited, I splashed cold water on my face. I thought about dabbing perfume on the pulse points of my neck.

He's married to someone else, you idiot, I told myself, and grabbed a Busch from the minifridge instead. I drained half of the beer and considered the perfume again.

What the hell! He deserved to feel lousy about the good thing he passed up. I finished the beer, then brushed my hair and my teeth, applied lip gloss, and spritzed myself with

Oscar de la Renta. Max knocked at my door.

"Thanks for seeing me. I feel so stupid about all of this." He looked longingly at my beer.

"Help yourself if you want a beer," I said, gesturing to the bar. "I'll take one too." He opened two bottles and handed me one. He sat down in the chair beside me, the no-stain slipcover crackling as he squirmed to get comfortable. His Adam's apple bobbed as he took a long pull on the Busch.

"How did you play today?" he asked.

"I played lousy," I said. "You came over here after ten years at this time of night to ask about my golf game?"

"You aren't in the mood to cut me any slack, are you, Cass?" I shook my head no. After three beers in quick succession, I wasn't holding back.

"You must think I'm a real rat." He sighed. "I know it looks bad — what happened after that night on the beach."

"No," I said. "It looked pretty good for you. It looked like you were out to get laid for the night, and you did. You got just what you wanted. I was a big, dumb sucker. End of story."

"That's not it, Cass. I loved being with you. I really meant to call you. I wish I could explain it now, I wish I could have then." He tore strips off the label of the beer bottle and balled them up while I waited for him to go on.

"Remember when we cut Mr. Romero's class and drove down to Savannah?"

"Dave wanted to kill both of us," I said. "Mom thought grounding me for life would be enough punishment."

"How about the time it snowed two inches and they closed school?"

"We drove all over town trying to borrow a sled," I said, laughing. "The trash can lids worked pretty well, though."

"We had a lot of fun together," Max said. He reached over and brushed a strand of hair off my forehead.

"Why are we discussing this now?" I said, pulling back out of his range. "I won't lie to you, you really hurt my feelings. But I got along fine without you. And you and Brenda have done just dandy, too, from the sound of it." Max winced. "We made a mistake. It's medieval history now." I stood up and strode to the door. "Thanks for your concern. I think you should leave."

Max followed me across the room. "But that's what I came to say. I don't think that night was a mistake. I've thought about it every day since then. You are the most beautiful woman I've ever known. You're strong." He squeezed my bicep. "And soft at the same time." His fingers barely touched my cheek.

Laura's warning about me and men reverberated in my head. Maybe I didn't give any guy a decent chance before I cut him off. On the other hand, Max was definitely married. A few beers could not obscure that basic truth. I knew getting involved with him in any intimate way would confuse me further and leave behind a legacy of shame. Still, I felt a powerful connection to him — same as I had years ago, but amplified by that abrupt and painful finale. I fidgeted, my stomach flip-flopping and my heart pounding. Max reached out to take my hand, and drew me close. I tugged my hand away.

"You can't finish this," I warned, "so don't even start."

"Shhh . . . It's okay." He pulled me back close to him. He kissed me, first gently, then with the fierce passion I remembered from our one night together. He ran his hands through my curls and down my back and over the curve of my buttocks. I hugged him tightly, filled with a mixture of piercing excitement and dread. He fumbled with the top button of my jeans and loosened the shirt from my pants. I traced the line of his jaw with my index finger. Kissing me again, he slid his hands under my T-shirt and massaged my back. All the while, one small, sober section of my brain looked on in disbelief.

"You're so beautiful, Cassie," he whispered. "Even more beautiful than you were back then." He unhooked my bra and cradled the soft weight of my breasts in his hands, brushing my nipples with his thumbs. Then the beeper in Max's back pocket shrilled. He pulled away, leaving my brassiere draped around my neck, while he sheepishly studied the number on the display window.

"It's Brenda," he said, his voice flat. I yanked my shirt down over my hips. He sat down abruptly, his shoulders sagging. For several moments, he was silent.

"I'm sorry," he finally said. "I came over to apologize for being a boor. Now what can I say? The truth is, as much as I wish it were different, I guess I should never have come."

I straightened my clothes, confused and drunk. "Just get the fuck out, Max." I had no pity for the agony in his face.

"I'm really sorry if I hurt you. I'm more sorry that what should have been a beginning had to end."

"Nice closing statement, Counselor." I walked to the door and jerked it open. "You didn't even bother with the fucking Boone's Farm Apple Wine this time."

"I'm sorry. I'm sorry." He stumbled slightly and caught himself on the doorjamb. "Good luck tomorrow. Take care."

I slammed the door closed behind him.

I won't think about this, I said to myself, my body rigid with anger and shame. It's best to go on as if this hadn't happened. I hooked my bra closed, tugged tight the corners of the bedspread, straightened the faded drapes, hurled Max's beer bottle into the trash. Three-pointer. I took a hundred practice swings in the mirror with the Ben Hogan nine-iron. Then I lay awake on the bed until almost four, searching for a way to block out my feelings.

Drapes: vertical. TV: horizontal. Highboy: vertical. Hide-a-Bed: horizontal.

But the lingering humiliation was strong — too powerful even for Joe Lancaster's mental techniques. Six a.m. could not come soon enough.

# 16

I sat with Walter Moore again at breakfast. Even his company seemed preferable to facing the thoughts swarming my own mind. I popped a couple of Advil and washed them down with orange juice.

"Look," I said. "Kaitlin's got the headline." I read aloud from the front page of the *Herald-Tribune*. "So Won Lee of Seoul, Korea, took the lead in the Sectional Qualifier at the Plantation Golf and Country Club. In second place, shooting sixty-eight, was Kaitlin Rupert of Myrtle Beach, South Carolina. Asked about handling the pressure of the tournament, Rupert said: 'I just hit every shot as though this was my last day ever playing golf.' "

I smiled at Walter. "I bet she got the quote because So Won's English isn't very good. She'll be happy with the publicity."

"But not the second-place finish," said Walter. "She's not satisfied eating some other girl's dust." He shook his head in admiration. "She's really something, isn't she?"

"Looked like she was hot at you yesterday."

"She understands that I have to run a business," Walter said. "She knows that what we have going between us means a whole lot more than a Deikon logo on somebody's bag."

I wasn't altogether certain he was right on that one, but I wasn't going to argue with him either.

"You're not eating much this morning," he said. I looked down at my tray. I'd forced down a few bites of Raisin Bran and half a stale blueberry muffin. Last night's overload of beer still bloated my system.

"Nerves," I said. "I'll get something later. See you over at the club."

"You look tired," said Laura when I arrived at the range. "Sleep okay?"

"Fine." No way was I going to tell her about the visit from Max. Bad enough that it happened, that I'd allowed things to go as far as they had. How could I explain that I'd let a guy who hadn't touched me or even talked to me in over ten years practically strip me half naked? And worse yet, that I might very well have slept with him, if his *wife* hadn't beeped him from home? So far, the cost of surviving the Q-school pressure cooker seemed to be the erosion of my better judgment.

Perhaps I'd sort out the events of last night later under Dr. Baxter's careful tutelage. Or maybe I'd never bring them up at all — bury them deep in my memory's back boneyard. In any event, I was determined that none of this would interfere with my golf round today.

"Walter likes a winner, doesn't he?" said Laura. She pointed down the range, where he stood talking to So Won Lee. He had one of her clubs in his hand. I imagined he was describing all of its many shortcomings.

"He's got good business sense," I said. "She may be the next Se Ri Pak. If he gets in with her now, she could be a major Deikon cash cow."

"Uh-oh. Doppler radar shows trouble on the horizon," said Laura in a low voice. We watched Kaitlin approach the practice tee where Walter was talking with the Korean golfer. She smiled and simpered, then gave Walter a full-length, lingering body hug, completely ignoring the presence of So Won Lee.

"The old 'catch more flies with sugar' approach," said Laura, shaking her head. "Come on, girl. Today's your day. I can feel it. You're going to tear this golf course up. Let's get over to the tee."

Julie and Heather, along with Heather's entourage, were already standing outside the ropes around the tee when we pulled up. Two enormous sandhill cranes, with red caps and long, knobby knees, preened on the tee box.

"Those birds are beautiful," commented Heather's little mother.

"You know they mate for life," said

Heather's fiancé. "Like us."

"They are so handsome," said Heather back. "Like you."

"Wait 'til they let out a squawk in your backswing." In my current wired state, the google-eyes were scraping on my nerves.

"Those birds would make a darned good feather duster," said Julie. Apparently the lovers were getting to her, too.

"Go on, scat! We have work to do here." Laura shooed the cranes off to the side of the tee box.

Having turned in the lowest score of our threesome yesterday, Heather took the place of honor on the tee vacated by the birds. She gazed down the fairway. "Keep an eye on this, honey," she told her caddie.

"You don't need to go for medalist," he said, winking back in our direction. "Play smart." She split the fairway with a long, screaming drive.

"Thank God," said her mother.

"That's a beauty! And you met your first goal," said the fiancé. "Hit the fairway on one."

Neither her tee shot nor her marital status have any bearing on your performance, I told myself.

Julie and I teed off in quick succession, her ball curving into the right rough, mine heading left. All three of us made par by hitting the green in regulation, followed by two putts.

"There's your second goal, par on the first," said the fiancé, as Heather plucked her ball from the cup. Julie and I rode in silence to the second tee.

I knew the best strategy today was to block the cut out of my mind. Heather's fiancé had it right. I could only play one shot at a time, and none of them would be executed well if I was thinking about the whole round, the whole tournament, or my whole life. I envied the woman who watched us from the screened-in porch around her pool as we climbed the stairs to the second tee. From where I stood, she had no stress at all.

We began to get a good idea of how fast the greens were on the second hole. Julie and Heather's drives both skidded across the green, passing the hole on their way. I dubbed my tee shot short, then chipped my ball by the hole along the same line I'd seen the others take. Two putts later, I carded my first bogey of the day.

We followed a long stretch of cart path and turned the corner into the third hole. The early morning sun hit the heavy dew on the fairway, making the grass almost indistinguishable from the lake that lined the left side.

"I'll be glad to be finished with this course," said Heather, after blasting another drive dead center down the fairway.

"Carpe diem," said her fiancé.

"I can't feel my swing," I muttered to Laura.

"Doesn't matter," she told me. "Don't worry about it. Just grind it out and it'll come."

So I ground. A scrambling par on three, a straightforward par on four, a bogey I felt lucky to manage on five, and my first birdie of the day on six. Julie, meanwhile, had begun to flail helplessly at her ball, finding bunkers, water hazards, and missed opportunities on almost every shot.

"We're being timed, girls," Heather said after I'd just missed a par putt on the seventh green. "The rules official is hanging out over there in the bushes. We're going to have to pick the pace up."

Though I knew my own play was not the culprit for our slow progress, I tightened up anyway. I swung too fast on the eighth tee and pulled my drive left. It hit the fairway hard and caromed into the pond.

"The swing wasn't all bad," said Laura. "It just took a rotten bounce."

"I'll walk," I said, waving her onto the cart with Julie. The expression on her face was grimly sympathetic. She knew better than to say anything more. Support, comfort, criticism — it would all be lighting a match to the brittle tinder of my nerves. Music wafted out from one of the condos on the right side of the fairway. Liza Minelli was joined by a chorus of yapping Spaniels from the house near where my ball had dived underwater.

"If you drop here, you can chip out past the trees. Then a wedge on, one putt, take your bogey and run," said Laura. I studied the palm trees that blocked the green. In the background, Liza invited me and her other chums to a cabaret.

"I can make it over these," I told Laura.

"It's not worth it," she said. "Just take your lumps and move on. We'll make a birdie later."

"No, it's worth a shot," I said. "I've got all the room I need."

"You're pressing too hard," she said.

"I'll be fine. I'll get my eight up fast and over."

She backed off. I swung hard. The ball soared up, nicked the last frond of the palm tree directly in line with the green, and plopped back down just twenty feet ahead of us. This time, without any further consultation, I chipped out into the open fairway, hit a wedge on, and two-putted for triple bogey.

"You'll never have to see that hole again," said Laura.

Now I felt a fierce concentration settle over me. I swore I would not make another dim-witted, bone-headed error. I was not exactly in what sportswriters call the zone, but it was a different territory compared to my jittery start. Nothing distracted me from my focus — not the endearments of Heather's fiancé, not the escalating prayers of Heather's mother, not Julie's rapidly disintegrating performance. She double-bogeyed three of the four holes of the Panther's Claw. I parred all of them, then birdied the par five sixteenth.

"Almost there, girls," said Heather's fiancé.

"It's all in God's hands anyway," said Heather's mother. "God has a plan for each of us." I thought she glanced at me and Julie with pity. As though her Heather was all set, but only God knew what our particular plans might be. Heather and I each drove safely into the fairway on seventeen. Julie pulled her shot just far enough left to catch the out-of-bounds stake marking the outside edge of the driving range.

"That's just the kind of day it's been." She sighed and teed up a second ball, which again rolled over the staked OB line and then dropped off into the pit containing the damaged irrigation pipe. She teed up and hit a third drive without comment.

"Don't even look for them," she called out to Laura, who had started over to search for the wayward balls. "I wouldn't play another stroke with those balls. Not even a shank."

I had lost count of her total score. I just recorded the scores she made on the individual holes. I hoped that avoiding her total would help keep me from thinking about mine. I knew I hovered close to where the cut line would fall. In that case, a birdie on one of the last two holes could very well mean the difference between heading home today or playing on toward a spot on the LPGA Tour.

I stood frozen over my first putt on seventeen, then, with a nervous jab, smoked it ten feet beyond the hole. I stared at the cup. Putter and I are one, I told myself while Heather and Julie putted. Then I lined up, closed my eyes, and stroked the ball toward Laura's feet. It wobbled on the edge, then dropped in for par.

"Good job back there," said Laura, handing me my three-wood on the eighteenth tee. "You had me scared for a minute." I breathed in slowly, chose a spot on the fairway to shoot for and swung.

"You made your second-to-last goal," Laura joked. "Drive in the fairway."

Though my seven-iron leaked a little right, I chipped up close to the pin, then sank a four-footer to make another par. Under other conditions, it would have been cause for celebration.

"I needed birdie. To have any chance now, the cut would have to go awfully low," I said.

"You were awesome," insisted Laura, pumping my hand and patting my back. "Let's just wait and see." I shook Heather's hand and offered Julie a consoling hug.

"It wasn't your day."

We rode over to the clubhouse in silence

and watched the volunteers record our scores. Eve and Mary, whom I'd eaten dinner with at Chili's Saturday night, arrived shortly after us. Eve's total, 145, looked to be safely inside the cut. Mary's 160 looked clearly out. The Bible study leaders, Nicki and Joanne, stood to one side, waiting for their scores to be posted.

I began to understand at a gut-twisting level how hard competition was among friends. I wanted these girls to do well — I knew how much it meant to each of them. But sitting on the bubble of the cut, I knew their performances were not independent of mine. Only the low seventy scores and ties would go on to play tomorrow. Go on to try to live the dream. This exhilarating, crazy dream we all shared.

"Let's get out of here," said Laura. "We won't know anything about the cut until the afternoon threesomes come in. We can't stand around here all day. We'll lose what little is left of our minds. Let's get some lunch. Maybe we can even catch forty winks."

# 17

"That's the English translation for my Indian name, you know," said Laura. "Lunch and Then a Nap. Don't you have to admit you feel better?"

I laughed. The tuna on rye had gone down great, but Laura's snores and my nerves had made sleep impossible. "I'll feel better when this is all over. Whatever the outcome." I parked the car in the only shade I could find at the back of the lot and we walked over to the clubhouse. A large but subdued group of golfers had gathered at the site of the scoreboard.

"How's it look?" Laura asked one of the officials.

"Should fall somewhere between 151 and 153."

I noticed that Kaitlin's 139 for the two rounds anchored her in second place, only one stroke behind So Won Lee. My 153, on the other hand, left me twisting not so gently in the hot afternoon breeze. If the cut came through under 151, I'd have to assume Kaitlin had been right that first day at the Grandpappy driving range: I'd been out of my mind to even try Q-school. If I just missed at 152, I'd be haunted by one shot, any shot, that could have moved me into the second half of the tournament. Maybe the stupid heroics I tried on the eighth hole today. Or any of the three-putts I'd muddled through yesterday. With the cut at 151, I could choose two shots to beat myself up over. The combinations would be unlimited.

An unsmiling official approached the scoreboard with an enormous pair of cardboard scissors. She held them up in the space directly above my name with one hand and extracted a roll of Scotch tape from her pocket with the other. Just then, I heard a commotion coming from the direction of the LPGA office.

"Hold off on that," called out Alice MacPherson as she hurried toward the crowd. "We need to make an adjustment. There's been a disqualification." The golfers around me broke out into excited chatter.

Alice smoothed the piece of paper in her hand and cleared her throat. "Ms. So Won Lee of Korea has been disqualified from the LPGA Sectional Qualifying Tournament for the use of illegal equipment — a nonconforming driving club."

The buzz from the crowd escalated, almost obscuring one high, piercing scream that had to belong to the Korean player. The scoring official peered at the paper Alice held out, then marched over to So Won's name. She wrote across it in large red Magic Marker letters: DQ. After consulting with the other officials, she picked up the cardboard scissors and taped them just below my name.

"I'll be damned," said Laura. "You made it!" She hugged me hard. "You made it, you crazy woman. We did it!" She began to perform a war dance around me.

"Excuse me, may I have your attention for another moment, ladies," said Alice MacPherson. "Members of the press are located in a tent next to the practice putting green for the Bobcat course. If they contact you, we urge you to provide an interview. While there is no penalty on tomorrow's round if you decline to speak with them, we will levy a hefty fine. This will be good practice for those of you who are playing on the Tour next year." She smiled, the first one I'd seen from her since I arrived.

I was stunned by the sudden swing from elimination to inclusion. I backed away from the other players and caddies to get some breathing space. From the fringes of the crowd, I saw So Won Lee, now alternately sobbing and screaming at Alice MacPherson. Another Korean golfer translated her despair into English.

"It's not my club," she said. "I've been set up. I've never seen this club before." She pointed to the driver Alice clutched in her hand. I moved a few steps closer. I believed I *had* seen the club before — being passed back and forth between Kaitlin Rupert and Walter Moore on the Palm Lakes driving range. The experimental Ball Hog/ Tee Warrior/Fairway Bruiser had somehow made its way into the golf bag of So Won Lee.

"This place is a madhouse," said Laura. "Let's get out of here. You need to putt. You need to work on those irons a bit — tomorrow's another big day. We want nothing but fairways and greens. We'll have time to celebrate on Friday."

We retrieved my clubs from the trunk of the car and walked over to the practice range.

"I can't believe it," I said. "How the hell did that happen?"

"You're not the only one who can't believe it," whispered Laura. "Take a look at that."

At the far end of the range, Walter Moore had taken Kaitlin by the shoulders. He shook her with a barely controlled fury. "How could you do this? How could you pull a stunt like this? You and me — we are finished. Washed up, sweetheart."

Kaitlin unfastened his hands from her arms and stepped back out of his reach. "First of all," she said in an ice cold voice, "I didn't do anything. I had nothing to do with putting that stinking club in that bitch's bag. Second" — she brushed off her shirt where his hands had gripped her shoulders.

"Second, you big, dumb oaf. We certainly are finished because we never were started. I can't believe you were stupid enough to think for one minute that I was interested in anything but your equipment. No, let me rephrase that to make it quite clear — not your equipment, your *golf* clubs. Now get away from me before I call security." She gave him the same quick shove she'd given her mother that first morning back in South Carolina. Only Walter, significantly larger and more solid than Kaitlin's mother, did not lose his balance.

I had never seen anyone look as angry as Walter Moore. The twitches that I'd noticed during our two breakfasts now resulted in bulging eyes and fierce jerking movements in his lips and cheeks.

"His birdie is cooked," I said to Laura. "He's lost two endorsement deals — So Won's out of the tournament, and Kaitlin's a nightmare. Plus, you know he's got to be in hot water over the discovery of the illegal club. He nearly had heart failure when I asked him about it. He wasn't supposed to have shown it to anyone yet. He was just grandstanding for Kaitlin's benefit."

"Do you think she really put it in So Won's bag?" said Laura. "Why would it mean that much to her to be in first place, halfway through the tournament? I could understand it a little better if all the rounds were over."

"I don't understand the girl, myself," I

210

said. "Maybe she didn't believe she could ever beat So Won fair and square." I felt the vibration of my cell phone in my back pocket, where I'd placed it after we finished the morning's play.

"Cassie, it's Joe —"

"Doc! You won't believe what's happening here. First of all, I'm in for tomorrow!" I accepted his excited congratulations, then explained about So Won Lee's disqualification. "I feel bad about how it happened," I said. "I only made the cut because someone else screwed up, or she got screwed, whatever the case may be."

"You did what you had to, that's all that matters," said Joe. "Listen, could you use another hand there?"

"Are you finally coming over? Even after what a grump I was last night? That's fantastic."

"Mike gave me the boot," said Joe. "Told me he couldn't take having me look over his shoulder for one more minute. That's just fine, I said. Cassie could use me at Q-school. I knew you'd make the cut. I just knew it."

"Joe's coming," I told Laura.

"I have one problem," said Joe. "I had a little accident and I'm in the hospital at Ocala."

"Oh, my God, are you all right? I'll come right up."

"I was hoping Laura could come and pick me up. I'm fine, but my arm's in a sling and the doctor won't let me drive. But you need to stay where you are, young lady. Let me speak to Laura." Laura took the phone and scribbled down directions for the hospital.

"I hate to leave you alone another evening," she said after she'd hung up.

"I did fine alone last night," I said. The embarrassing memory of Max Harding's visit flashed through my mind. This time, I'd stay in the motel room. Completely alone.

"He figures it'll take me three hours to get up there. Four tops, if I hit traffic," said Laura. "I'll be back snoring in the other bed by midnight."

"I'll be fine," I said. "Go. Take the car. I can catch a ride over to the motel. I'll work a couple hours here, eat a good dinner, and turn in early. We don't tee off tomorrow until later in the morning anyway."

I worked at the practice range until dusk, mostly sticking to the plan Laura and I had agreed on. No last-minute grip shifts, no new swing thoughts, just a couple hours of smooth tempo and visualization of success on the course. Ha. Okay, so there were a few negative thoughts regarding the fact that every iron I had hit today leaked right. And how the hell could I have skulled two chips when I hadn't produced a line-drive trajectory that plug-ugly since the eighth grade? Not to mention the small matter of one-third of my attempts on the short grass resulting in three-putts. I tried to push away the doubts that whispered I didn't belong in the contest tomorrow. I'd show myself and everyone else that my place here had been earned and was deserved.

One of the volunteers flagged me down on the putting green. I wasn't in the mood to talk. A pounding headache and my fragile grip on an optimistic outlook for round three took the urge for chit-chat with a stranger right out of me.

"Cassie," she said. "Aren't you Cassie Burdette? Did you hear that Kaitlin missed her interview this evening?" She had the breathless voice of someone who couldn't wait to tell you their news, because the more people she told and the more personal details she had to tell, the more important she felt. "They looked for her everywhere. Do you have any idea what happened to her?"

"I have no clue," I said. "We're not friends."

The volunteer scurried off, I assumed in search of someone who'd turn out to be a more sympathetic listener and less of a grump. I ambled over in the direction of the clubhouse to look for a ride home to the Starlight. The headache I'd woken up with this morning still pulsed uncomfortably. I couldn't wait to get back to my motel room, take a couple of Advil, and sink into the oblivion of sleep.

On the short walk back to the clubhouse, Kaitlin's missed interview began to nag at me like a paper cut on my trigger finger. I couldn't get away from it. No one missed an interview in the professional golf world unless they'd pitched a major temper tantrum. Sponsors took note of that sort of acting out and adjusted their deals downward accordingly. Fans and tournament officials knew every detail about which golfers were a pain in the butt. It added pressure to a career path that was already difficult enough.

I knew Kaitlin was aware of this. And I knew that someone as fiercely competitive and frantic for attention as she would not miss her interview for anything less than a serious emergency. Maybe she'd developed food poisoning so immobilizing she couldn't even pick up the phone to call over and alert the tournament officials.

Or maybe she got called home this afternoon for a death in the family. Nah. She'd finish the tournament, then go home, figuring the dead person wouldn't care whether she showed up that night or a couple days later.

I scolded myself for being catty and decided I'd stop by her condo to atone for my uncharitable thoughts. In the process of being a Good Samaritan, I might get lucky and catch a ride home from her more agreeable brother. I could use a little cheering up.

# 18

As dusk fell, I walked to Kaitlin's condo by way of the Bobcat's eighteenth fairway. Earlier today, I'd assumed I would never see this hole again. Now I had two more shots at it. I cut through a hedge and found the Ruperts' entranceway. Inside the vestibule, the door to their apartment was just cracked open. My knock echoed in the tiled hallway.

"Kaitlin," I called. "Hello. Gary. It's Cassie. Kaitlin! Anybody home?"

No answer. I knocked and called three more times.

The Ruperts' neighbor stuck his head out from his door. "Time to take a hike, girlie. Either they aren't home or they don't want company. Whichever it is, scram." He slammed his door shut.

Now, a dilemma. The last time I stepped uninvited through someone's open doorway, I'd discovered a dying, soon to be dead, man. One of those in a lifetime was enough. On the other hand, if either of the Ruperts was in trouble and I hadn't checked on them, I knew I'd feel responsible. And finally, I had to admit that a small part of me welcomed the chance to snoop.

I opened the screen door and walked in. The condo was similar to the one where I'd attended Bible study, with a combination living area/kitchen, decorated with rattan furniture, pastel colors, and tropical prints. I nudged each of the bedroom doors open and peered in. Gary's room was spotless; the only personal item in evidence a copy of *Into Thin Air*, which lay open on the bedside table. Kaitlin's bedcovers slopped onto the floor, blending with a pile of what I assumed was dirty laundry. I stepped over the pile and opened the door to her closet. No funny business there either. I decided to use the bathroom before heading home.

I pushed on the partly open door. It was jammed in place. I pushed harder, wedging my shoulders and head through the opening until I could look into the bathroom. There was nothing remarkable other than a cosmetic salesperson's dream supply of beauty products and a pile of dirty towels and clothing so substantial it blocked access to the facilities.

One of the many reasons I was thankful not to be Kaitlin's roommate. I turned to leave, feeling I'd done my duty. Maybe they'd simply forgotten to lock the door on the way to their dinner. In any case, it was really none of my business. Then I noticed a note left on the kitchen counter.

"Gone to pick up Mother and Pop at the

airport. I'll drop them off at their hotel and be back after ten. Hope you had a good dinner and made things nicey-nice with Walter." Signed with a *G* and a smiley face.

The only mystery remaining was which Rupert had forgotten to close and lock the condo door. My money was on Kaitlin. I did also have to wonder how she'd feel about her parents arriving at Q-school, given the bad blood between them. And how she could possibly manage to make things "nicey-nice" with Walter Moore, given the lather he'd worked himself into this afternoon.

I walked back to the clubhouse to look for a ride home. The only light shone from a room near the dining hall, which had been turned into a temporary first aid station for the Q-school contestants.

"Can I help you?" asked the young man seated at the desk just inside the room. He smiled and gestured to the book he'd been reading. "Anatomy," he told me without my asking. "I'm starting medical school in the fall and I want to have a head start before I get there. They say it's brutal the first year."

"Sorry to bother you, then," I said. "I was hoping to catch a ride back to my motel."

The student ran his fingers through his blond brush cut. "As far as I know, everyone's gone home for the day. It was a happenin' scene here, I suppose you heard. Everyone was bushed. Would you like me to call you a taxi?"

I nodded. This guy might not know anything about medicine yet, but at least he had the makings of a good bedside manner. I hoped his years in med school wouldn't wipe that out. He dialed and spoke to the dispatcher at Triple-A Taxi.

"All the cabs are out at the moment, but they'll send someone over ASAP. It might be half an hour," he told me after he'd hung up.

"Damn," I said. Then belatedly, "Thanks." I felt too antsy to just sit and wait. "I guess I'll go over to the range and pace off some distances. The accuracy of my irons wasn't all that great today." Not that he cared about my golf game. "Could you send the taxi over if they show up before I get back?" The student nodded and returned to his anatomy text.

I walked across the road and past the Panther putting green and pitching area to the driving range. I paced across the field, visualizing precisely where I should be hitting each of my clubs. Joe would be proud. Fifty yards, one hundred, one fifty, two hundred, two fifty, three hundred, the markers read. Fairways and greens were my goal for tomorrow's round. And, getting all those putts to the neighborhood of the hole. Nothing was more demoralizing than a birdie putt left short.

Just ahead, I saw the pit that had been dug to repair the Panther's irrigation system. I suspected that pit, with its ensuing speedy putts, would be featured in a lot of nightmares in the year to come. I wondered why it had taken so long to get the replacement part. The course could lose its greens altogether if the new widget didn't arrive soon. I wondered if Julie's ball from this morning's round still lay in the pit. Two shots out of bounds on one hole — there was some really lousy luck. I leaned over and looked into the excavation.

"Shit!" I yelled. The pale form lying in the hole was definitely not a golf ball. I punched 911 on my cell phone. "There's a woman in the pit on the driving range. I think she's badly hurt. We need help right away."

The operator inquired about the location of the incident and then took my name. "Stay where you are," she said. "We'll send someone by."

I pressed end and glanced back in the direction of the pit. Hell if I was going to wait here alone. I sprinted over to the first aid office where I'd seen the student working.

"Help!" I said, struggling to catch my breath. "There's a body in the pit over on the range!" He looked doubtful. I tried to appeal to his status as Future Doctor of America. "Please hurry. We might have the chance to save her life."

He closed his book slowly, marking his place with a brochure for Busch Gardens. I grabbed his hand and dragged him to the driving range.

The medical student and I approached the pit. He held out a small penlight attached to his key ring. I flashed it over the bottom of the hole. A woman's body lay crumpled in one corner. In spite of the dim light, I was quite sure it was Kaitlin Rupert. I directed myself to observe the scene clinically, as Sheriff Pate, or even Joe Lancaster, would have done. I would not give into either the wave of nausea that flooded me or the powerful urge to scream and run.

A skimpy white lace brassiere and underpants had been stripped from Kaitlin's body and lay tangled on the loose dirt beside her. Along with her white-gold hair, they were saturated with blood. A golf club appeared to be embedded in the side of her head. The medical student nudged me aside and peered into the pit. There was a moment of stunned silence.

"I haven't finished reading the chapter on the brain," said the student. "But I'd say it's a nine-iron to the parietal lobe."

"It's not a nine-iron," I said. My voice came out tight and shrill. "It's a driver. It looks a lot like the Fairway Bruiser. Titanium shaft and illegally inflated coefficient of restitution, creating a springlike effect in the club face. Or on someone's brain. Outlawed according to Appendix II, 5a, the USGA Rules of Golf." And Kaitlin said I didn't know the rules.

"Are you feeling all right?" the student asked. He grabbed my forearm, guided me back from the edge of the excavation, and began to grope for my pulse. "Put your head between your knees if you feel faint. It's not uncommon for the layperson to feel woozy when they encounter the scene of an accident."

"This was no accident," I said.

The student keeled over and did a face plant into the grass.

From the rear seat of a Sarasota Sheriff's Department cruiser, I watched officials drape yellow crime scene tape around the end of the driving range containing the pit and Kaitlin's body. By the light of the flashing strobes on the police cars, I saw the medical student in the back of a second cruiser. Even from a distance, and even granting that intermittent blue lights would not do favors for anyone's complexion, his skin appeared sweaty and pale. I could not picture him handling a bloody ER assignment with the requisite gruff detachment.

"Kindly step out of the vehicle." The curt voice of one of the officers startled me out of my reverie about the medical student's future. I faced three more policemen when I emerged from the car. "Why were you out here?"

"It sounds weird," I said. "It was just a feeling I had, that somehow Kaitlin was in trouble. I can't really explain it all logically." It sounded more than weird. Even to my own ears, my explanation sounded weak, suspicious, and completely unconvincing. I forged ahead anyway, describing hearing about the missed interview, going to the Ruperts' condo, and then pacing off distances at the practice range while I waited for a cab. Finally, I described how I'd spotted the body and returned to the club to enlist the aid of the medical student.

Just then, Sheriff Pate swaggered up. Ignoring my wave, he drew the other officers several yards away from me.

"Pate says this is the second body you've stumbled on in two weeks," said the man who had been interviewing me, when he returned from the conference with Pate. "Interesting coincidence."

"Interesting is not how I'd describe it," I said. "Grisly, terrifying . . ." The wall that had risen inside and blocked my feelings about discovering Kaitlin suddenly gave way. I sank to a squat beside the cruiser and began to cry.

"Get back in the vehicle," said Pate. "We're going to take a ride to the station."

At the sheriff's department, my interrogation did not wind down until after ten o'clock. I reviewed my movements during the entire evening for two different officers. Their questions took two unpleasant turns. First, the following irrefutable fact was established: I had found not one, but two, dead bodies in the short span of two weeks. No one knew this more vividly than I did.

Second, I had benefitted from So Won Lee's elimination out of the golf tournament. Because of the illegal golf club found in her bag, I had squeaked into the second half of the tournament. Making me a logical perpetrator for the misplaced club. And now that same golf club had turned up as an apparent murder weapon. Were these events connected? I had no clue. I had no reasonable explanation for either of them. I reported in detail my conversations over the last week and a half with Walter Moore and Kaitlin herself, hoping they might shift suspicion from me to someone else. At this point, anyone would do.

"Sheriff Pate," I began.

"Sheriff Pate?" hooted one of the other officers. "In his dreams, he's Sheriff Pate. Low-down-on-the-totem-pole Deputy Pate, to you." Pate squirmed with discomfort as several of the deputies taunted him.

Why the hell had he lied to me about his title?

"We are not intending to arrest you tonight, Miss Burdette," said the only deputy who had not participated in razzing Pate. "But you may not leave this county until we inform you that you may go. Is that clear enough?"

I nodded. This implied threat made Detective Maloney's desire to keep in touch after I'd found Bencher's body feel positively chummy. Evidently, the police had not been impressed with my protestations of ignorance and innocence. Although any number of people may have wanted Kaitlin Rupert dead, I looked like one of them. As I shuffled out to the vestibule, I felt scared, tired, confused, and ravenously hungry.

Walter Moore was slumped in a chair in the corner of the entrance area. He leaped to his feet when he saw me emerge from the hallway.

"Cassie! What's going on? Did they find the bastard who killed her? I didn't do it. I swear I didn't. Did you tell them I wouldn't hurt her?" If he'd looked wild as he shook Kaitlin on the practice range this afternoon, he'd downshifted into near-demented now.

"Just tell them the facts, Walter." I figured that would be good advice whether he'd murdered her or not. Either way, I desperately wanted to have confidence that the authorities I'd been taught to believe in would find the truth. Doubtful, though, with Pate on board.

I pulled my phone out to call for a taxi back to the Starlight Motel. It vibrated before I could dial the number.

"Cassie! It's Jeanine Peters. I've been trying

to reach you for hours."

"I've been a little busy."

"One of the golfers from your tournament was murdered!"

"I know —" She interrupted me as I began to tell her that I'd had the bad luck to find the body.

"There's something you should see over at the office. I went back earlier this evening to get my makeup and I overheard some stuff. Dr. Turner is clearing out his files later on tonight. You wanted me to call you if anything came up."

"What is he clearing out?"

"I don't know exactly. It has to do with the False Memory Consociation — Turner's been worried about their plans to teach Kaitlin Rupert a lesson. Now that she's turned up dead, that plan is going to look really bad for him."

"How does he know she's dead? They only found her a couple of hours ago."

"I have no idea. You told me to call if I heard something. I'm just keeping my word. If you wanted to look at any of his papers, it's now or never."

"I'm glad you called. Let me think a minute, it's been a crazy night." I was not in any mood to snoop around someone's office. I was in deep shit with the authorities already. On the other hand, my father always said, if you're in a hole and someone hands you a shovel, shut up and start digging.

"First problem," I said. "I'm at the sheriff's department and I don't have a car."

"No problem there. I live right around the corner," she said. "I'll pick you up in a few." She didn't give me time to elaborate on problems two, three, four, and five, all related to reasons why I ought to just go home and mind my own business.

# 19

"This is a big risk you're taking," I told Jeanine as she parked her Civic behind the strip mall housing Turner's office. "You could lose your job if we get caught. Or something much worse."

"I told you I wanted out of that place anyway," she said. "Hey, if you introduce me to Rick, I'll owe you forever. This is the least I can do. And if Turner shows up early, I'll just tell him I forgot my wallet or my mascara or whatever. He has this idea all blonds are dizzy, so he'd believe anything I told him." She giggled and glanced at me. "Besides, I bet he'd be so pleased to see you here, he wouldn't bat an eyelash. He talked about you all day yesterday."

"Talked about me how?" This did not sound like good news.

"He seemed taken by you." She unlocked the back door leading into Dr. Turner's office. "He kept asking me questions about you."

"What kind of questions?"

"Just stuff about what I'd noticed when you were here. What we talked about."

"You didn't tell him I was pretending to be a patient?"

"Of course not!" Jeanine frowned. "I was so excited about the golf, I did tell him about your being here for the tournament and how you were going to help me meet Rick. Was that all right?" It didn't feel all right, but she looked too upset to scold.

"Let's take a quick look around," I said. "And then get the hell out of here. What exactly do you think we'll find?"

"I'm not certain myself. But he was talking about the Rupert suit. I heard him tell some guy on the phone that they needed to clear everything out of the office tonight. They're supposed to meet here after midnight." She looked at her watch. "That gives us almost two hours."

"Does he make hard copies of all his documents, or should we start with the computer?"

"Gosh, the girl who comes in on Fridays is forever filing, so I know there are records in those cabinets." She waved at the row of green metal file cabinets against the far wall. "Rupert starts with *R*. I'd start there, if I were you. Turner's a logical kind of guy. In some ways, anyway."

"Great. Why don't you keep an eye out for trouble?"

Jeanine moved to the front room and peered through the dusty slats of the Venetian blinds in the waiting area. I began to flip through the files in the top drawer of the third cabinet. Halfway toward the back of the

228

drawer, I found "Rupert, Kaitlin/Peter." It was a thick folder, stuffed so full I could hardly pull it out, even using two hands.

"There's someone pulling into the parking lot!" Jeanine's voice shook.

"What kind of car?" I asked.

"Looks like a maroon Mercedes. And a black Lincoln following. Shoot! That's Dr. Turner." All her reassurances about how she'd handle a crisis in the event Turner showed up evaporated. "Oh, my God, he'll kill me if he finds us digging through his stuff!"

Jeanine dove into the inner office and shut off the lights. As I jammed the file I was holding back into the cabinet, we heard the scrape of the key in the front door.

"We don't have time to get out," said Jeanine. "He'll hear us leaving."

"Is there a closet?"

Now mute with fear, Jeanine pointed to a door in the corner of the room. We crammed ourselves into a narrow space left between cartons of computer paper and toner. Pressed up against Jeanine in the dark, I could smell her flowery perfume and the scent of bubble gum on her breath.

"I'm sorry," she whispered. "This was a dumb idea."

"Shhh!" We heard heavy footsteps as Dr. Turner and another man entered the office and walked across the room to the back door.

"Don't you think we should call the police? It looks like a break-in to me — the door open and the alarm off," cautioned Turner's visitor.

"Nah. No cops. That dumb broad must have left the goddamned door unlocked. She's done the same thing a half dozen times. If she wasn't easy on the eyes, I swear I would have fired her long ago." I gritted my teeth. I'd been so far off with my assessment of this guy, it wasn't funny.

We heard a door slam shut. "Why are we suddenly packing things up?" asked Turner's companion.

"It's gotten too hot," said Turner. Now I recognized the subtle edge of urgency and panic in his voice. "With the Rupert girl dead, the cops are probably gearing up to search the place. I can't risk leaving this stuff here."

"Somebody tipped them off?"

"Christ, Vinnie. Everyone's gonna know we backed her father financially. It won't take a genius to make the connection. Besides, there was a girl here Monday snooping around, asking questions about the organization," said Turner.

"So who killed Rupert?"

"How the hell would I know?" said Turner.

"Could it have been Atwater? I told you that guy was nuts. All those damn crazy Bible verses. I told you not to get involved with him. . . ."

"You're a fucking genius, looking backward. We all are. Shut up and get to work."

"We need empty boxes," said Turner's companion. "We can't carry all this out loose."

Jeanine clutched my hand. She must have had the same thought I did: the logical — the only — place to look for boxes was in our closet. And from the general tone of their conversation, I could guess they wouldn't take discovering us in here with grace.

"I brought a couple in my trunk," Turner said. "Take the keys and I'll start pulling things out." I let out a long, slow breath.

"So lay it out for me, Will," said the second man when he returned. "What's your plan?"

"One, we need to move this stuff out. And two, shut that nosy girl up. The second job is yours."

"You think someone sent her? You think she saw something while she was here? Why the hell did you let her in?"

"Shut up, for Christ's sake. I'm not playing twenty questions. Do your job and it won't matter what she saw or why she came. With both Rupert and Bencher dead, the only thing that could blow us out of the water is this snooping bitch."

"It's gone too far already. . . ."

"You owe me this. I've paid your inflated

legal fees for years. Now I need you to come through for me or your daughter's story may find its slimy way to the newspaper."

There was a long moment of silence. I was beginning to feel nauseated with claustrophobia, the sharp edge of a box of supplies digging into one rib, and Jeanine's heaving chest pressing in on the other side.

"I'm sorry about the way things are turning out," said the second man. "But I won't stoop to hurting someone. I'm a lawyer, not a mobster."

"Christ, I'm sick of your bullshit! It's a little late to be taking the high road." From the noises outside the closet, it sounded like the men had started to scuffle.

"There's no need to get violent!" said the second man. A heavy object crashed into the closet door. Jeanine parted her lips to scream. I clapped my hand over her mouth.

"What in the hell? Did you hear something?" asked Turner.

"No, I didn't."

"I think someone's in here!" insisted Turner. "We'd better have a look around." We heard him walk to the rest room and fling open the door. Jeanine inhaled sharply and grabbed my hand as the footsteps approached our hiding place. The odor of sweat expanded to fill the small space. What story could we possibly concoct to explain our position? At the exact moment one of the men rattled the knob on the closet door, Jeanine reached forward and pushed in the lock button.

"That dumb bimbo must have locked the door again. Where the hell are the keys?" Turner moved away from our closet. I heard him opening and closing drawers and rustling through their contents. "Look at the shit she keeps in here. It's like a goddamned beauty spa. Half the time, we can't even use the copier because the paper's locked away and she's forgotten where the goddamned keys are. She'd lose her own tits if they weren't right under her nose."

"Look, Will," said the second man in a conciliatory voice, "the place is empty: your nerves are getting the better of you. There's no one here but me and you. I'm going to do what I can to take care of the situation. I've been along for the ride every step of the way. But don't ask me to hurt someone. I can't do that."

"No blood, pal. Just scare the hell out of her. We're in this together, buddy, like it or not. Let's get out of here."

"One more thing," said the second man. "Do you think Jeanine would go out with me?"

"You're joking." Turner's voice was incredulous. "That girl is an intellectual zero."

"She has other charms." The man laughed. "Two of them, to be exact." Their footsteps faded into the distance. We heard them leave the front office and lock the door behind them. Jeanine let out a deep breath.

"Can we get out of here? I like you and all that, but these are tight quarters."

I flung the door open. "You were brilliant, turning the lock at just the right minute. I had no idea how we were going to explain ourselves."

"Just sheer reflex," she said, following me out into the dim shadows of the office.

"That guy's a pig. How long have you worked for him?"

"He's a horse's behind, all right, but he isn't around that much," laughed Jeanine, giddy with relief. "And for the money I make, I let his idiotic comments wash right over me. I guess the trick with painting two colors of foundation in your cleavage works pretty well."

"Disgusting pigs," I said. "Just say no, that's my advice. Do you know Turner's buddy?"

Jeanine shrugged. "Not really. Vinnie something or other. He's come in the office once or twice, that's all."

"Do you think Turner murdered Bencher and Kaitlin?"

"He told Vinnie he didn't know who killed her."

"He's no fool," I said. "He's not going to admit he murdered someone, especially not to a lawyer. We've got to look around a little more. . . ."

"No way!" said Jeanine. "We're out of here. I'm not spending one more minute in this office."

"But we came all this way and had the living daylights scared out of us. I can't see leaving without looking a little further. Just give me a few minutes."

"Absolutely not." Jeanine blocked my path to the file cabinets. "We're leaving now." Reluctantly, I agreed. We exited the building, locking the door and setting the alarm behind us.

Jeanine dropped me off at the Starlight Motel. I raced up the back stairs and inserted my key card into its slot.

"My God, Cassie. Where have you been? You gave us the worst scare." Laura hugged me hard, then stepped aside for Joe.

"It's well past curfew, young lady," he said after he'd released me.

I stood back to admire his familiar rumpled khakis and deep dimples. Other golf shrinks seemed to dress like the players they coached. Joe tended to the professorial — all he needed was a pipe and a corduroy jacket with suede patches on the elbows.

"Laura said you were going to bed early. I figured we wouldn't see each other until tomorrow."

I ignored his accusatory tone and ran my hand down the length of the blue sling that held Joe's left arm. "Are you okay?"

He nodded. "Where have you been?"

"It's a long story," I said. "Unbelievably long. First of all, Kaitlin's been murdered."

"*Kaitlin's* dead? No way! What happened?"

"I don't know what happened. Naturally, I found the body and the cops think I killed her." I explained about finding the corpse in the pit, lying next to what I believed was the illegal driver that had resulted in the elimination of So Won Lee. For a moment, I wrestled with whether I should confess about my break-in to Dr. Turner's office. It was late, I was beyond exhausted, and I knew Laura and Joe would want every detail. And then they'd pepper my narrative with horrified reprimands.

"There's more, isn't there?" said Laura. "You've got a very strange look on your face. A guilty one."

I sighed. "I just came from Dr. Turner's office with Jeanine. We listened to him spend the evening clearing files out that he doesn't want the police to see."

"Who's Jeanine?" asked Laura.

"Dr. Will Turner? Of the False Memory Consociation?" asked Joe at the same time. "What do you mean you *listened* to him?"

I sighed again. I explained to Joe how I'd masqueraded as a patient yesterday. Then I described tonight's adventure — Jeanine's call and our eavesdropping on Dr. Turner from the closet inside his office. "He's working with some other guy, a lawyer. He wants this guy to scare me off the trail."

"What trail?" said Laura. "I don't get what Turner has to do with any of this."

"You shouldn't have gotten involved with him," said Joe. "I told you I'd look into it when I got here. The guy's a fanatic." He turned to Laura. "He's the head of this organization that supports parents whose kids have accused them of abuse. They target therapists who work with what they call memory recovery techniques. In most of these cases, the sexual contact was not recalled until the victim got into therapy. So Turner's organization attacks what they call false memories of abuse. They provide financial help, picketers, publicity, whatever's needed."

"I guess this guy who was helping him tonight also had trouble with his daughter," I said. "Turner threatened to expose him publicly, if he didn't help."

"Are the accusations true, then?" Laura asked.

"Some yes, some no," said Joe. "Both sides have merit. You can't generalize about this — you have to look at the situations case by case. Real victims need permission to speak up about what happened to them. At the same time, innocent people need protection from damaging, unfounded accusations.

Turner and his crowd don't want to allow any leeway for the possibility that incest exists. Or, I should say, that memories of incest can surface in the process of psychotherapy. As a particularly vocal shrink, Bencher was a major target. That is, until he died last week."

"But do you think Turner killed him?"

Joe tugged on one ear. "He's driven, he's brilliant, he has a lot at stake. But on paper, I wouldn't have thought he was capable of murder. On the other hand, he's a clear link between the two deaths. And he has other people in his organization who are not nearly as smart or controlled."

"Unfortunately, I'm a link to both the murders, too," I groaned. "Or that's what the cops see." I collapsed on my bed and pulled the spread up over my face.

"Look," said Laura. "There are a million other possible suspects. So Won Lee had an obvious motive to club Kaitlin to death. Walter Moore did, too."

"I saw him at the sheriff's department, waiting to be questioned," I said from under the bedcovers. "According to the note I saw in the Ruperts' condo, Walter was out to dinner with Kaitlin right before she died. Then there's that Leviticus guy. He was in the immediate vicinity of both the murders. And he fits into your category of a not-too-smart, but loose, cannon. Turner and his buddy mentioned his name tonight. They're worried about him, anyway, whether the cops are or not."

"Didn't Pate tell you yesterday that one of Bencher's patients already confessed to killing him?" asked Laura. "In that case, the two murders aren't even connected."

"Time out, ladies," said Joe, pulling the bedspread off my face. "Can we all agree that you need to focus on tomorrow's tournament?" Laura and I both nodded. "As I see it, ruminating about who killed Kaitlin is not congruent with that goal. So here's the plan. Close your eyes, both of you." I shut my eyes. "Now picture carrying a heavy load, something so heavy you can hardly stand up holding it." I imagined my arms full of a large package. My thighs and forearms ached from the effort of carrying it. "Now you see me come into the picture," said Joe. "My arm is fine. I look strong and solid."

"What are you wearing?" asked Laura. "Are you naked?"

"Jeans and a golf shirt, O you of the dirty mind," he said. "Now picture me taking the burden from you." I visualized handing over my heavy package. "You feel light. You feel relieved," said Joe. "Open your eyes now. In that load were all those questions about the two murders. That worry is mine now. Your only concern is your golf game. Agreed?" We both nodded again. "Then I'll see you at the range at eight. In the meanwhile, Laura, stick to this girl like Crazy Glue. We don't want anything to happen to our favorite LPGA prospect."

# 20

In spite of the late hour we'd finally gotten to sleep, I woke up at 5:30 a.m., muscle fibers twitching and brain cells spinning. Maybe a vigorous run would settle me down. I'd learned by painful experience in the first round that it didn't pay to arrive at the golf course too early. I got up and pulled on my running clothes in the dark.

"Where the hell are you going?" asked Laura, her voice muffled by two pillows.

"Out for a jog. I'm too anxious to just sit around."

"You'll stay around the motel, then?" said Laura. "I don't want anything happening to you on my watch. Doc said you weren't to go out alone."

"So come along."

"Gimme a break. Not a chance I'm going jogging in the pitch dark. Can't you use the gym downstairs?"

"Their equipment is pathetic," I said. "And I'll lose my mind if I wait around here until tee time." I knew Laura and Joe both meant well, but the weight of their good-natured worry had begun to feel an awful lot like living at home with Mom.

"Just be careful," said Laura, rolling over and stretching. "I'm going to snooze for another twenty minutes or so. Hey, I had the weirdest dream. I have to remember to ask Doc what it means. I dreamed they canceled the rest of the tournament because a whole flock of Canadian geese landed in the parking lot and linked wings. None of the officials could get to the golf course from their cars because of all the honking and flapping."

"You don't need an advanced degree to interpret that," I said. "You feel guilty that you didn't stop the goose hunt last winter at your course in Connecticut." Then it hit me. "Oh, my God. They may have really canceled the tournament, with someone murdered on the grounds." I strode over to the bedside table. "I'm going to call the office and find out."

"It's five-thirty, Cassie. They won't be sitting around waiting to take your phone call at five-thirty." I dialed the number I found on the information packet Alice MacPherson had given me on the day I arrived. Busy signal.

"You see," I said, placing the phone back in its cradle. "There is someone there."

"You go out for your jog, and I'll call them again in twenty minutes, I promise," Laura said. "When you get back, I'll have all the latest news."

I started down the stairs. By the time I'd reached the parking lot, it no longer felt like

I had the patience to wait even half an hour to hear about the status of the tournament. I had to know now. I retrieved the spare key from under the wheel well of the Pontiac and drove over to the Plantation Golf and Country Club. If the tournament was status quo, I could jog on the Panther course while I was there: it would be prettier than running out by the Interstate. If the tournament was canceled, to hell with the exercise. I knew Laura could be talked into my favorite breakfast at the Cracker Barrel — cheddar cheese omelet with ham, sausage, *and* bacon, plus sausage gravy and biscuits on the side. A truckload of heart-stopping sludge, yes, but just what the golf doctor would prescribe to help cushion the collapse of a long-time dream.

As I pulled into the parking lot at the club, my headlights flashed over a hunched figure hurrying toward the clubhouse. I stomped on the brakes and lurched to a stop next to Alice MacPherson. She appeared distracted, unaware that my rented Pontiac had nearly flattened her.

I rolled down the window. "It's awful news about Kaitlin Rupert." Wouldn't pay to appear only interested in my own concerns.

Alice nodded. "Unbelievable." She continued walking briskly toward the clubhouse.

"Is everything still on here?"

She nodded again, calling back over her

shoulder, "No changes. Lucky for us, the crime scene is contained to the other golf course so we'll be able to proceed as planned on the Bobcat. I'm telling all the girls, you'll need to make yourself available to the sheriff's department for questioning, as they request. Oh, and we will be holding a memorial service for Kaitlin after the afternoon round. I'm estimating sometime around four, depending on the weather this afternoon. And speed of play." Just mentioning the possibility of slow play brought a scowl to her face. She rushed off in the direction of the anxious-looking group of volunteers huddled at the entrance to her office.

I locked the car, crossed the road, and started off at a fast clip down the Panther's first fairway. Laura would kill me when I got back. But the conversation with Alice left me feeling like I needed to see the site where I'd found Kaitlin's body. This time in the daylight.

I circled the perimeter of the front nine, staying close to the cookie-cutter condominiums and small resort homes that defined the boundaries of the golf course, and let my thoughts wander. Kaitlin's death had freed up another spot in the tournament. I wondered if the officials were planning to fill it with one of the girls who'd missed the cut. It was bad enough to have slithered in on the basis of So Won Lee's unfortunate elimination. I couldn't imagine how it would feel to advance because someone else had died. Been murdered. This line of thinking reminded me that another suspect could be added to the list of possible murderers: whichever golfer had the score that fell one shot higher than mine.

Ridiculous train of thought.

I ran past a hand-carved sign on the eighth fairway: "Wetland Preserve Area: Keep Out!" None of us players had had any desire to flaunt the rules. But in spite of our best intentions, I bet a dozen balls at least, and possibly the girls who'd sliced them, had gone into the wetlands over the past two days. I noticed that I already felt calmer about today's round than I had about playing the two days previous. Maybe due to a sense of fatalistic optimism, if such a thing existed. What will be, will be. Could my serenity have been the influence of Heather's annoying little mother? Since God has a plan and he's in charge, why the hell should I work so hard on promoting my idea of how things should go?

Or maybe my equilibrium had to do with Joe Lancaster arriving in Venice — a reassuring belief that he would not allow me to disintegrate into a mass of pulsing, three-putting nerves. I could already imagine his advice.

"Today and tomorrow we're going to be patient. You have thirty-six holes to play. Don't force any shots, just play one at a time. Think about your routine for each shot and the results will come."

Really, there was nothing in those words that I couldn't have thought of myself. That I hadn't already told myself, for that matter. But Joe had a way about him, as soothing as a cat's purr, a well-worn baby's blanket, warm milk.

You're losing it, Cassie, I told myself.

I picked up the pace until I was breathing hard and hoarse. I passed a sign near the ninth green. "To Help Save the Earth, We Are Using Reclaimed Water." A few lights had begun to flicker on in the condos adjacent to the nature preserve and I heard the buzz of a stone saw from inside one of the new homes-in-progress. My watch read six o'clock. In fifteen minutes, Laura would begin to worry. I sprinted for several minutes until I reached the wooden bridge leading through the marsh to the thirteenth tee. Although the early morning sky had begun to lighten from black to an eggplant purple, a thick overhang of swamp maples reduced visibility in the marsh. I thought I recognized the haunting call of a pair of sandhill cranes. Maybe the same fellows we'd chased off the tee yesterday. Then, over the clip-clopping of my Nikes, I heard a loud rustling noise in front of me. Just ahead, an enormous alligator crawled across the walkway and plopped into the water. I couldn't help myself: I screamed.

"Shut up, Cassie," I said aloud. "You're

scaring the hell out of the wildlife."

I continued to run the length of the board-walk, now imagining the echo of a second set of footsteps. I looked behind me, but saw no one. I thought of Dr. Turner instructing his companion to frighten me. No need for that — I could do it perfectly well for myself. I glanced over my shoulder a second and third time. It would have been easy enough to hide in the shadows of the vegetation, but not so easy to follow me on the walk — unless you didn't care whether you were seen or heard. Now every woodland sound resonated with the possibility of danger. Damn, I wished I were back at the motel spinning on that shaky stationary bicycle.

I burst out of the woods and loped the length of the fourteenth fairway, then back along the catwalk leading to fifteen and the safety of the access road. I'd had enough. Viewing the pit where Kaitlin's body had lain was a lousy idea anyway. I could hardly re-member what my point had been. Some kind of personal or existential farewell? Just get me out of here.

By the time I reached my car, I was drenched in sweat. The parking lot was buzzing with the arrival of the first wave of today's golfers. The atmosphere felt charged, partly due, I supposed, to the shock of Kaitlin's death. And partly to the death of the hopes of half the women in the field after yesterday's cut. Awesome golfers, nice girls, decent people — none of that mattered if they hadn't shot two solid rounds of golf over the last two days. And in two more days, only thirty of us would survive to move on to the final stage of Q-school; more corpses strewn along behind. Sheesh, I was getting morbid.

I retrieved my cell phone from the glove compartment and called Laura. "The tournament's still on. I'll be back shortly," I said, and hung up before she could begin to scold. I leaned against the car to stretch my calves.

"Morning, Miz Burdette."

"Oh, my God, you scared the hell out of me." I turned to face Deputy Pate. His ugly leer lingered on the contours of my body, making me feel like I was outfitted for a wet T-shirt contest, in spite of the unkempt hair and the eau-de-Nike I was sure I reeked.

"You seem jumpy."

I shrugged and pulled my left foot up into a quadriceps stretch.

"Finding a dead friend would do that to you, I suppose," he said. "Or was she a friend?"

"Is that a rhetorical question, *Deputy?*"

"This is a murder investigation, Miz Burdette. The question was quite serious."

"Then no, she was not a friend. Which is not to say that I wanted her dead or killed her, either one. She was a difficult woman.

I'm sure you are finding many others who feel just the same way in the process of your investigation. Why did you tell me you were the sheriff, Deputy Pate?"

He stared at me, his eyes revealing nothing more than a cold reflection of my own. It had probably been a bad idea to confront him, to flaunt his embarrassing exposure the night before.

"If it were up to me . . ." He paused for dramatic effect. Though as far as I was concerned, the only effect the pause had was to underscore how powerless this little twerp had turned out to be. "If it were up to me, you would be under arrest, Miz Burdette. The circumstances of being the closest person to two freshly murdered bodies seem entirely too coincidental."

"Excuse me, but I thought you said one of Dr. Bencher's patients had confessed to killing him?"

"The guy turned out to be a wack job. Big surprise, eh? Finding a fruitcake in a shrink's office. So we're still looking." He stared me down for several seconds. "Good day." Then he swaggered off, leaving me in a now-too-familiar state of heightened panic. Tournament or not, I had to help find the real killer. Regardless of whether Pate occupied a ground-floor rung in his bureaucracy, he clearly intended to stir up trouble.

My surrogate parents waited back in the

motel room. "I'm fine. I need to shower. Let's talk at breakfast," I said, sweeping past Laura and Joe and into the bathroom in my best imitation of adolescent disdain.

"Here's the deal," I explained later over corn flakes and wheat toast. "Pate says the patient who confessed to killing Bencher turned out to be a fraud. So we're back to two unexplained murders. Unfortunately, I was the wretched soul who discovered both of them. I need help here, guys. We can't just sit back and wait for that lardbutt to find the real killer. He isn't looking very hard, except at me."

"The most important thing is that you tee off in ninety minutes," Joe began.

"I understand we can't take care of this now," I said. "But Turner's threat has me worried, too. The whole time I was running, I imagined hearing someone sneaking up behind me. I know my concentration will improve if we make a plan before we leave for the golf course. Something a little more detailed than imagining I'm handing over a heavy load." I smiled at Joe. "No offense intended."

Laura pulled out her Bobcat yardage book and opened it to the last page. "Fine, let's make a list. I always feel better with a list."

"The obvious suspects would be So Won Lee, Walter Moore, Mr. Atwater, and Will Turner," I said. "Other than me, and I promise I didn't kill either one of those people."

"Just to be thorough," said Joe. "Let's add anybody else who could have been at both of the crime scenes."

"That's not so easy," I said. "Maybe Julie Atwater? But why would she kill the guy she had a consultation with? Why would she kill a friend, for that matter?"

"What about Kaitlin's family? You said Gary had gone to pick them up at the airport. Could the note have been a cover-up?" said Joe.

"The girl was found with her underwear ripped off and her head bashed in. That doesn't sound like a family affair to me."

"But it doesn't rule them out," said Joe. "Stranger things have happened. Do you think she was raped?"

I shrugged. "I have no idea. Incest, rape, who knows? I guess we should include all of them, whether it really makes sense or not. We can eliminate possibilities as we go."

"I'll take Turner and both Atwaters," said Joe.

"I'll look into the Ruperts and try to talk with the folks at the Deikon headquarters," said Laura. "That leaves you Walter Moore and So Won Lee." Laura picked up her tray and headed for the trash can.

"Look, Kaitlin made the headline again," I said. I read from the front page of the *Herald-Tribune*. " 'Kaitlin Rupert, a participant in the LPGA Sectional Qualifying Tournament at the Plantation Golf and Country Club was discovered dead on the grounds yesterday evening. Cause of death appears to have been head trauma by blunt instrument, reportedly a golf club.' "

I folded the paper in quarters. "The club used to kill Kaitlin bothers me," I said. "It wasn't a casual choice. When you think about it, an iron has a sharper blade — it would make a much better weapon than a wood. So it had to be someone who knew what had happened on the course earlier. Someone connected with the tournament. Or someone who understood the meaning of the experimental driver."

"Or someone who knew enough about all that to throw the club into the pit and confuse the hell out of the scene," suggested Laura.

"It's pathetic, when you think about Kaitlin's quote in the paper yesterday," I said. "She said she played every shot as though it was her last. And they *were* her last golf shots. She just didn't know it."

"Time for you to play golf, young lady," said Joe. "We'll work on these problems later this afternoon."

"I have other questions, too," I said. "Like why is Max Harding really in town? I didn't buy what he said when he was over the other night."

Laura frowned. "Max Harding was over the other night? You didn't mention that."

"I'm going to call Detective Maloney in Myrtle Beach, later, too," I said, ignoring her question. I hadn't meant to mention Max's visit at all. "I'm sure not going to get any inside scoop on any of this from Imposter Pate."

# 21

The LPGA commissioner was holding a press conference in front of a small group of reporters and spectators when we arrived at the golf course. "This has been shocking news, absolutely unthinkable. Kaitlin Rupert was part of our golf family." He removed his glasses and polished the left lens with the end of his tie. He set the glasses back on his nose. "We have made the decision to continue on with the tournament in spite of the tragedy. We hope you will all demonstrate your support to Kaitlin's family by attending the memorial service. The service will be held next to the practice green at approximately four o'clock this afternoon. Questions?" He pointed to a small, thin woman in the crowd who had raised her hand.

"Are the rest of us in danger?" she asked in a trembling, reedy voice.

"The police have assured me that if they had a specific, reliable reason to believe the community was at risk, they would so inform us. They assure me that maintaining our safety is their primary duty. To that end, additional officers will be assigned to patrol the Plantation Golf and Country Club until the matter is resolved." Which did not sound altogether reassuring to me. I left the crowd and headed over to the range.

Both Joe and Laura stood by while I warmed up — I stuck with the routine I'd seen Mike use for nine months. Maybe it was pure superstition, but changing anything now felt like asking for trouble. First I checked the placement of my right elbow, then the extension of my left forearm, finally the clearing movement of my hips — all the technical details that had tripped me up at various points in the past. Details that now I knew by heart. Then, starting with sand wedge, and on up to three-wood, I hit exactly eight shots with each club. Finally, I tackled the important but elusive job of developing a smooth tempo for today's round. Easy rhythmic swings that might help me coast through a lifetime's worth of frayed nerves, all packed into one morning.

Although quiet while I worked at the range, Joe stepped forward when we reached the putting green. "Start with some lag putts here," he said. "Let's get a feel for the speed of the green." He stationed himself on the other side of the practice area and tossed the balls back to me after I rolled them toward the hole.

"Looking good," he said. "I'm going to make a call and see how Mike's doing over at Ponte Vedra. He should have made the turn by now. Finish up with two-footers, so you have the sound of the ball dropping into the cup in your mind when you tee off."

I'd sunk fifteen short ones in a row and was verging on pretty darn hopeful, when Gary Rupert and his parents approached my bag.

"Cassie, I think you've met my folks, Peter and Margaret?"

"Oh, God," I muttered. My putter dropped to the ground with a muffled thunk. "I'm so sorry about Kaitlin. This must be so awful for you." I hugged Gary and touched his mother softly on her hand. Margaret Rupert began to cry — from the condition of her mascara, I could see this was not the first time she'd wept today. Tears crowded my own eyes. I needed to back off emotionally and narrow my perspective from sympathetic acquaintance to skeptical observer. "If there's anything I can do . . ."

"Thanks," said Coach Rupert. "Since Kaitlin can't be here, we'd love to see you play well today." He startled me by gathering me into an awkward, one-armed embrace. "I know this is none of my business," he said. "But don't be a stranger to your father. Life is too short." Whatever ugliness had passed between him and Kaitlin, the sharp pain in his voice was real. Though Gary wouldn't be carrying a bag on the golf course today, he had the far more difficult job of tending his family's grief.

Once they'd left the practice area, I tried to step away from the feelings that had washed over me and review what I thought I'd seen: three family members devastated by the death of someone they loved, the pain made sharper by the rift that had existed between them before she died. Hard to find the face of a murderer there.

I stopped by the bulletin board to check the pairings. I would be playing with cheery Jessica from Michigan, and a woman I did not know, Maria Renda. My 153 still anchored the rock-bottom position in the field. The powers-that-be had apparently decided not to admit another golfer in Kaitlin's place. So much for that potential suspect.

"Mike's hanging in there," said Joe when we met up on the path to the first tee. "He and his caddie aren't getting along too well, but it doesn't look like it hurt him to have me out of his way."

I chuckled. Even though I believed personality clashes and Mike Callahan went together like thunder and lightning, I was relieved to hear that I wasn't the only caddie who'd gotten on his nerves. A little mean, but I couldn't help myself.

When we reached the tee box, I greeted Jessica and her father. I recognized our third player as the tall woman Kaitlin had infuriated just before the thunderstorm in the first round.

"Maria Renda," she said, thrusting her hand in my direction, eyebrows raised like black boomerangs. "You haven't played in this kind of tournament before, have you?" I shook my head no. "Good luck, then." The tone of her voice said a lot more than that. Like, Good luck, you poor dumb bastard. And, What are you doing out here anyway? And, Stumble around as much as you like, but stay the hell out of my way.

"She's got a bug up her butt," said Laura, once Maria had returned to her cart.

"She lost her card two seasons ago," whispered Jessica.

"So she was already on the Tour?" I asked.

Jessica nodded. "She played for two years with the big girls, then her game went South. Just imagine the pressure she feels — reduced to struggling through the Q-school sectionals with us."

I broke into a commiserative cold sweat just thinking about it. How bad would that be — surviving two levels of Q-school, then flunking out of the real thing and having to come back and do it all again?

"Time, ladies," called out the starter.

Flashing a wide smile at her father, Jessica hit her tee shot down the center of the fairway. Maria teed off next, firing a towering hook that cleared the fairway bunkers to the left and died in the deep rough on the side of a mound. She stomped away from the tee, wearing the same fierce look she'd had two days ago in the lightning shelter. Her blond caddie, again dressed in his good-guy cavalry costume, trotted off behind her.

"Hope she pays that caddie better than you pay yours," said Laura. "Now go get 'em, girl!"

The sense of well-being I'd experienced earlier this morning had evaporated. My three-wood felt like a baseball bat, my arms like stuffed sausages — all fat and gristle and no muscle, certainly no sign of the muscle memory that should have carried me through this kind of panic. Choking, I believed they called it — no matter what sport you happened to be in the process of screwing up.

"Let it go," said Laura.

"Let it flow," urged Joe.

"Let it snow," I said, suddenly hysterical. What the hell? At this point, there was no place to move but up, up, up. I was a double murder suspect, the very worst golfer in the field, and an object of pity to even the second worst. DFL, the caddies on the Tour called it. Dead Fucking Last. Why not swing freely? My drive landed twenty yards behind Jessica's, with a flat lie and a clear shot to the green.

"That's a beauty," said Joe, beaming with relief.

"It's a sucker pin," said Laura, "right on top of the trap. Just go for the fat of the green."

Maria Renda located her ball lying dangerously close to the out-of-bounds line. She took a fast swipe at her second shot.

"See what I mean," said Laura as the ball dribbled into the bunker in front of the green. "She cut it too close." Maria screamed at her caddie in Spanish.

"I'd hate to hear the translation of that," said Jessica, covering her ears with her hands. The two of us hit our second shots safely on the green and two-putted for easy pars. Maria Renda left hers in the sand on the first try and carded a double bogey.

"I feel bad for her," I said.

"Won't help her or you one bit," replied Laura. "You can buy her dinner later if you really feel sorry for her. But right now, eye on your own ball, please."

By the third hole, we began to understand the serious disadvantage of teeing off as the last threesome in the field. With three bogeys on the second hole, we'd set no records for speed. But we still had to wait five minutes before the third green cleared. Jessica knocked her ball just short of the green.

"Stay below the hole," said Laura. "It looks like murder coming back down." My ball landed just past Jessica's and rolled five feet from the cup.

"You're the tops," said Joe.

Maria Renda glared in his direction, then yanked her shot left. It caromed off the stone wall lining the water hazard and plunked into the brackish pond. She let loose a barrage of enraged Spanish and sent her caddie off in search of a rules official. We waited by the green, assuming she wanted a ruling to determine the most advantageous, while still legal, drop. Of course, she had to know the rules of golf like her mother's face — we all did. But calling the official over was conservative play. At this point, nobody wanted to give up the slightest advantage or pull some dumb stunt that would add penalty strokes.

"Mike's two under after fifteen," said Joe as he returned to our group and slid his cell phone into his pocket. "But his caddie's threatening to quit."

"Who's feeding you these details?" I asked.

"One of my buddies is following Mike's threesome. He promised to keep me posted."

The rules official consulted with Maria, then approached the green and motioned Joe over to the cart. "Excuse me, Dr. Lancaster, but Ms. Renda is distracted by your commentary," he said. "While there is no rule against speaking with spectators, we would appreciate it if you would take care not to inconvenience the other golfers."

"Of course," said Joe. "I'm sorry." He backed away from the green.

"Joe knows etiquette better than any professional golfer on the Tour," I said to Laura once the official drove off. "Her game would be in the toilet even if Bob Rotella and David Leadbetter were both standing by to patch her up. What a pain in the butt." We marched on in silence: I was just mad enough to birdie three and four, and eke out ugly pars on the next three holes. Jessica played steady, unremarkable golf, and Maria Renda dug her own trench deeper and deeper.

"Somebody has a sense of humor here," said Laura, pointing to a hand-carved sign in the garden by the eighth tee: "Time to Stop and Smell the Roses." Nice sentiment, but not likely today. Besides, it was hard to smell anything other than the bleach used by workers powerwashing the windows on the adjacent pink condos.

After both Jessica and I had planted our drives in the fairway, Maria stepped onto the tee. She pantomimed her swing twice in slow motion. From the particular attention she paid to the position of her elbow, I gathered she was trying to correct her string of snap hooks. After shifting her feet to point slightly right, she blistered her longest drive of the day. Straight down the middle. No duck hook there — not even a gentle draw. However, with the combination of the adjustment in her setup and the fact that the fairway took a dogleg to the left, her ball headed toward a finger of the same pond she'd encountered on the third hole. It skipped through the rough and hopped into the water. Maria stalked off the tee and slammed her driver against the Stop and Smell the Roses sign. The club head flew off the shaft and clocked Laura just above her left ear, knocking her to the ground.

"Oh, my God, you've killed her!" I yelled.

Laura cracked one eye open. "Not dead, just stunned. Give me a minute and I'll be fine." I rushed over to where she lay. A large red welt that reproduced the grooves of Maria's driver had begun to swell along her hairline.

The rules official who'd scolded Joe on the third hole drove back up to our group. He squatted down next to Laura and peered into her eyes. He asked her name, the date, and her current whereabouts, all of which she answered cheerfully and correctly. Then he turned to Maria.

"I hope you have a fruitful day. Because you can expect notice of a fine for unprofessional conduct when you return to the clubhouse." She slunk over to retrieve the club head from a rose bush, apologizing a second time to Laura on the way.

"I know you didn't hit me on purpose," said Laura.

"I'm going to take you in and have the nurse on duty check out that lump," said Joe. "At the least, you could end up with one hell of a shiner."

"I don't plan to see anybody except you guys tonight," protested Laura. "I don't want to leave Cassie."

"I'll be fine until you get back," I said. "You should get some ice on that." They rode off to the clubhouse with the official. On the way to my ball, I walked the length of the hole with Maria's caddie, who appeared to be maintaining a safe distance from his boss.

"She's a bit of a hothead," I said.

He grinned. "She is a lot of work, but it makes for an exciting ride. And there are other advantages." The sudden loft in his pale eyebrows suggested involvement in off-course activities, the details of which I preferred not to know.

By the time Laura and Joe rejoined us on the tenth tee, I had carded another birdie on eight and was flying high.

"I just missed the lag putt on nine or we'd be three under," I said. "Let me see the damage." Laura removed the ice pack from her temple to show me the thin slit of her swollen and discolored left eye. "Whoa, baby. That's a doozy."

The remainder of the round flew by without incident. A simple par on ten, a splendid birdie on eleven involving a seven-wood out of the fairway bunker and a long downhill putt from the back of the green. On the par-three fifteenth, I took a free drop away from mole cricket damage on my short drive and chipped in for bird from the improved lie. Maria's face told it all — a hearty disapproval for my taking full advantage of the local rule. Or was it anger at her own miserable display of putting? Whatever the facts of her inner turmoil, the fight appeared to have drained out of her after her tantrum on the eighth tee.

A small crowd gathered as we approached the eighteenth green. I remembered the scene I'd pantomimed in the moonlight before the tournament started. I executed a close approximation of the drive and approach shot I'd imagined, and just missed the long birdie putt. The spectators who waited under the shade of the live oak clapped enthusiastically as we walked off the green.

"A sixty-eight, you animal! You shot a sixty-eight!" yelled Laura. She picked me up and whirled me around until I begged to be released. I couldn't stop smiling. The sixty-eight, which threatened my best score ever in competition, meant an express ride away from the rock-bottom position where I'd started the morning.

# 22

A reporter gestured to me as I entered the roped-off scoring area. "Could you stop by the press tent when you're done here? We'd like to talk to you a few minutes about your round."

"Never thought I'd hear those words," I told Laura.

"They may get more than they bargained for," said Laura. "You don't have to describe every shot."

"Lay off, it's my fifteen minutes. Let me bask a little."

By the time we reached the press area, four reporters were shouting questions at a member of Deikon Manufacturing's brain trust. Which is to say, not Walter Moore.

"We are well aware that our equipment did not meet USGA specifications regarding the coefficient of restitution," he said. "For the layman, excuse me, layperson, that means the club's face did have a springlike effect due to the construction of its layers. In other words, it will fly one hell of a lot farther than anything else out there on the market."

He laughed, then cleared his throat solemnly.

It appeared that he, too, was enjoying his short burst of fame. "In fact, however, this club had not yet been released, or should I say, unleashed, on the public." Another grin broke through, then he recomposed his serious expression. "We regret that our marketing representative did not follow company policy when he allowed the piece of equipment to be utilized ahead of its scheduled release date. He has been relieved from employment with our company." Poor Walter. The golf gods were really piling it on.

"Are you aware that the club was used to murder a golfer yesterday?"

Definitely a marketing nightmare.

The Deikon representative frowned. "We deeply regret Ms. Rupert's death and extend our sincere sympathy to her family. Otherwise, I have no further comment." He ducked under the ropes and stalked away from the press tent. The reporters turned to me.

"How was it out there today?" asked the reporter from the *Herald-Tribune*. Kind of a dumb question, but almost an obligatory opening for most golf interviews, and one I was delighted to answer.

"After the first few holes, I started to have fun, even though I left a few birdie opportunities on the course. But overall, my swing felt good, like I was hitting the sweet spot. Wow, what a time for that to happen!"

Who was this talking? The reporters laughed with me.

"Maria Renda had a rough day. How did that affect your round?" asked the reporter.

"Yeah, she struggled." I searched for something nonconfrontational to say. Truth was, on top of nearly sending my best friend to the great golf course in the sky with her temper tantrum, she'd been a royal pain in the ass. And here was my chance to let her have it. On the other hand, the women's golf world was a small community, and I did not need to juice up the intensity of her bitterness. "I've been there. I tried not to think too much about her. Just play my game while I had it rolling."

"Any thoughts about how you'll handle tomorrow's round?"

"Fairways and greens, then roll in some putts," I said. "Is that a brilliant plan or what?" The men laughed again. I was beginning to like this public relations business.

Just then Laura approached and tapped me on the shoulder. "The memorial service has started. I hate to interrupt your chance to wax on about the high points of your round, but . . ."

I thanked the reporters for taking the time to talk to me and we jogged back toward the clubhouse. There, the reality of the upcoming service was enough to subdue my euphoria.

"Keep your eyes open," I said to Laura.

"In all the murder mystery movies, the killers always show up at the funeral. Maybe they have some twisted need to check out the results of their handiwork. I'm certain Joe could explain it."

A somber crowd had gathered near the putting green, where Kaitlin's makeshift memorial service was in progress. A sprinkling of the players had already begun to weep, their brightly colored golf clothes contrasting with their tears. TV personnel from Sarasota Channel 10 News murmured into their microphones, no doubt describing the scene to their viewers. The conspicuous presence of ten or so sheriff's deputies around the perimeter of the small assembly reminded all of us that Kaitlin's death was both unnatural and unresolved.

"Today, we celebrate the life of Kaitlin Rupert," said a minister in black cloak and clerical collar who stood next to Gary and his parents. Mrs. Rupert sagged into the consoling arms of her son and husband. The grim set of Gary's mouth reflected the sadness of the moment, sadness that would linger in the weeks, months, and years to come.

"A beautiful young life was taken from us yesterday, prompting us to remember that we do not always understand the mysterious ways of God. Jesus was no stranger to grief. He told us: 'In my Father's house are many mansions; if it were not so, I would have told you. I go to prepare a place for you.' " An edgy, lonely feeling filtered through me as I listened to the preacher's words.

"I'm going to look around a bit," I whispered to Laura. "I see Jeanine on the other side — I want to say hello. I'll meet you later at the car."

I needed to move around, and not just to scan the crowd for murder suspects or chat with Jeanine. A lapsed Presbyterian, I was just no good with death. I wished I had the unquestioning beliefs of my Catholic friends from childhood: go to church, take Communion, confess your sins, and presto, you had a place reserved in heaven. That kind of blueprint could take the sting out of dying. But much as I wanted to believe it, I didn't. I couldn't get the picture of Kaitlin lying cold and lifeless on the ground out of my mind. Or worse yet, incinerated to a handful of ashes and stashed in some hideous, but pricey piece of pottery. Maybe you'd expect it when someone old died — that was the natural order of things. But with a person like Kaitlin, so young and full of expectations for her life . . . well, even if she'd been annoying as hell while still alive, her death cast a shadow that blurred all the edges of what I could understand.

A representative from the administrative office of the Futures Tour introduced herself to the crowd. "We did not have Kaitlin with us long," she said. "Yet she left behind many strong memories of her short career."

In the present circumstances, that seemed like a safe enough generalization. I spotted Julie Atwater standing with a cluster of golfers. She leaned against one of them, tears leaking from under her dark glasses and down her face. Why was she still here? If I'd missed the cut yesterday, as she had, I would have been gone, baby, gone. Plantation Golf and Country Club a speck in my rearview mirror. Maybe she had left, then returned when she heard the news about Kaitlin's murder.

The minister led the crowd in a unison recitation of the Twenty-third Psalm. "Yea, though I walk through the valley of the shadow of death, I will fear no evil; for thou art with me . . . ," I mumbled.

This was the other part that stunk about death. Each time someone I knew died, all the other sadness from my life piggybacked on the recent one. Just now, I had Coach Rupert's unexpected advice about my father fresh in my mind. I struggled to push back the memory of watching Dad's truck vanish down Cherry Lane, only black smoke from his cracked muffler and a fine silt of dust left behind. As I wiped my tears on my shirtsleeve, Jeanine tapped my shoulder.

"Hey, Cassie," she said.

"Hey."

"This is really hard. I didn't even know her, but I feel awful about this." I nodded, another tear running down my cheek.

"Gosh," she said. "I didn't realize you felt that close to her."

I shrugged, deciding it would be both too complicated and beyond rude to explain that my grief was really for fatalities in my own past, not for Kaitlin. The minister read a final blessing and the crowd began to disperse.

"Are you busy later?" I said. "Why don't you join Laura and Joe and me for dinner — meet us sometime around seven at the Starlight?" I gave her a quick hug and headed back to the car, where I'd planned to catch up with Laura.

"I need a nap," she said. "I've got a big goose egg and a headache to match."

"Can you find a ride home? I wanted to try to catch Tom Reilly, the publicity guy, before he leaves. Ask him a few questions about So Won Lee."

I snaked my way through the cars in the parking lot toward the LPGA office. In the row closest to the clubhouse, I saw the Deikon honcho unlocking the door to his SUV. "Excuse me," I called and trotted over to his vehicle. "I'm Cassie Burdette, one of the golfers. I've been very impressed with your equipment this week."

The Deikon man smiled and shook my hand.

"We're always pleased to find a new customer. Did you have a good day today?" He perked up when I told him about my sixty-eight.

"I'm going to need woods and irons," I said. The rep's face crinkled into an even wider smile. "Who should I contact about trying some clubs? I take it Walter Moore's on the way out."

"He's out, not just on the way out. I'll give you my card, you can call me at headquarters," he said.

"How long did Walter work for you? It must have been a shock when all this happened."

"A couple years," answered the rep, his smile gone now. "I warned my boss not to hire him."

"You predicted trouble?"

"It didn't take a brain surgeon," said the rep. "A guy comes to you with work experience as a bouncer and a used car salesman, plus a manslaughter charge in his curriculum vitae. You be the judge."

"A manslaughter charge?"

"I have to get back," said the rep, sliding into his front seat. "Give me a buzz and I'll be sure you get fitted for those clubs. I can't promise we'll sponsor you, but a sixty-eight is a darned good start." He winked and slammed the door shut.

I continued on to the LPGA office and found Tom, alone, typing furiously on his laptop. "Give me a minute," he said. "I need to send out the quotes from today's round. I see from your interview that you hit the sweet spot."

I laughed and wandered back out into the hall to peruse the players' bulletin board. The Bible study notice and list of nonconforming drivers were still posted. The Fairway Bruiser brouhaha continued to puzzle me. Why would Kaitlin Rupert have put the illegal club in the Korean golfer's bag? Was the elimination of So Won both from Q-school and Walter Moore's elite stable of sponsored golfers worth the risk Kaitlin would have been taking?

I tried to picture the scene around the building where the carts were stored, where she could have tampered with So Won's golf bag. There would have been a crowd of milling golfers, as well as volunteer expediters, and club personnel tending to the carts. Easy enough to slip the driver into someone's bag, presuming you weren't caught in the act by its owner.

Then it occurred to me that So Won's golf bag looked a lot like Kaitlin's Deikon monster — dark green plaid with brown leather piping, and a forest of expensive woods sprouting from the lip. Maybe someone had intended to place the club in *Kaitlin's* bag and chose So Won's by mistake. Standing behind So Won's bag, an observer might not have noticed that the Deikon logo was missing. And I could make a long list of girls who might have enjoyed seeing Kaitlin knocked on her ass for breaking a USGA rule. In fact, there'd be a catfight to get top billing.

"I'm ready for you, Cassie," said Tom Reilly, poking his head out into the hallway. "How can I help? I hope you're not here to complain about your write-up — it's already been e-mailed to headquarters and posted on the website."

"I'm sure it's fine," I told him. "I'm just curious about So Won Lee."

"That was a darned shame," said Tom. "From what I saw, she was a nice girl, and a nice player."

"I know you can't show me her profile," I said. "But could you look it over and tell me if you see anything unusual, anything that might possibly connect her to Kaitlin's murder?"

He brought out a thick notebook containing the profiles from the entire Q-school field. Mine would be there, too. Husband, no. Children, none. Hobbies, none I cared to make public. Organic gardening made me sound like a dork, and I didn't want someone goading me to perform hot licks on a banjo I hadn't touched in years. Lowest score ever, sixty-five, Palm Lakes Golf Course, Myrtle Beach, South Carolina. Lowest score in competition, sixty-eight, Seminole Golf Course, Tallahassee, Florida

— a flat, wide-open layout that took some of the bragging rights out of the number. If I had planned on playing here next year, I'd be able to replace that score with today's round. Teachers or individuals having influenced your career — this blank was remarkable only for the absence of my father's name.

Tom interrupted my thoughts to read from So Won's page in the notebook. "She was born and raised in Korea, has been playing on the Futures Tour this year, enjoys time with her family, shot a sixty-two at her home course in Seoul, sixty-three this year at the Lincoln Futures Golf Classic in Avon, Connecticut. I don't really know what you're looking for, there's no question asking whether you'd cheat or kill somebody to make it onto the LPGA Tour. Point is, she didn't need to do either. You could see from her scores the past two days, she's one of the ones who's going to make it. Unless this whole illegal golf club affair brings her down."

"I hope not," I said. "Thanks anyway, for looking."

"You might try speaking with Jung Hyun Ro — she's the gal who does most of So Won's translating. I saw her earlier on the range."

I accepted a second round of his congratulations and best wishes and left the office. I stopped again at the players' bulletin board and read the Bible study notice and list of illegal drivers for the umpteenth time. I wondered if

Maria Renda was out shopping for a club to replace the driver she'd destroyed earlier today. I still didn't understand how her caddie tolerated her over the long haul. Some quirk in his personality — masochism maybe — allowed him to interpret her volatile nature as part of her charm.

Which again brought Kaitlin to mind. Loving Kaitlin either took someone half-cocked, and I'd place Walter Moore squarely in this category, or a person who took the "love your neighbor as yourself" commandment very much to heart. Like Julie Atwater. Former Bible beater and possible lesbian. I no longer knew what to think of her. No way around it: her friendship with Kaitlin seemed odd, her calm presence a major contrast to Kaitlin's turbulence. And despite her explanation, I didn't understand the bad blood between her and Gary.

I grabbed my putter from the trunk and trotted over to the practice area, my mind running loose with possibilities. Suppose Julie had developed a crush on Kaitlin after Kaitlin helped her out with the referral to Dr. Bencher. What if Kaitlin gave her the cold shoulder and the crush evolved into a jealous rage once Kaitlin turned her advances down? This theory would raise Julie to the status of murder suspect, as well as explain Gary's dislike for her.

I found Jung Hyun Ro at the Panther putting green. She nodded politely at my greeting, then refocused on her putting stroke. "How is So Won Lee holding up?" I asked, dropping three balls down onto the short grass. "It was such a shame, what happened to her."

"She was very sad," said the girl. She sunk two three-footers. "It was not her golf club that they found in her bag." Clunk, clunk, two more balls deposited in the heart of the cup. "But she is at peace, if it is God's will. And she has forgiven those who have wronged her." I looked carefully to see whether Jung Hyun Ro was including me, the obvious beneficiary of So Won's misfortune, in that company. Her face was blank. I rolled a putt well past my targeted hole.

"Is she still in town?"

"She left for Orlando yesterday afternoon."

So much for the theory of So Won Lee as killer. It's hard to have a murder pinned on you if you were miles away from the immediate vicinity.

I returned my putter to the trunk, slid into the driver's seat of the car, and pointed it to the Starlight — home away from home. None of my ruminations fit just right. Walter Moore, with a manslaughter charge in his history, was developing as a solid suspect. Other than that, my latest brainstorm about Julie Atwater made as much sense as any of the other theories we were working with. Not a lick.

# 23

It was twenty to six when I arrived back at the motel. Walter Moore ducked into the reception area ahead of me.

"Walter!" I called out when I reached the vestibule. He turned back from the elevator. Every crease in his face contributed to the intensity of his scowl. "Do you have a minute?" I tipped my head toward the empty breakfast nook. Manslaughter charge or not, I figured he was unlikely to hurt me in full view of the motel lobby.

"Make it snappy," he said. "I'm on my way out of this stinking town."

"You've had a rough week. That was hard, the service for Kaitlin. They did a nice job, though." Now I was babbling. Frankly, I was surprised the cops would allow him to leave the area.

He clenched his teeth until the small muscles around his nose and eyes began to twitch, but said nothing. Either he was struggling to contain his sadness or really, really angry.

"Let's see, I've lost two contracts, a girl-friend, and my professional credibility. Plus, the cops are on me like flies on a cow's ass. Rough week? You make the call."

"What's next for you?" I asked after several silent moments. It was a clumsy question, but I couldn't think of a casual entree into the subject of his plans.

"If I knew," he said, spittle forming little hills of bubbles in the corners of his mouth, "if I knew, I don't believe I would pass the information along to you. Some people are better than others about keeping quiet about subjects that are none of their fucking business." The last few words were more hissed than spoken.

"I didn't say anything —" He stood up and shut down my objections with a sharp wave.

"Well, good luck," I said to his back as he strode out of the room.

I flipped on the TV and surfed through reruns of Maury, Ricki Lake, and Queen Latifah. From this quick review, it appeared I could choose between programs about dictatorial husbands and fathers, gender-bending affairs, or two-timing gold-diggers. Who watched this garbage? And more to the point, where did they find the losers willing to expose their bizarre problems to public ridicule? I shut the television off — I was wound way too tight to sit through any of the available nonsense. The conversations with Walter's boss and Walter had turned the screws a little tighter still.

Returning to our room was not an option yet. Laura would kill me if I woke her up ahead of schedule to yak about my murder theories. That left pulling the trigger on the cocktail hour ahead of the others — not the smartest move just before the final round of Q-school. Or I could work some of my tension out in the miserable motel gym.

The desk clerk waved me over on the way through the faux green lobby to the small room that housed the exercise equipment. "I have two messages from your mother," she said, holding out a pair of Starlight-logo sticky notes. "She told me she hadn't been able to get through to you. She asked me to deliver these to you personally."

"Is something wrong?" I wasn't particularly worried. Mom's baseline level of hysteria tended to escalate when I'd been out of touch for more than three days.

"She just said she hadn't heard from you. She thought maybe there was a problem with both your voice mail and your cell phone." She shrugged apologetically. "You know mothers."

I sure knew mine. I thanked the clerk and continued on to the gym. The room was dim and empty, the skeletons of the equipment lit only by the flickering television that hung from the ceiling. I slid my key card into the slot, opened the door, and flipped on the overhead lights. The previous patron had left the TV volume blaring. Maury was attempting to intercede between a snotty teenaged girl wearing black lipstick and double nose rings and her enraged father. Unable to find the channel changer or reach the volume button on the television, I left him holding forth and turned to the exercise equipment.

Having run this morning, I skipped over the selection of cranky aerobics machines and went straight for the weights. No LifeMaster computerized machines here. The motel had provided an unlikely assortment of free weights — two pounds and three pounds, then skipping directly to fifty. I knew bicep curls with the fifty-pounder would leave me crippled, probably unable to swing my clubs higher than shoulder level tomorrow. The lighter weights were not worth the effort, even with multiple repetitions. The only other selection was a vaguely familiar Smith press bar, this one produced by EZ-Fit. I read the description and instructions from a faded printout on the wall. The bar targeted pecs with bungee cord counterresistance and had a built-in spotting system that eliminated the need for a lifting partner. Who wouldn't want firmer pecs?

I squinted at the faint numbers on the upright sidebar. The weight on the EZ-Fit was set for forty pounds, which seemed ambitious but not unmanageable. As instructed, I lay on my back on the bench, with my chest centered under the barbell. I grabbed the bar with the overhand grip illustrated on the wall, disengaged it from its selectorized safety system, and lowered the weight to my chest. I braced my feet against the footholds at the end of the bench and slowly extended my arms to lift the barbell. It felt refreshingly heavy.

By the third repetition, the muscles in my arms and chest had begun to shake with the exertion; I was no longer feeling refreshed. Either I wasn't as strong as I liked to think, or the EZ-Fit could use a recalibrating tune-up. I needed to reduce the amount of weight on the barbell, or else quit. Quitting sounded good.

I extended my arms again and pushed the bar up and over into the safety slot. Instead of catching when I flipped the barbell over, the entire weight dropped and banged down toward my chest. By sheer reflex, I absorbed enough of the impact with my hands to avoid being knocked breathless or cracking a rib. I stared up: the selectorized safety spotting system had apparently failed, and the bungee cord cable supporting the weights had snapped in half.

"Stay calm," I told myself. "Breathe easy." Not so simple with forty pounds pressing on your windpipe. The scene on the television came into focus as I regrouped. Maury motioned the studio audience and the father for quiet.

"I'm seventeen years old," shrieked the

teenager with the nose rings. "He can't tell me how to run my life." The gem-encrusted ring in her exposed, pierced navel glinted in the studio's harsh light.

"I will not allow my daughter to behave like a common slut," said the father. "As long as she's in my house, she'll live by my rules." He slammed his fist down on Maury's flimsy studio desk. At first glance, he had long ago lost the battle of controlling this girl.

Three more times, I positioned my sweaty hands on the barbell and heaved up. But I did not have enough strength left to move the weight more than an inch above my quivering pecs. Breathe in, breathe out . . . now on the TV, Maury and the teenage she-devil had agitated the dictatorial father into a seething rage, which reduced him to speechless grunts.

"You've put my brother down all his life," said the girl, pointing at her father with a long black fingernail. "He's a failure, a fucking flop." The audience hissed at her use of the f-word. "You've told him that every day of his life until he finally bought it. You're not going to do the same thing to me."

A small contingent of the audience rose to their feet and began to chant: "Loser! Loser! Loser!" Where the hell was the girl's mother? Couldn't she pull the plug on this embarrassing display? I glimpsed a janitor passing by the small window in the gym room door.

"Help!" I yelled. "Help!" The fight on the television obscured my screams.

I studied the safety clips that dangled several feet above me. Even if I was able to summon the strength to lift the bar again, the latches hung uselessly from the poles. Next plan: if I could roll left and tip the barbell sideways onto the floor, I thought I might have room to slide out from under it. I shifted my body right. The legs of the bench collapsed, slamming my head against the floor. The barbell bounced off my windpipe and rolled up under my chin.

I lay stunned and choking, my eyes filling with tears. I fought back the urge to struggle against the weight across my neck. My left leg had caught under the bench as it fell. Each movement I made increased the pain. I wondered how long I had to lie here before another motel resident had the bright idea to work out. Certainly from the looks of the wall-to-wall, grime-gray carpet, the housekeeping staff did not often visit the gym.

From down near my hips came a familiar buzzing noise. The cell phone had dropped out of my pocket during the collapse of the bench and lay vibrating with the news of an incoming call. Although my hands were free, the phone was out of reach. The chatter of the vibrating phone stopped, then started up again. I shifted my body toward the phone, ignoring the sharp pain in my leg, and rolled over onto the talk button with my right buttock.

"Hello!" I screamed. "Hello!" I could barely make out the small, tinny voice on the other end.

"Cassie? Is that you? It's Mom."

"Mom!" I yelled down in the direction of the phone. "I need help!"

"I can't hear you. Turn down the radio. You'll damage your hearing with all that noise."

"Listen, Mom, please," I shouted. "I'm trapped in the gym under a piece of equipment. I need you to call the main desk and tell them to come and help me."

"This connection is terrible," said Mom. "It sounds like you're breaking up. Call me back when you get out of the dead zone."

"Mom!" I screamed. "Don't hang up!" Too late. The phone lay silently blinking. Even if she called again, I doubted I could stand the pain involved in rolling my hip over the talk button a second time.

Maury signed off today's program, insisting that the father and daughter hug before they were allowed to leave the studio. The audience cheered and booed.

I had begun to feel faint and woozy when the door to the gym burst open.

"Oh, my goodness!" said the desk clerk.

"What are you doing here?" said Laura.

"The thing collapsed on me," I croaked. "My leg's crushed and I can't breathe. Please get it off."

"I'm going to get the manager," said the desk clerk as she ran from the room.

"Thanks a lot," said Laura. She squatted down, lifted the left side of the barbell, and eased the weight off my neck. The purple goose egg on her temple throbbed with her effort. She thumped the weight down on the floor beside me. I sat up, slid my leg out from under the bench, and gulped for air.

"Are you all right?" Laura asked. She studied the Smith bar. "What were you thinking of, trying to bench ninety pounds?"

"I was thinking you would kill me if I woke you up too early," I said, annoyed by her scolding tone. "I thought it was set for forty. The numbers are almost worn off. See if you don't think it looks like forty."

The motel manager rushed into the room with the desk clerk. I reviewed the details of the incident.

"The safety catch is not working and the cable snapped. It's very dangerous," I said, fingering my swelling neck. "Besides all that, you can't read the damned numbers on the bar. I'd recommend you spring for a new piece of equipment."

"We need to call the police," Laura insisted.

The manager looked horrified. "We'll take care of it," he said. "We'll look into it. We don't need the police. We'll give you one night's stay free for your bother."

"You don't understand," Laura said. "Someone's threatened Cassie. This machine has been tampered with."

I crawled over to lean against the wall. "I think it was just a fluke," I said. Laura had already punched 911 into my cell phone and begun to explain the situation to the operator.

"I'm calling an ambulance, too," said the manager, apparently now committed to displaying his concern for my condition.

Several minutes later, the sheriff's deputy who had worked with Pate at the scene of Kaitlin's murder was shown into the exercise room by the desk clerk. "Not you again."

I smiled politely and explained my altercation with the Smith bar. The detective crouched down to examine the flattened bench.

"Why do you think this was done deliberately? This equipment looks like it could use some updating."

"Updating!" Laura snorted. "That's the term they use in real estate when the kitchen appliances were manufactured and installed in the Stone Age."

"All of our guests sign a statement when they check in," interrupted the manager. "The athletic equipment is provided for the convenience of our guests and all use is strictly at your own risk. Let's go somewhere more comfortable." He ushered us out of the gym and down the hallway into the breakfast area, away from the sight of the offending equipment.

"You're going to have to tell the detective about the closet," said Laura. "Tell him about Turner's threat." Joe and Jeanine arrived in the lobby as I finished reviewing the details of our foray into the False Memory Consociation's office.

"So the second man, whose name you do not know, was instructed by this Dr. Turner to scare you off, is that accurate?" said the deputy. I nodded, shrugging apologetically at Jeanine. "And you were hiding in the closet because . . ."

"Because, Sheriff, I mean Deputy, Pate was making me feel like you guys weren't looking very hard in any direction except mine for either Dr. Bencher's or Kaitlin Rupert's killers. One more thing," I said. "I don't mean to tell you how to do your job, but Walter Moore is not too crazy about me either." I reported our earlier conversation. "I saw his boss in the parking lot earlier today — he says Walter was charged with manslaughter."

"When?" said Laura. "Who did he attack? Was he convicted?"

"I don't know the details."

"Hmm," said Joe. "I don't like the sound of that at all. One of the best predictors of violence is a violent history."

An ambulance attendant, who had hovered

in the background while we spoke, stepped forward and palpated my neck and upper chest, then examined my leg. "Nothing broken, as far as I can tell," she said. "Looks like some soft-tissue bruising, which you can expect will swell and discolor. I'd recommend you stop by the ER just to be on the safe side."

No way was I going to spend the evening in some emergency room. "I really feel fine. Except for thirsty and hungry. Are we finished here, Detective?"

He nodded. "We'll be in touch. Stick around until you hear from us, will you?"

I'd heard a lot of that lately. "I'll be playing golf again tomorrow," I said. "Final round."

"Ice and rest," called the ambulance attendant on her way out the door. "I didn't say anything about golf."

# 24

Jeanine parked the car in the Chili's lot. She turned to assess her passengers: Joe in his blue sling, Laura with a bruised and swollen face, me with the thick, red, striated neck of a professional wrestler. Though the V-necked U.S. Open T-shirt I had chosen did not constrict or irritate my sensitive skin, it definitely failed to disguise the ugly swelling.

"All of you people look like you belong in an infirmary, not a restaurant," she commented.

"Nothing a few cocktails won't fix," I said. Once we were seated, with drink orders safely delivered to the waitress, Joe addressed Jeanine.

"How did you get involved with this person?" he asked, pointing to me.

"Oh, we met at Dr. Turner's office. Cassie was practicing putting while she waited to see him and we got to talking." She smiled in my direction. "She told me that her friend Mike Callahan would introduce me to Rick Justice if I'd help her get some information about the doctor. I am so excited about this weekend. Will you excuse me, I need to run to the ladies' room." She popped up as if just the thought of meeting Rick created unbearable pressure in her bladder.

Laura and Joe turned to stare me down as she threaded her way across the room. "You told her Mike would introduce her to Rick? Our Mike Callahan? Are you nuts?"

"I didn't exactly promise." It was hard to imagine what I could say that would not sound lame and predatory. "I told her . . . I don't remember exactly what I told her. I was desperate for information, and I admit it, I probably led her on."

"You have to come clean and tell her the truth," Laura said. Jeanine returned to the table and slid into her seat.

"Truth about what?"

"Mike isn't going to have the time to socialize this weekend, if he makes the cut," Joe explained. I flashed him a grateful look. "But if you do come up to the tournament, look for me and I'll show you around. I'd be happy to introduce you to Rick Justice."

"That is so sweet," said Jeanine, batting her heavily mascaraed eyelashes over her green eyes. No wonder Joe was so eager to help me off the hook. I considered offering him a napkin to mop up his drool.

"By the way," he continued. "Mike shot a sixty-seven today, so unless he really chokes tomorrow he'll definitely be playing this weekend. How do you like that — Mike Callahan finally makes the cut in a major."

"That's fantastic," I said. "Of course the asshole had to show me up and shave a stroke off my brand-new tournament round record." That came out harsher than I'd meant it to. I knew I was annoyed more at Joe than Mike. I liked to keep my reactions toward Joe anchored in the just-plain-friends department. My irritation over his admiration of Jeanine suggested I hadn't been a hundred percent successful.

"Mike probably hit from the ladies' tees," said Laura. "Besides, he's been a professional golfer for over a year now; he's supposed to know how to play. You're just getting started."

"Look out, here comes Kaitlin's family," I said.

Joe jumped to his feet as the Ruperts reached our table. "Mr. and Mrs. Rupert, I'm Joe Lancaster. I'm so sorry about your loss."

Gary took Joe's offered hand first. "Gary Rupert. Thanks for the kind words."

I introduced Jeanine and Laura. Gary and his father accepted their condolences graciously. Margaret Rupert remained silent.

Then Gary noticed my neckline. "What the hell happened to you?"

"A little altercation with some exercise equipment." I explained the bench-pressing incident in the motel gym.

"I've never seen that happen," said Coach

Rupert, frowning. He appeared relieved to move away from conversation about his daughter's death. "Sometimes my players disengage the counterbalance because it causes the weights to bind, but I've never seen the safety catch fail on one of those machines."

"Could it have been vandals?" asked Gary. His fingers grazed my neck. "Are you sure you're all right?"

"Fine." I smiled and did a little eyelash batting of my own. Mostly for Joe's benefit, I told myself — he'd asked for it. "I may not be able to talk a lot tomorrow, but in some circles that would be counted as an advantage."

"There's vandalism everywhere these days," said Jeanine. "People are just plain mean. They don't seem to think about how their actions will affect someone else. Like that club they put in the Korean girl's bag." She realized what she'd said as soon as the words left her mouth. "I'm sorry, that was so thoughtless."

Gary and Coach Rupert grimaced with identical thin smiles.

"Not to worry," said Coach. "We don't believe our daughter would have done something like that. Though I don't suppose it matters anymore." Mrs. Rupert sagged visibly toward her husband. The claws from the high school mascot Nighthawk tattoo emerged from Coach's sleeve as he reached around to prop her up.

"We need to get going," said Coach. "It's been a hard day. Have a good dinner. Nice to meet all of you."

"Take care, Cassie," said Gary. "No more exercising tonight, I hope."

"I am so stupid," said Jeanine after they'd moved across the room out of earshot.

"You weren't thinking," I said. "It's okay."

"That's just what Dr. Turner is always saying," she said, her eyes beginning to fill with tears. " 'You don't think before you speak, Jeanine. The most absurd things come out of your mouth. God gave you big boobs to make up for a shortage in the brains department.' "

"I can't believe he'd say something so cruel." In truth, I was mostly surprised that she would have stayed in that job and put up with his crap. And even more surprised at her willingness to repeat those hurtful comments to the general public. I turned to Joe. "Speaking of that jerk, did you find out anything new about his memory association?"

"I spoke to a colleague in the American Psychological Association central office," said Joe. "Turner had developed a particular vendetta against Dr. Bencher. Bencher saw Turner's daughter in therapy several years ago and, according to him, encouraged her to accuse her father of incest."

"Gross me out!" said Jeanine.

"Wow," I said. "That explains why he's so invested in this false memory organization."

"Turner's daughter's story is similar to that of Kaitlin Rupert and Julie Atwater," explained Joe. "Once she'd had several sessions with Bencher, she turned on her father, claiming to have remembered that he abused her sexually."

"Julie said Bencher never encouraged her, he just listened," I said.

"Whatever the truth, Turner was a senior lecturer in his college physics department at the time. The publicity finished his career there. Who wants a child molester on staff? First his application for tenure was denied, then they asked him to resign. He fought it for a year, but in the end, he quit and started the FMC."

"So he isn't a shrink at all," said Laura. "Cassie, you said he listed himself in the phone book as a therapeutic consultant."

Joe shook his head. "He has no mental health training of any kind. And he'd made life hell for Dr. Bencher up until the day he was shot. The FMC featured Bencher many times in their monthly newsletter column — 'Dangerous Liaisons.' Each month several former patients would talk about their interactions with a so-called charlatan shrink. Bencher's name got to be a regular there. Somehow, they tracked down his list of patients and found the ones who were dissatisfied with his services."

"How did they find out who were his patients?" I asked. The idea of someone contacting me about my own therapist, or him about me, gave me the serious creeps.

"With the records kept by managed care companies these days, privacy is a lot less private than it used to be," said Joe.

"I don't get this Bencher dude," said Laura. "How come he got involved in so many crazy cases?"

"I don't believe he was a charlatan," said Joe. "But he did enjoy the excitement of a high-profile, high-risk case. And once you get involved in something like that, you get the reputation for being able to handle difficult patients and situations."

"Word of mouth." I nodded. "Like Kaitlin sending Julie Atwater to see Bencher."

"It also looks like the FMC arranged to have Bencher picketed," said Joe.

"You mean they paid Julie Atwater's father to picket?" I asked.

"I don't think they had to pay Atwater much, if at all," said Joe. "He had his own axe to grind. He was convinced Bencher was a high priest in a satanic cult that took hold of his daughter and implanted her with these traumatic memories."

"I really can't believe I worked for Dr. Turner," said Jeanine. "He sounds worse and worse." She wrapped her arms around herself and shivered.

"Besides that, I managed to get in touch with Turner's daughter — the one who started the whole ball rolling."

"How did you find her?"

"How did you get her to agree to speak with you?"

"I found her on the Internet," said Joe. "She lives in Tampa. She moved there before Turner set up his office in Sarasota. She wouldn't say a lot — she wasn't happy about me tracking her down and asking her to excavate her history. She did say Turner was violent and cruel and she's still scared to death of him. She's barely left the house since he moved to Florida."

"Bottom line," said Laura. "Nothing you learned would eliminate him from our pool of suspects. Everything you've told us fits with what Cassie and Jeanine overheard in the closet. He might have gotten someone like Mr. Atwater to do the dirty work, but he sounds capable of anything, even murder."

Joe nodded and looked at me. "He also sounds paranoid enough to have someone follow you around and do something destructive to get you to quit snooping in his business. I'm not buying the accident-in-the-weight-room hypothesis."

"Turner would have had no idea I was going into that gym," I protested. "I had no idea I was going in there until five minutes before I went." I swallowed the last inch of my beer and motioned for the waitress. "I'm having one more," I told Laura before she could argue. "I deserve it."

"What about Walter Moore, then," said Laura, frowning. "Could he have known you were going to work out? You said you talked to him just before you went into the weight room."

"Why would he be mad at you?" asked Jeanine.

"We overheard a big shot from Deikon telling the press that Walter is history with their company," Laura explained.

"He has this idea that I was involved in exposing the experimental club," I said. "He knows I saw him showing it to Kaitlin back home, and I guess he thinks I ratted on him. Maybe he even thinks I teamed up with Kaitlin to put it in So Won's golf bag."

"Well, you are the one who benefitted most clearly from her elimination out of the tournament," said Joe. "Believing that, the guy definitely had motive to hurt you, whether or not the thinking was twisted. He's lost everything. So he had nothing to lose. He could have set up the bench press accident. With the manslaughter charge in his background, I'd put my money on Walter."

"But at the time I spoke to him, I didn't know I was going to the gym. It's not like I posted an announcement: Cassandra Burdette will be working out at six o'clock."

"What about the other possibilities?" said

Joe. "Did you dig up anything on So Won Lee?"

"Nothing," I said. "I got nowhere. I just can't see her beating Kaitlin to death, even if she had a good reason. And I did talk to her friend Jung Hyun Ro — she claims So Won had already left town before Kaitlin died."

The waitress slid my bacon cheeseburger and a mound of Chili's fries in front of me.

"I did have another idea while I was over at the office," I said, arranging mustard and onions on the bun. "What about Julie Atwater? Suppose she had a crush on Kaitlin and Kaitlin shut her down. Julie seems stable, but between the Bible study stuff and her crazy father, there's been an awful lot of upheaval in her life. She could have snapped, just like Maria Renda did today on the golf course." I took a huge bite out of the cheeseburger and sighed with satisfaction.

"It sounds far-fetched," commented Laura. She pulled the list she'd made yesterday out of her pocket and smoothed it open on the table in front of her. "I'm sorry to say, I didn't do my part. I got distracted by a blow to the head." She lowered her voice to a whisper. "What do you think about one of the Ruperts?"

"I don't see it." Joe shook his head. "Other than Mom, who's very hard to read, they seem pretty normal. Sad, tired, shocked, but still able to make a normal connection. Or, in Gary's case, slobber all over a pretty girl."

I glared at him. "I'm pretty sure Mrs. Rupert belonged to Turner's false memory group," I said. "And a reporter yesterday asked Kaitlin how she felt about the organization funding her father's defense."

"I'm wondering about the two different murder methods," interrupted Laura. "First, a guy gets killed with a bullet to the throat. In the throat, for God's sake. That seems really unprofessional. Then Kaitlin gets stripped, maybe molested, we don't know that for sure, and beaten to death with a million-dollar club. I don't see the connection. Maybe there isn't one."

Joe swallowed a mouthful of garlic mashed potatoes. "Try this one out. Supposing Turner had Mr. Atwater kill Bencher. Then later, when Kaitlin didn't bow out of the lawsuit against her father, he paid Atwater to rough Kaitlin up a little, just scare her away. But Atwater got overexcited and finished the job. If he molested his own daughter, I imagine he'd be capable of the same thing with a stranger."

"I'm feeling a little queasy," said Jeanine. "Do you think we could talk about something else while we eat?"

"Do you mind just one more question about the experimental golf club?" I asked. Jeanine nodded assent. "I'm not so sure Kaitlin really put that club in So Won's bag yesterday. Their bags look so much alike — maybe someone wanted Kaitlin eliminated from the tournament, not So Won Lee."

"Interesting," said Joe.

"Who do you have in mind?" asked Laura.

"That's the hard part, she'd made so many enemies. How to choose?"

"New subject," said Joe. "Are you planning to play tomorrow?"

"Of course! Why would you ask that?"

"Just wondered how you felt after the Smith bar thing."

"I'm already feeling better," I said, cramming the last bite of cheeseburger into my mouth. "After this and a couple Advil, I'll be good as new."

The phone rang just as I had moved into the twilight between wake and sleep.

"It's for you," said Laura, rolling back under her pillow. "It's Charlie."

"Hey," said my brother. "Mom told me you're pulling out of the tournament. Just called to say I'm sorry to hear that. I hope you're okay."

"Mom's wishful thinking got mixed up with reality again," I said, laughing. "I shot sixty-eight today. She couldn't pry me out of this tournament. Where are you?"

"D.C. Still at the office. Big trial starts tomorrow. But tell me about your day." I began to review the round for him in detail.

Laura lifted the pillow off her head and rolled her eyes. "I hope you plan to pay him caddie fees for this." I ignored her.

"Your hard work finally paid off," Charlie said when I'd finished describing the day. "Congratulations. Mom also told me Kaitlin Rupert got murdered in the motel gym. Is that true? Are you safe there?"

I laughed again. Mom had a way of butchering facts almost beyond recognition. I told Charlie about finding Kaitlin's body the night before and getting trapped today under the bench press. "I honestly don't think someone set that up," I said. "No one knew I was going in there to work out." I shifted the conversation away from me. "From what you remember about Coach Rupert, do you think he would have molested Kaitlin?"

"I've been asking myself that question since I heard about the lawsuit. He was like a second father to me, but easier to get along with than Dad. I could please Coach without taking on Dad's baggage."

"Which baggage do you mean? Our father didn't travel light."

"Dad so badly wanted me to be successful in a way that he hadn't managed. It was too much pressure. I had to get away. Getting close to Coach was the only way I figured out how to do that. It wasn't subtle or kind to Dad, but I was only sixteen."

"That doesn't really answer the question."

"I know, I know. I'm getting there. Bottom line, Coach was really a lot like Dad. Hard on his players, expected nothing but the top performance we could produce. Underneath the crustiness, we knew he really cared."

"What about with his kids? His daughter? Dad pretty much gave up on me after you bailed out." I wished I'd been able to keep my voice from cracking.

"I'm sorry about that." He was silent for a moment. "I think it was different with Coach. He was disappointed that Gary wasn't much of an athlete, but really excited about what he saw in Kaitlin. I just can't imagine him hurting her. In any way, but especially that one."

"Lights out, for God's sake," Laura grumbled.

"I gotta go," I said. "Caddie Snow is giving me hell."

"Good luck tomorrow," said Charlie. "Be safe. And play well for you, not for Dad or anyone else."

I lay awake a long time, sad about our conversation. I missed Charlie. I missed my father, a fact that didn't too often surface through my anger. As I drifted off to sleep for the second time, I remembered that I had not called Detective Maloney. I'd put it on my list for tomorrow, after I finished the final round of the tournament.

# 25

After a quick breakfast of half a roll of Tums and three bites of Rice Krispies, I finished my warm-up routine at the driving range by 6:45. My still swollen neck had proven to be an advantage of sorts — any undisciplined swing provoked a painful twinge, which forced me to retreat to an easy tempo. Laura watched me grimace after a particularly wild tee shot.

"You sure you want to go through with this?" she asked.

"I did a lot of thinking lying under that barbell," I said. "Thinking about why I'm here and what this all means. What my brother said last night really pulled it together." Laura raised her eyebrows. "This is for me. I need to go out there and do the best I can. For me. I need to find out if I have what it takes to make it on the Tour. This is the best chance I'm going to get." I took a deep breath. "So I'm ready."

Laura gave me a hug. "Then I'm with you. Let's go warm up the flat stick. Getting a couple of putts to drop today could be big."

"Ladies and gentlemen, this is the final round of the LPGA Qualifying School, the seven-forty-five starting time. On the tenth tee, from Myrtle Beach, South Carolina, Miss Cassandra Burdette!"

With the booming voice and the full-court-press introduction, I figured the starter must have had aspirations for announcing a bigger tournament than this one. The only fans available to respond to his broadcast were Joe, Jeanine, and the boyfriend of one of my playing partners. Their cheers produced a jolt of excitement that ran through my body, top to bottom. Smiling with encouragement, Laura fished the three-wood out of the bag and handed it to me. I rehearsed my preshot routine: sight the target, two quick practice swings, one final glance at the target. Then I nailed my drive down the middle of the fairway.

"You corked that one!" Laura yelled. I moved to the side of the tee for the other golfers in our group. Eve Darling hit a solid drive, as did Kelly Faison, our third playing partner. As we started down the fairway, I spotted Gary Rupert in animated conversation with Max Harding on the far side of the practice putting green. Thank God they weren't following us. I felt a backbreaking pressure already, even without a bigger gallery. Then I realized that I'd forgotten to add Max to the list of suspicious characters we drew up during dinner last night.

"What are you thinking about the approach

shot?" Laura asked. I didn't admit I hadn't been thinking about the approach at all.

"I'm going with an easy seven-iron. Pin's in back, right?"

Laura checked the pin placement sheet — the players' guide to today's hole locations. The Plantation staff had saved the most precarious pin positions for our last day, just like in the real professional tournaments. That way, we had to choose between playing conservatively to protect our current standing, or straining to hit the riskier shots that could advance us in the field. Whether we succeeded and rolled our balls up close to the hole for easy birdies, or failed, and slam-dunked them into water hazards for bogeys or worse, this system made for great final-round drama. Not to mention final-round terror for the players involved.

"Yeah, pin's in back. You clocked the drive almost two fifty. That's one of your best! Seven-iron looks good." I waited for Eve and Kelly to hit their shots, then stepped up to my ball and swung.

"Just what you wanted. You're on the dance floor," Laura said. Her words came just a beat late, reflecting the same disappointment I felt as I watched the ball stop well short of the hole. Given the long drive in the middle of the fairway, I'd had a chance to stick the second shot close to the pin. Instead, I left myself a fifty-foot birdie try. I sized up the putt without consulting Laura and rolled it close enough to drop the next one for par. We moved on to our second hole, the par-four eleventh.

My legs and arms felt heavy, my neck hurt, my stomach churned. Too little sleep, too much fear, too many hopes tied to this one round. "I've hit the wall," I told Laura. "I can't even hit a simple seven-iron."

"Don't think about it. You just hurried the swing a little. You're a player. Like Joe says" — she winked in his direction — "real players take it one shot at a time." She held out my three-wood and gave me a little shove toward the tee. My head throbbed from the effort of trying not to think. I managed two average swings and two medium putts, and with relief, scribbled another four on the scorecard.

"Do you have anything to eat in your bag?" asked Joe as he walked beside me to the twelfth tee.

"Didn't you get enough breakfast?"

"I want you to eat something," he said.

"I'm not hungry."

"Trust me, it'll keep you going," he said. "You have a lot of holes left to play."

I rustled through three pockets before surfacing with a partially fossilized Power Bar. Gnawing on the end of the bar, I watched the other two golfers tee off. No major challenge here — I'd made birdie and par the previous two rounds. A smooth five-iron would take me home.

But my mind kicked in with another agenda: a poise-sapping, fast-backward review of all the trouble I'd found anywhere during the first three days of golf. And then a quick, but also lethal, review of the trouble my playing partners had encountered. Any partners, anywhere. An ugly parade of shanks, hooks, worm-burners, rainmakers — all of which cost strokes, confidence, and tournament position — flooded my brain. IMRAS. Inexperienced mind run amok syndrome. I'd seen Mike struggle with the same thing during his rookie season.

Swing through it, damn it, I told myself. Shut it out.

Too late. My muscles had already tensed in reaction and my tee shot plopped into the pond in front of the green.

I trudged toward the hazard where I would hit my next shot, remembering the only tournament that I'd caddied for Mike where he came in the money. We were in Cromwell, Connecticut, the final round of the Greater Hartford Open. We'd reached seventeen, the signature hole at River Highlands. From the championship tee, the fairway curved gracefully around a lake to a small green packed with spectators. Even for the pros, it was a hard hole. The landing area looked no wider than a two-lane highway. Pull your drive left, and you were in thick rough or a nasty sand trap or a difficult downhill lie. Push it too far right, you were wet. If you got lucky enough to keep your tee shot in play, the crowd salivated for your second. They loved a perfect approach that landed softly near the pin, almost as much as they loved to see golfers destroyed by a second shot into the water.

That day, Mike fell in the second category. He started out well — blasting his drive down the middle of the fairway. I'd handed him his wedge, then hustled to move the bag out of his line of sight. That's when I'd noticed that his hands shook a little, a slight tremor that matched the quiver in his lower lip. Then he tightened his grip. With that simple adjustment, he murdered the shot — hit it fat, choked the zip out of it, sent it cannonballing into the pond, identical to the shot I'd just hit. The crowd moaned, filled with a conflicted mixture of sympathy and self-righteousness. Let's face it: most of the amateurs who'd played the course had made several ball donations to that pond, and most never even finished the hole. That didn't stop them from turning to the guy standing next to them.

"Hell, I know how to hit *that* shot!" they'd say. And in their imaginations, with just a little work on their putting stroke, they'd have taken Mike's place in the tournament. That day Mike dropped a second ball near the pond's edge and hit a beautiful wedge to within inches of the cup, setting himself up for a tap-in putt and a nicely recovered bogey.

That's what I directed myself to focus on — the recovery shot. Leave the screw-up behind me on the last tee and hit this one close to the cup, maybe even drop it in for a natural and unexpected par. Stop the bleeding. Build momentum. Even before I hit the thing, I imagined it arcing up over the water, dropping down on the brown patch I'd picked out on the green, and rolling up next to the pin. And it happened that way — amazing.

I sunk that bogey putt, then eked out a bushel of pars and one lone birdie on the third hole. I'd long since lost track of where I stood in relation to the field. And Laura knew better than to bring it to my attention. There was no advantage to reminding me that the entire direction of my professional life rode on these last few holes.

As I stood on the eighth hole tee box, we heard voices raised from the direction of the clubhouse. I stopped in midbackswing. "What the hell's that all about?"

"Don't hit until you feel ready," said Joe. "I'll go take a look." He jogged off, returning to our group after I'd putted out.

"You won't believe it. They hauled Walter Moore away in handcuffs. It took three deputies to bring him down." Then Joe put his competitive, no-nonsense game face back on. "We'll find out more when we get in. Just put a smooth cut on this last drive. You're almost home."

Too tired to think about Walter's arrest or to try harder than was good for me, I hit the green three shots later, producing my second birdie opportunity of the day. I left the birdie putt short, but sank the par. A grin split my face as the ball clunked into the cup. After the other golfers putted out, Laura slung me over her shoulder and began what she called her signature Choctaw victory dance. "You were awesome!" she shouted as we whirled around.

"I left a few shots out there. . . ."

"Don't even start with that nonsense. We are finals-bound. LPGA Tour — look out!"

"Put me down, you'll throw your back out," I said. "Nothing's official yet. We have to wait for the other girls to come in. And I'm not leaving the scoreboard until the last number's posted."

"Well, I'm ravenous," declared Laura. "I'm going over to the dining room. Shall I bring you something back?"

"I'll get a bite later when we go to celebrate." I stretched out in the shade, with a full frontal view of the scoreboard one hundred yards to my left. As Laura carried my clubs off to the parking lot, my cell phone vibrated.

"Cassie, it's Jack. Jack Wolfe."

"You don't need to say your last name, you idiot." I laughed. "Wow, I can't believe we're really talking. Your timing is amazing. What time is it there?"

"Midnight. I guess it's tomorrow by your calendar. How'd you do?"

"I'm pleased," I said, reluctant to brag. My cheeks ached from smiling. "Unless the whole rest of the field comes in under par, I'm guessing my seventy-two puts me somewhere around fourteen or fifteen."

For several minutes, Jack flooded me with questions and congratulations.

"Are you coming back to the States anytime soon? I miss you," I said, surprising myself with my daring. Up to now, any intimate feelings we had for each other had been seen only a little, and heard even less. At this moment, I felt good enough to step further out on a limb with him.

"Probably not before Christmas," he said. "But I called for another reason, too." I recognized the sound of a sharpening saw, its teeth bruising the bark on the branch I'd just stepped out on. "I don't know how to say this, so I'll just lay it on you. I got married last week."

The tree limb thumped to the ground with me on it.

I scrolled through my mental storehouse of etiquette according to Mom. I thought I

313

remembered one saying appropriate for the new bride and something else for the groom. Maybe "Congratulations" for guys telling you about their weddings? Or was it "Best wishes"? Whatever. I certainly couldn't repeat the parade of expletives that had rushed into my mind.

"Congratulations," I said finally.

"Gosh, I'm relieved you're taking it so well. I was scared to death to call you. It sounds crazy, happening so fast and all. But when I met Masako last month, I just fell head over heels. She's really different from American girls. Not that you aren't the greatest," he added quickly.

"I'm no geisha." My only wish now was to wind this miserable conversation down fast.

"That's just it," he said. "She has a totally different idea of how the relationship between a man and a woman should be. It's like the women over here get what they need because they are serving the needs of the man."

And why wouldn't that appeal to him, a lovely Asian suck-up tending to his every whim.

"I know it's not feministically correct. It sounds crazy, but she explained it all to me."

"So she speaks English?" Obviously he struggled with the fine points.

"Some," he said. "She's learning."

She'd be learning a lot.

"Will she travel with you?" I felt a sick

fascination with the details of his impulsive commitment.

"That's the beauty of the marriage deal," he said. "She doesn't work, so she can go with me anywhere and make sure I eat good stuff and get whatever else I need."

"Hmm," I said. Like get laid on a regular schedule.

"I'm so glad you understand. You're a doll, Cassie. I've been too embarrassed to tell you this was going on. I used to imagine us together — I even thought you could be my caddie. Who knows where it could have gone? But with both of us on Tour, it wouldn't have worked out in the end."

"Yeah, great. This phone call must be costing you your week's earnings." I couldn't resist that one sucker punch. I'd read in the *Herald-Tribune* today that he'd missed another cut, so his week's earnings were zero. Again. I hoped Masako didn't eat much.

"I gotta go — the press wants to talk to me," I said. A total lie, but it sounded good. "So good luck." I punched the end button with more vigor than was necessary, cutting off his second round of effusive congratulations.

At some primitive operating level of my brain, I had known that the relationship with Jack had been more fantasy than real. Hell, we barely knew each other. The fierce physical attraction had been fueled by the improbability of its consummation. With the sudden clarity of vision that comes with being dumped, I recognized that I probably wouldn't have liked what I found, knowing Jack better. But I'd needed something to hang on to, to help get through these hard weeks. Something to keep me floating while I navigated the disappointment of Mike's permanent dismissal, the serious stress of living back home, and then, the trauma of qualifying school. But the relationship with Jack should have come with a warning label: do not mistake this for a life-saving device. Just now, it felt like the air had whooshed out of my water wings, and I found myself dogpaddling alone.

I sat up cross-legged and returned to watching the other players as their numbers were inscribed on the scoreboard. Anything to shut Jack out of my mind. Despair, elation, rage — those girls showed every reaction you could find a name for. I imagined the volunteers manning the Magic Markers were glad they had a table between themselves and the golfers.

"Cassie," said Gary. "I almost fell over you. Congratulations! I'm so happy that you played well."

I smiled. "Thanks. There's only a couple threesomes left, so it looks like I'm definitely moving on up."

"Have you had lunch? Can I buy you a drink?"

"I'd love that, but I have plans with Laura

and Joe. Can I get a rain check?"

"I'll call you when we're back in South Carolina. Great job!" He kissed me on the cheek.

On my way to meet Laura at the car, I dialed the Myrtle Beach Police Department. Detective Maloney picked up his own line. At the sound of his voice, I felt a rush of the rage I'd suppressed all week. "It's Cassie Burdette."

"How did it go?"

"Fine. It looks like I'm in. But I'll warn you, I'm pissed. That jerk you sicced on me this week not only made life miserable, he nearly ruined my shot at this tournament. He harassed me every chance he got. And he masqueraded as the sheriff when in fact he's a freaking peon."

"Slow down," said Detective Maloney. "Take it easy. Pate called me this morning and admitted you mistook him for the sheriff." He began to laugh hysterically, which did nothing for my mood.

"It's not funny. It's probably grounds for a lawsuit. And that idiot would not come off well in front of a jury."

"Easy, Cassie," he said. "I'm sorry. I don't think you'll be able to squeeze a lawsuit out of it — he just failed to correct your mistake." He began to laugh again.

"I can see this phone call was a waste of my time," I huffed.

Maloney's voice grew serious. "Sorry, but the idea of Arthur making sheriff is so unlikely. Now tell me how you played."

"Well enough to move on to the finals," I said. "No thanks to Pate."

"I'm sorry. I screwed up," he said. "Arthur's my wife's sister's husband and she's always pressuring me to give him a hand, give him a chance to move up the ladder. I figured this would be a way to keep an eye on you and do my family duty, all at once. I had no idea he'd dress up like the sheriff. How can I make it up to you?"

"How about telling me what's going on with the Rupert murder case? And what's up with Walter Moore?" Maybe I could squeeze some inside info out of him, while he was feeling contrite.

He hesitated. "This isn't official."

"Come on. You owe me."

"The whole thing's about to be wrapped up. They arrested him for Kaitlin Rupert's murder just an hour ago. And attempted murder, in your case." A chill coursed through my body. "Thanks to your tip, they found his fingerprints on the Smith bar and a smudged print on the illegal golf club, too. He's denying everything, but the evidence is strong."

"Wow," I said. "I thought he was a little crazy, but I never had the feeling he'd really murder someone."

"That's not all," said the detective. "We're closing in on Will Turner for Bencher's shooting."

"Wow," I said again. "Two different killers. And I stumbled into both of them." I noticed Laura weaving toward me through the crowd of golfers around the scoreboard. I accepted Maloney's third apology and signed off.

"Guess what?" said Laura. "Mike's caddie just quit — couldn't take the heat."

"That doesn't surprise me one bit."

"So Joe and I are leaving right now — driving up to Ponte Vedra so I can carry Mike's bag tomorrow. Joe talked Jeanine into coming, too. Come on along and we'll buy you dinner at Sawgrass."

My gut erupted into queasiness. "Nah." There was no logical reason Laura shouldn't take the job with Mike. But I felt sick anyway. Dr. Baxter would have had a field day with the feelings that wcrc making their ugly appearance. "I already booked a flight out early this evening. I'll watch for you guys on TV tomorrow."

"What are you rushing home for? Come with us."

"I'm exhausted," I said. "I need to just collapse. In my own bed."

"Any words of wisdom about carrying Mike's bag? I'm nervous. This is important stuff."

"Keep it simple," I said. "Use the old

319

caddie maxim: Show up, keep up, shut up. The less you say, the less he can blame you for. Just don't take any crap from Mike. It's not good for him, and it won't help you either." This I knew well from my own excruciating experience.

"Don't worry. He'll think you're a pussycat when I finish with him." She hugged me. "Thanks."

I pulled away. "Thanks for carrying me through this week."

"You sure you'll be okay here alone? I feel bad about bugging out and leaving you here."

I didn't really feel okay about being left alone. But it was time to grow up and depend on myself, not lean on an entourage of old friends, supposed boyfriends, and headshrinkers. "Don't worry about it. You helped me get the job done. I'll be fine. I just talked to Maloney — he said they've arrested Walter Moore for Kaitlin's murder. They found his fingerprints on the Smith bar."

"No way. That's great. I feel better leaving you then." She turned and scanned the crowd, then waved to Joe. "I've gotta go. We're catching a cab to the Hertz office. I'll call you tomorrow. And don't worry, baby, we have some unfinished celebrating to do."

I watched her wind her way back through the crowd. I hadn't had the chance to tell her about Jack getting married to the Japanese sucker. We hadn't had a victory toast. We hadn't laughed about every stupid shot I made today or reviewed the great ones, the few we'd find to agree on. And my so-called pal Joe had left without a word. Talk about double-crossed.

I ran out to the parking lot to look for Gary. As he backed his car out of its parking space, I waved at him to pull over.

"Is the offer for lunch still good?"

"Absolutely," said Gary. "Hop in." Gary might not have been an athlete, a smooth-talker, a gorgeous hunk. But he seemed real, and he was available. Right now, that meant a lot.

I buckled my seat belt.

"Ready?"

I nodded. I was ready for something; we'd find out what.

# 26

Gary followed my directions to the little French place Laura had discovered the night she'd arrived in Sarasota.

"I have something to celebrate today, too," said Gary, after we'd been seated. "They nailed that bastard Walter Moore for Kaitlin's murder."

"That's great," I said. "Joe saw him get dragged off the course in handcuffs today." Gary's face looked sad. I fumbled around for the right words. "I don't mean it's great that they had to arrest anyone. It's not great that it happened."

"I know what you mean." He patted my hand. "I told her from the beginning that signing with him would cause trouble. Those clowns at Deikon thought they could pull her strings — tell her what tournaments to enter, what she could wear, you name it."

"Gosh, Kaitlin didn't strike me as the kind of girl who'd follow anyone's instructions, unless she saw something really big in it for her."

"You didn't know her the way I did." A tear swelled in the corner of his eye. He blinked it away. My turn to pat his hand.

"Anyway, the sky's the limit, champ," he said. "And I'm ordering the best bottle of wine on the menu."

"After the week we've had, it might take two," I said, mostly joking.

"I'll make sure they have a second one standing by." He motioned the waiter to approach our table.

"My name is Evan. I'll be your server today." His hands and his voice shook slightly. He hooked a wisp of streaked blond hair behind his ear. I wondered whether ours was the first table he'd ever waited on.

"Tell me about your selection of Chardonnays, Evan."

"I'll get the wine list," said the waiter.

"I'd prefer to hear it from you."

Evan the waiter, who looked as though he'd be more comfortable surfing than discussing the finer points of white wine, stumbled forward. "Well, we have a nice, fruity Fetzer."

Gary grimaced.

A red flush appeared on the waiter's neck and slowly spread across his face. "Let's see, the Woodbridge is popular, too. Our female guests seem to enjoy it." He grinned at me.

"I've never liked their whites," said Gary.

"How about the Sutter Home?" said the waiter, beginning to sound desperate.

"Nothing nicer than that? This is a big celebration."

The waiter's face lit up. "We just got in a

case of Robert Mondavi Coastal Chardonnay."

"Fine," said Gary. "Bring it on. And set aside a second bottle to chill." He turned back to me. "You'll like this, even though it's probably a little heavily oaked. In my opinion, all the American Chardonnays spend too much time in the barrel."

"I'm sure it will be fine." Wine was wine, in my experience. "If it doesn't come with a screw top, I know it's special."

Gary laughed. He thought I was kidding.

"Where are your parents? How did they take the news about Walter? I feel so bad for them."

"I put them on a plane back home this morning," said Gary. "I doubt they've even heard yet. I'll call later this afternoon. If they're anything like me, first they'll be thrilled. Then they'll remember that Kaitlin's still stone cold dead, no matter who killed her or how many years he spends in jail."

"I'm sorry. What a mess."

"Anyway, let's move on to happier subjects. What happened to your lunch with Laura?"

I frowned. Not a happier subject. "Mike Callahan canned another caddie, so he talked her into pinch-hitting for the weekend at the PGA Championship."

"Wow, that's big time." The waiter arrived with the Robert Mondavi Coastal Chardonnay Gary had ordered and poured him a splash. "You swirl, then sniff for flavors," he explained.

"The bouquet on this one is lemony and oaky." He motioned the waiter to fill my glass.

I sipped. "Much smoother than my usual Sebastiani from the jug."

"And it's not even in the same universe as Boone's Farm," he said with a smile.

I laughed. "Did you drink that poison, too?" I took another sip. "Delicious. I don't really get the bouquet thing, though. I guess my palate's not too sophisticated. I can tell the difference between red and white, though."

Gary chuckled. "You make me laugh, Cassie."

I drank quickly, a little embarrassed, and noticed an immediate reduction in the level of my tension. I hadn't realized just how tight I'd gotten over the course of the morning.

"Tell me how it felt being the player this week instead of the caddie," said Gary.

"Good question. There's a world of differ-ence." Gary refilled the empty glass as soon as I set it down on the table. "As a caddie, you do every bit of planning you can to make sure each swing turns out right. You check the yardage, you test the wind, you read the green. Then you have to step back and let someone else swing the club. When you're a player, your caddie can help as much as she likes, but in the end you're alone with the club and the ball. It's weird. It felt incredibly weird."

The waiter delivered my chicken salad on croissant sandwich and a cup of ham and white bean soup, then poured me a third glass of the Chardonnay.

"Do you mind talking about Kaitlin?" I asked.

Gary shrugged. Now under the influence of Robert Mondavi, I ignored Gary's lack of enthusiasm and forged ahead.

"I was talking to my brother last night," I said. "I just don't get why Kaitlin thought your father had molested her. I didn't know Coach that well, but it makes no sense. Not to Charlie either."

"I can't explain it," said Gary, motioning to the waiter to bring the second bottle of wine.

"Are you sure we need that?" I asked.

"How often have you made it through Q-school?" Gary said. "It's a no-brainer."

I was on the edge, high but not yet drunk. I'd lost just enough judgment to be easily convinced both that I deserved more wine and that more wine would make me feel better.

"So back to Kaitlin," I said, after the waiter had removed our dead soldier from the table.

"My parents always spoiled her. Whenever she had a problem, they bailed her out.

She's the baby, they'd say. You have to love her. It was the same when I was growing up." I detected a note of bitterness in his voice. "Frankly, I don't think they did her any favors. She never felt responsible for her own problems."

"So when she was unhappy, she looked around for who to blame. This time it was Coach."

"I guess," said Gary. He drained his glass and pushed his half-eaten croque monsieur away. "Could we talk about something else? This is depressing."

"I'm sorry," I said. I arranged my silverware in an even row next to my empty plate. "So what's up next for you?"

"Find a job. Preferably not as a caddie. I'm not into heavy labor and I don't enjoy prima donnas." He laughed. "Though I'd carry your bag anytime."

He picked my hand up off the table and massaged the lifeline that ran down the center of my palm. Reflexively, I pulled my hand back. Too hot. Someday I'd figure out what I felt about this guy, but not today. Nothing felt clear in the confusing aftermath of the week's events. Old boyfriends, new boyfriends, no boyfriends. Missed the cut, made the cut, made the big cut. And dead bodies everywhere. I excused myself to go to the rest room. As I walked down the hallway, I noticed both a definite level of euphoria and a tendency toward lurching.

"Did you ever find out what happened with that barbell yesterday?" Gary asked when I returned.

"The cops think that was Walter, too." From the curious looks of the couple at the table next to us, I assumed the volume of my voice had veered too high. "If he killed Kaitlin," I whispered, "he'd already crossed the line once. He wouldn't have hesitated to do me in if he thought he needed to protect himself." I took a large bite out of the chocolate mousse cake that had arrived during my absence. "Mmm. You know, while I was trapped in that gym, I was forced to listen to the Maury show. Have you ever watched that?"

Gary shook his head.

"It was unbelievably bad. There was this crazy teenage girl who spent the entire hour screaming at her father. I kept thinking, Where the hell is the mother in this picture? Why is she allowing them to humiliate the whole family?"

"I'll remember to skip it."

I was aware that Gary had requested a moratorium on my amateur psychoanalysis of Kaitlin. But halfway through the second bottle of wine, curiosity overran politeness.

"So this girl kept talking about her brother — how she wouldn't let the father treat her the same rotten way he'd treated him. I know

I'm straining the analogy, but I wonder if that's what bugged Kaitlin. Somehow she felt compared to you. It's hard to have a perfect older brother, I can tell you that from personal experience."

"I doubt that was it," said Gary. "I was far from perfect. There was very little to compete with. If anything, she was the perfect child. She won every athletic and scholastic award that Myrtle Beach High offered. Don't get me wrong, she deserved what she got — she had talent, but she worked hard, too."

"She might have been a contenda'." I giggled, hearing my words beginning to slur. I struggled to pronounce each one distinctly. "I guess I'm not a good detective. I just wouldn't have ever picked Walter as the murdering type. Plus, he was so into his career. Single-minded and a little crazy, that's how I would have described him. But not really dangerous."

"One never knows," said Gary. "People are strange."

"If they hadn't arrested Walter, I would have placed my bet on your mother as the killer."

Although I definitely surprised myself by blurting out this unexamined and tipsy insight, Gary was speechless. "My mother? Where in the hell does that crazy idea come from?" he finally croaked.

"Maybe I spent too much time with Pate

this week," I said. "But let's say she was mad at Kaitlin for accusing Coach of the abuse, and she tried to talk with her, but it didn't go well. Kaitlin refused to drop the suit. So then they got into a scrap and your mom hit her harder than she meant to." Gary opened his mouth in protest. I held my hand up to cut him off. "There's precedent for my theory — I saw them tussle on the Grandpappy driving range. Though Kaitlin definitely had the upper hand in that incident. Can't you picture it?"

"No, Cassie, I can't."

"Hey, do you suppose it's possible that someone else in your family molested Kaitlin? She seemed so sure it happened. I think I read a book like that once, where the girl thought her father abused her, but it was really her uncle." I laughed. "Maybe she even suspected you!" I warbled the music that introduced *The Twilight Zone:* "Doo, doo, doo, doo . . ." The couple at the next table stopped eating to stare at me again. "Hey! I bet that's what my dream was trying to tell me — that Bencher's lips were saying *Rupert, Rupert!*"

"I think you've had enough, young lady." Gary reached for my wineglass and drained the last inch of Chardonnay. "You're starting to hallucinate." He frowned and signaled for the waiter to bring the bill. It didn't take a genius to see that my teasing had gone too far.

"Sorry, sorry," I said. "Speaking of hallucinating, I saw you talking with Max Harding this morning on the golf course. You never did like him."

"He stole my girl." Gary snorted, a little drunk now, too. "That's you, you know. Then he broke her heart and ruined her for anyone else."

I tried to deflect the conversation far away from his "my girl" reference. "That bozo Max came to my room the other night, but I told him to take a hike."

"What did he want?" Gary leaned forward and took my hand, squeezing it tightly.

I was hit with a sharp wave of queasiness and dizziness. "I think I might upchuck."

"Let's get out of here. You've had a rough week." Gary paid the check and helped me outside and into the car. "You need a nap," he said. "When's your flight?"

"Sheven o'clock." I groaned and slumped against the window. "I don't feel too good."

"Crack the window, get some air," he said. "You rest for a while and I'll come by later and drive you back to the club to get your car."

"You're an officer and a gentleman," I said. "Thanks, pal."

# 27

I woke from a restless sleep, splayed out crossways on the motel bed. I was fully dressed, though wrinkled and sweaty, with a dry mouth and a heaving stomach. The alarm clock read four o'clock. The drapes were pulled shut and the room was dark. Was it afternoon or middle of the night? Damn. I had a bad feeling I'd missed my plane.

The details from my lunch with Gary began to take fuzzy shape in my mind. I was immediately grateful that he'd been gentleman enough to deposit me in the motel room and leave me here, alone. I remembered informing him that his mother would have made a logical murder suspect. How embarrassing was that? Next came the memory of teasing him about who actually perpetrated the abuse of Kaitlin. God help me. He had not been amused.

Someone pounded on my door. I stumbled across the room and peered through the peephole. Gary leaned against the door frame, looking fresh and cheerful, with damp hair and clean clothes. I cracked the door open.

"I came to give you a lift back to the club.

Are you feeling any better?"

I opened the door wider. "I made an ass out of myself, didn't I?"

"Don't be silly. You're just as charming drunk as sober." He smiled. "Ready?"

"Come in just a minute. I need to wash my face." I retreated to the bathroom and tried to repair the damage done by too much wine and a hard nap. I took a big slug of chalky pink Pepto-Bismol, brushed my teeth, and splashed my face with cold water. I looked in the mirror. There was no quick fix for the hair.

As I stepped out of the bathroom, Gary grabbed both my hands and drew me uncomfortably close. He smelled of mint toothpaste and stale alcohol.

"Gary, please. I'll miss my plane." I laughed. "Besides, I'm in no shape for a romantic encounter."

I tried to pull away, but he tightened his grip on my wrists and leaned in to kiss me. I turned my head. "I'm not ready for this. Maybe later . . ."

He pushed me onto the bed and lay sprawled across me, stroking my hair. "There isn't going to be a later, Cassandra. So it has to be now." He ground his lips and teeth into mine, making hoarse sucking noises as he kissed me. I could feel the hard shape of his erection through the thin khaki shorts. The sharp taste of bile rolled up the back of my throat. The unformed thought that had hovered in the back of my mind since waking took its full and frightening shape: Gary had killed his sister.

I pulled my mouth away from his face and tried again, summoning my firmest voice — the one I used at the driving range to correct wayward junior golfers. "I'm just not ready for this, please, Gary. I can't believe you're ready either, with all that's happened this week."

He began to massage my chest through my blouse.

"Please, Gary. Let's take it slow, get to know each other, spend time together back in Myrtle." At this point, I had no intention of spending any time with him, ever. But neither did I want to throw gasoline on the fire of his madness.

He rolled over and rested on one elbow, his other hand still clutching both of mine. He brushed a matted curl out of my eyes. "You couldn't leave things alone. Theories about my mother, analysis of Kaitlin's motives, you couldn't let it rest. My mother, a murderer?"

"I'm sorry," I said, now summoning my most earnest and reassuring inflection. "I had too much wine. I promise you I will never bring the subject up again."

"You and that fucking Harding." He leaned in and kissed me again, hard. Then he stroked my bruised neck with an unexpected tenderness. Both wrists ached from the tightness of his grip. "Why did he come to your room the other night?"

"He said he wanted to apologize for dumping me. I told him it was too late. That's it, really, that's all we said."

"Did he show you the photo?"

"What photo?" I was really confused.

"You're a lousy actress, but beautiful anyway. I regret to have to break this pretty neck," he said. "God, that sounds like dialogue from a bad movie." His laugh seemed almost normal. "What I mean is, if the Smith bar had finished you off, I would be spared the trouble. Though we'd have missed this fun."

"You set up the Smith bar to fall on me?" I was first furious, then very afraid.

"Of course not. It would have been a convenient, though unfortunate, end." I began to struggle to get away from him. Despite his pudgy, unathletic build, he was very strong. He rolled on top of me, pinning my hands under his weight. He fastened his teeth around my upper lip and sucked gently. "Don't fight me, Cassie. I don't want to hurt you more than I have to."

He ran his tongue across the contour of my cheekbone and into my left ear. I suppressed a sudden urge to gag. "It doesn't have to be this way. You don't have to force this. Let's take it slow."

He shook his head. "Too late for that. You had to keep pushing." He shifted into a falsetto impersonation of me at lunch. "Why did Kaitlin think your father molested her? My brother and I don't believe it." He nuzzled my neck and chest, then rested his head on the bedspread just inches from my face. "I asked you to stop with your stupid questions. They'd arrested Walter. He'd take the fall and it would all be over. Yes, there were still problems. I would have had to keep a close eye on you. What did you see in Bencher's office in those files? I didn't know. My name in his appointment book? The file on Kaitlin? Did you see me leaving? Did Bencher tell you my name? I didn't know."

I realized then that Deputy Pate had been right — Gary had been very worried about me stumbling into that crime scene.

"I didn't see anything. Just papers everywhere. I told you that on the first night we met down here. I was only joking about the dream, Gary. You can let me go; I didn't see or hear anything."

"I can't," said Gary. He unbuttoned my shirt, pulled it open, and began to lick the exposed skin. "You know I killed her, so I can't."

I felt a new rush of horror at his confirmation. Keep him talking, Cassie. Buy some time. Act nonchalant. The air-conditioner compressor lurched on, sending a blast of musty, frigid air across my stomach and chest.

"Why did you kill her? You must have had a good reason."

He stopped rooting at my neck and stared at me. "After Kaitlin went to see Bencher, she thought she started to remember things about being molested by our father. I couldn't let it go on. Sooner or later, they would have blundered into the truth. I thought if I got rid of the shrink, the whole thing would fade away. But she was obsessed."

"So you did molest her."

He squeezed my wrists together harder. "It was harmless. Just kid stuff. But she made such a big deal out of it. She filed a goddamned lawsuit, for Christ's sake. I would have been ruined once she remembered it was me. My father would have seen to that." At the mention of his father, his voice dropped to an angry hiss. "I felt sorry, but there wasn't a choice. She forced it to happen. Same as you have. But we'll have some fun first, too." He began to kiss my face, then my neck and chest, all the while grinding his hips into my pelvis.

"Gary, stop!"

"What's the matter? I know you're no virgin. I saw you and Max on the beach that night. I even took pictures."

"You took pictures?" I was confused, then furious. Though under the circumstances, the news of this intrusion was hardly meaningful. "Why?"

He laid his head alongside mine and smiled. "I wanted you for a long time." He trailed his fingers between my thighs, then squeezed my crotch. "We would have been good together."

I squeezed my legs closed and struggled to push his hand away. "It wasn't going to happen, Gary. I was in love with Max."

"That's why I persuaded him to dump you."

I'd had a lot of theories about why Max quit calling me, most of them related to my shortcomings. Or his, with Dr. Baxter's nudging. This new information boggled my brain. "You made him break up with me? How?"

"I told him about the pictures. Your private little after-prom party. I said they would be posted on every bulletin board in the school unless he dropped you. The guy had no backbone, Cassie. He wasn't good enough for you."

He ripped the button off the top of my shorts and tugged at the zipper. I inched toward the edge of the bed.

"Don't fight me, baby," he whispered, still grinding his weight into my pelvis.

As he rolled his body slightly left to get better leverage on my zipper, I dropped my arm over the edge of the bed. My fingers closed around the training grip of the Ben Hogan nine-iron. I might have one shot. With no weight shift and a poor angle of approach, it would have to be more of a pitch shot than a full swing. And no do-overs.

As Gary yanked down the zipper of my shorts, I held my breath and swung the club. It bounced off the side of his head with a dull thump. He went limp. I rolled his body off the bed and ran for the door, gulping for air, zipping my shorts, and buttoning my shirt as I went. I rushed out into the hallway and slammed into Max Harding.

"Am I too late? Are you all right? The cops are on the way."

"Your timing has always been lousy," I said, scowling at him. "That scumbag Rupert is in there. I think I knocked him cold, but I'm sure not waiting around here to find out."

Max followed me downstairs to the lobby and sat next to me on a bench across from the reception desk while we waited for the police. He reached down between us, his hand brushing my thigh.

"Don't even consider touching me." I glared at him, my eyes and voice as cold as I could make them.

"I wasn't," he said. "I wanted to show this to you before the police come. I wanted to finally explain." He pulled a Polaroid from his hip pocket and offered it to me. "This is why I stopped calling."

I accepted the photo. It was faded and creased, the white borders yellowed with age. The dark shadows of two figures barely materialized from what appeared to be sand dunes behind them.

"Hello, Max. This could be anyone. This could be anything."

He pointed to a white splotch in the center of the picture and cleared his throat. "I don't know how to be delicate about this. That's your bum."

I looked again. "It doesn't look like anything. No one would have known it was me and you."

Max looked sick. "I didn't know that. He said he had others. He said he would ruin your reputation permanently if I didn't back off. I believed him. I didn't know what else to do."

"Couldn't you have discussed it with me? Maybe I would have liked to have some input on being dumped."

"He told me not to. He threatened to hurt you. I'm sorry. Then it got to be too late. . . ."

"Not too late to come on to me the other night, right, Max?"

Two sheriffs' deputies burst into the motel lobby before Max could answer. Not that I would have allowed him another word.

"Gary Rupert's in my room," I said, scrambling to my feet. "*He* killed his sister, not Walter Moore. I knocked him out — nine-iron to the parietal lobe, if you want the technical terminology. I'd be careful, though, he might be coming around about now. And plenty pissed, I would imagine."

They drew their guns and raced up the stairs, me and Max trailing behind. One of the deputies knocked on the door to my room. "Come out with your hands up!" one deputy shouted. There was no answer.

"Stand back," said the second deputy to me and Max. "Get out of the way. We're going in."

Fifteen minutes later, Gary regained consciousness. He spat at us and swore as they wheeled him out of the room, handcuffed to the paramedics' gurney. Max and I were transported to the sheriff's department to give statements.

"How did you become involved in this, Mr. Harding?" inquired the sheriff.

"Cassie and I go back a long ways with Gary," Max explained, meeting my eyes with an embarrassed shrug. "I talked to him earlier today at the golf course. I couldn't put my finger on it exactly, but I had the feeling he was losing his grip."

"What were you doing with him Saturday night?" I asked.

"Saturday night?"

"I saw you chatting with him in the bar at Chili's."

Max looked confused. "I was in Myrtle Beach on Saturday." He shrugged again. "Anyway, when I saw you drive away with Gary, I got worried." He extracted a handkerchief from his pocket and blew his nose. "So I followed you."

"You *followed* me?"

"Go on," said the sheriff.

He turned deep red and swallowed. "I waited outside the restaurant and tailed you back to the motel. I was going to leave after he left — I could tell you were a little tipsy and I figured you needed to sleep it off."

Deputy Pate, who'd skulked outside the interview during Max's questioning, broke into a wide grin. I scowled as hard as I could in his direction.

"When Gary came back a second time, I decided I had fooled around long enough. So I called these guys. And well, you know the rest."

"Where are you headed now?" asked Max once we'd been cleared to leave the sheriff's department.

I looked at my watch. "I missed my plane hours ago. I guess I'll just drive the rental car home. I can stop in Daytona on the way and look over the golf course where I'll be playing the second round of Q-school in October."

Never mind that useful reconnaissance of

the golf course features would be impossible by the time I got there in the dark. Truth was, I needed friendly faces around me — not the kind that would hover over me saying, "I told you this was a bad idea" — like my mother. Or the kind who would hang around saying, "I really messed up, how can I make it up to you?" — like Max.

I called Joe's cell phone and left a message telling Laura to expect a roommate arriving after midnight.

# 28

I slept until late morning, when Laura bounded into the room and shook me awake.

"I don't know how you put up with Mike for almost a year," she said, flinging herself on the bed next to me. "That man is a beast."

"How'd he play?"

"He shot seventy-four. He's certainly not scaring the leaderboard. And talk about walking on eggshells — it's more like broken glass when you're carrying Mike's bag. My hat's off to you. You're either a saint or a masochist."

I laughed. "He's not so bad. Just remember, you're a mallard in the rain, babe, a mallard in the rain."

She stuck her tongue out. "Are you ever getting up? We're dying to hear all the gory details of what happened with Gary Rupert. Joe's over at the putting green watching his guys. Can you meet us there in twenty minutes?"

I reached the practice area half an hour later, and worked my way around the enthusiastic fans crowding the putting green for a glimpse of their favorite players. Sheesh. This was a different world than the low-key buzz at the Plantation Golf and Country Club. Joe grabbed me from behind and folded me into one of his trademark bear hugs. All my plans to act standoffish washed directly down the drain.

"I owe you an apology," he said. "I didn't get a chance to congratulate you. I'm so proud of you." He hugged me again. "You must have thought I didn't give a hoot. We looked all over for you before we left, but you'd already gone to lunch with Gary."

I wasn't going to admit how bad I had felt about being left alone yesterday — lousy enough to have gotten trashed and practically thrown myself into a murderer's arms.

"I wanted to celebrate with someone. Maybe I jumped the gun a hair going off with Gary. It was not a good afternoon." I glanced over at Laura. "Jack Wolfe called just before you left to tell me he's gotten married."

"Who in God's name would marry him?"

"Easy, girl," I said. "This is my ex-boyfriend you're talking about." Laura lifted her eyebrows at that. "Anyway, her name is Masako and she doesn't speak much English."

"Which explains everything very nicely," said Laura.

"Time out, ladies," said Joe. "Tell us about Gary."

"We were having a pleasant enough lunch." I thought back over the sequence of yesterday's events. "He was a little snotty to the waiter, but other than that, things were fine. Right up until the moment I suggested his mother made a great murder suspect."

"You what?"

"I still think it was a good theory. We" — I gestured to the three of us — "never really talked about her, even though she looked suspicious all the way along. She belonged to Turner's wacko organization, she had a lot of conflict with Kaitlin, and she acted squirrelly whenever we ran into her. Call it sexism, call it ageism, but for some reason, we didn't consider her as a killer."

"I can't believe you told Gary that!"

"I'd had a glass or three of Chardonnay — my tongue was a little loose at that point. Anyway, he dropped me off at my room, then showed up later and attacked me. So I beaned him with the nine-iron. That's pretty much all there is to tell."

"What was Harding doing there?" said Joe.

"Gary had been blackmailing him for years. He made him stay away from me by threatening to expose an old photo." I held both arms up in my best Richard Nixon/Bill Clinton imitation. "Don't ask me anything else about it. I'm not talking."

"So Max got suspicious of Gary and showed up at your place?"

I nodded. "He saw us go to lunch and watched Gary come back to my room. By then, I'd already cold-cocked the guy and didn't need the cavalry."

"I don't understand why he didn't try to kill you right away," said Laura. "Why did he wait until later to do the job?"

"Even though I was teasing him about which words Bencher might have been trying to communicate to me, he must have thought it over and decided I couldn't be trusted."

"I bet if you had some hypnosis, you could remember what Bencher really said," said Laura.

"I don't want to know." In fact, after this week, they'd have to tie me down to hypnotize me. And I'd fight going under every step of the way. Right now I knew as much as I needed to know about my life — except for the future. And that would require a crystal ball, not a headshrinker.

"I followed up with the sheriff's department this morning. Right now, Gary's not admitting anything," said Joe. "But his mother has been talking. Apparently she suspected that Gary was molesting Kaitlin years ago. She knew she should have done something. But Coach was always so hard on Gary; she thought he'd go crazy if she told him what she suspected. So she told herself boys will be boys."

"She knew about the abuse and she didn't do anything?" I said. "That's outrageous."

"But not unusual," said Joe. "People overlook the most incredible evidence in the name of protecting someone else in the

347

family, or themselves, for that matter."

"I don't get it. Why would Mrs. Rupert have joined that kooky false memory outfit if she knew Kaitlin had really been molested?" Laura asked.

"She wanted to protect Gary, but she didn't want Kaitlin to get her father in trouble. She knew Coach hadn't done anything. I guess she hoped Kaitlin would just drop the charges, with enough opposition."

"She's got a forklift load of garbage on her conscience now," said Laura. "How's she going to live with herself?" She shook her head in disbelief. "I have to say, Gary Rupert surprised me. I really had my money on the phony Dr. Turner."

"If Turner didn't kill Bencher," I said, "why was he so intent on scaring me away from his office?"

"He'd mounted such a campaign of harassment against Bencher, he must have worried someone would take legal action against him," said Joe.

"Besides which," said Laura, "he made a darned good murder suspect. He was smart but sleazy and his tactics were just this side of guerilla warfare."

"Hit some short putts now," Joe called over to the golfer he'd been observing. "You want to start the round with the sound of the ball hitting the cup in your mind."

"Now that sounds familiar," I said. "How

much is that guy paying you for that canned line?"

"Someday, I'd like to hear more about the session you had with Turner," said Joe, ignoring my teasing. "He's an interesting character."

I nodded, glad Joe didn't have the time to spare now. I was still digesting the ideas he'd raised about my own family. The glass half empty, the glass half full.

"So who put the club in So Won Lee's bag?" asked Laura.

Joe shrugged. "No one's come forward." They both looked at me. We all knew that I had benefitted most from that maneuver. Did someone want Kaitlin out? Or me in? I'd probably never know.

On the far side of the practice green, I spotted Jeanine. She wore deep purple short shorts and a matching low-cut tank. She was animated, sexy, and drop-dead gorgeous. Through the crowd, I could just see the base-ball caps of two men clustered around her.

"Who the hell is Jeanine talking to?"

Joe laughed. "I may have created a monster. She's got Mike Callahan and Rick Justice fighting over her like it was their last chance at a meal. Or a birdie putt."

"Some girls have all the luck," I said. "I'm off guys for the time being. Hey, didn't I hear someone say something about buying me lunch? I'm starving."

# About the Author

ROBERTA ISLEIB is a clinical psychologist and avid golfer who lives with her family in Connecticut.

Visit her website at www.robertaisleib.com.

We hope you have enjoyed this Large Print book. Other Thorndike, Wheeler or Chivers Press Large Print books are available at your library or directly from the publishers.

For more information about current and upcoming titles, please call or write, without obligation, to:

Publisher
Thorndike Press
295 Kennedy Memorial Drive
Waterville, ME      04901
Tel. (800) 223-1244

Or visit our Web site at:
www.gale.com/thorndike
www.gale.com/wheeler

OR

Chivers Large Print
published by BBC Audiobooks Ltd
St James House, The Square
Lower Bristol Road
Bath BA2 3SB
England
Tel.   +44(0) 800 136919
email: bbcaudiobooks@bbc.co.uk
www.bbcaudiobooks.co.uk

All our Large Print titles are designed for easy reading, and all our books are made to last.